To one of my favorite people,

Carolyn Cohn

Port Fulton

C.C. Cohn

Copyright © 2009 by C.C. Cohn

All rights reserved. No part of this book shall be reproduced or transmitted in any form or by any means, electronic, mechanical, magnetic, photographic including photocopying, recording or by any information storage and retrieval system, without prior written permission of the publisher. No patent liability is assumed with respect to the use of the information contained herein. Although every precaution has been taken in the preparation of this book, the publisher and author assume no responsibility for errors or omissions. Neither is any liability assumed for damages resulting from the use of the information contained herein.

This is a work of fiction. Names, characters, places, and incidents either are the product of the author's imagination or are used fictitiously. Any resemblance to actual events or locales or persons, living or dead, is entirely coincidental.

ISBN 0-7414-5548-X

Published by:

INFINITY
PUBLISHING.COM

1094 New DeHaven Street, Suite 100
West Conshohocken, PA 19428-2713
Info@buybooksontheweb.com
www.buybooksontheweb.com
Toll-free (877) BUY BOOK
Local Phone (610) 941-9999
Fax (610) 941-9959

Printed in the United States of America
Published November 2009

This book is dedicated to my husband, Arnold,
and my friend, George Coolidge.

CHAPTER 1

SITTIN' THE GEORGIA LEE

"Hey, Calvin. Wait up. Wanna make a few bucks?"

"Sure. So far 1928 has been a terrible year."

"The boys heard you quit college and your job all in one week."

"I didn't know everybody in the Mound City Boatyard knew my life story. If you don't mind Lymon, I'm going to take my boat upriver. A boat ride clears my head."

"The job pays fifty and you can still take a boat ride."

"I'm listening."

"The big cheese, Leroy McMillan's got boat problems."

"What happened? The mechanics had Georgia Lee in perfect condition last week."

"The boat's intact as far as I know. Leroy beached her on a sandbar this side of Alton. He rowed his dingy to town and rang me up to send a tow."

"Leroy McMillan never could read the river."

"Look Calvin, I know you don't like him, but he's a rich pompous ass and I need someone to sit the boat tonight. Leroy doesn't want her vandalized. Are you interested?"

"Of course I'm interested."

"Good. I'll send Captain Drake with the tow to drag her off tomorrow."

"Could you throw in a couple of cans of gas?"

"Sure. Bring your cans to the pump. And Calvin, get a move on so you can get to Alton before dark."

"No problem Lymon."

"Here's the money. Take care of it and be discrete. I don't think Leroy was alone."

"Leroy McMillan's a jackass. Why do women follow that guy around?"

"He's got money, Calvin."

Calvin Johnson slicked back his unruly hair. "You mean young and handsome doesn't count for much today?"

"In 1928 you got to be rich to attract them fancy women."

"It's my plan to be rich and famous."

"Yeah. Yeah. Look Calvin, when you get to the boat, you make sure the main cabin's locked up. Leroy don't want any reporters from Alton nosing around."

Calvin sighed and rolled his eyes. "Is there anything else?"

"There is Calvin. Don't be no damn hero and try to get Georgia Lee off the bar yourself. Let Captain Drake tow her back on Sunday."

"Lymon, if the current grabs her and Georgia Lee floats free. I'll have no recourse but to grab the helm and steer her right down to St. Louis."

"No damn hero stuff. I'll see you Sunday, kiddo."

"You bet."

On the gas dock Calvin filled both gas cans from his sixteen foot boat called Baby Wildcat III. He hopped in and rope started the engine. His vintage outboard purred in the water as he untied her lines. Skillfully he maneuvered through the bustling river traffic at Mound City Boatyard. As he set a course upriver, he lit a stogie and sat back. It was relaxing to watch the muddy Mississippi ripple gently like a mill pond on a lazy afternoon.

Rounding Mobile Point, just below Alton, Calvin scanned the horizon with his binoculars. In the distance he focused on a white speck near the West Alton side of the river above the railway bridge. As he barreled under the bridge, the forty foot Richardson appeared grounded on the sandbar like a wounded swan. He slowed down and played it safe. Since he wasn't sure how much water stood under the big boat, he brought his outboard upstream and then drifted down with the current to the Georgia Lee.

After anchoring upstream, Calvin tested the water depth on both sides of Georgia Lee with his paddle. Unfortunately the boat was sitting crossways in the current with only about two feet of water on the upstream side. As the current whipped around the bow and stern, it made a hole on either end about waist deep. If this phenomenon persisted, the big boat would dig herself off the sandbar and proceed downstream on her own.

Tossing his line over the Richardson's cleat, Calvin tied off his sixteen foot outboard. He climbed over the rail and headed for the bilges to check for water. Assuring himself that the Georgia Lee's bottom was dry, he hurled the anchor over the bow. Now if the big boat started moving the downstream, the anchor would slow her progress.

As he entered the cabin, the woodwork, polished with fragrant lemony oil, made him pleasantly dizzy. As Calvin checked the Captain's spacious aft cabin he noticed black lacy undergarments with ostrich feathers scattered over the bed. He chuckled and locked the door.

Walking toward the bow, Calvin noticed the door open to the cheerful forward cabin. As he looked in, it seemed cozy, so he pulled his boots off and stretched out on the fresh sheets. Before long the sun peeked through the port hole into his face. Nap time was over. He sat up and slicked back his hair. His sweaty feet slipped into his boots as he headed for his outboard. Before dark, Calvin needed to make a trip to Captain Fluent's Dock in the shadow of the Alton railroad bridge at the foot of Henry Street. The dock was the only bank-side fuel stop for motorboats between St. Louis and Grafton. Captain Fluent sold gasoline and lube oil in milk bottles as well as bait and delectable turtle soup.

It was a short boat trip to Captain Fluent's Dock. Walking on the creaky boards Calvin noticed the freeboard of the old telephone pole deck was down four inches. He could see Captain Fluent's fishy pets swimming just below the surface. Charlie McCarthy and Mortimer Snerd, the biggest garfish in the Mississippi, gobbled up all the garbage around the dock and viewed visitors with an icy stare.

Captain Fluent waved and hobbled down the dock as the water sloshed over his shoes. "Well hello, Calvin. Long time no see."

"Good evening, Captain. Your dock's a might low, in case you haven't noticed."

"I noticed. I was plannin' to add another layer of poles. Just ain't got round to it."

"Don't wait too long or you'll be sitting on the bottom. You got some oil and water?"

"Oil is in bottles behind the stove. Help yourself. It'll cost you ten cents. I just filled the barrel from the river. Water's nice and clear."

"You don't happen to have some of that sanitized stuff from the St. Louis water plant, do you?"

"Calvin, there ain't nothin' wrong with my water. I've been drinkin' this here river water neat for eighty years and I'm healthy as a horse."

"What about turtle soup? Got any for a hungry friend?"

"Nope. I ate the last bowl this afternoon."

"That's too bad. When I saw that twenty-gallon lard can on the stove, my mouth started watering. That turtle soup of yours is better than any fancy St. Louis restaurant."

When he wasn't working, Captain Fluent lived a modest life aboard Tiger, his thirty foot-long, twelve-foot-wide wooden shanty boat anchored between the dock and the bank. Topsides was painted buff with green window boxes where the old man planted petunia seeds in spring. The river was Captain Fluent's life. He knew her intimately. Rumor had it that Cap' never walked past the land side of Broadway in Alton. He had no time, money or manners for a wife, but Cap' possessed an uncanny knowledge of the river. As Calvin loaded his oil, he watched as a fisherman checked with the old man for the latest forecasts.

"Howdy, Cap'. Fish biting today?"

"Sure thing, Alvin. You just motor up to Piasa and fish them rocks."

"What kind of bait should I use?"

"Dough bait, a course. Linseed and molasses catches the biggest catfish. Just happen to have some fresh. I made it up this mornin'. A jar costs you two bits. Did you hear about your fishin' buddy, Mack Rogers?

"No. What happened?"

"Yesterday Mack fell off his boat round Pearl. I helped the sheriff find the body."

"Where did he go down?"

"Well after I made some calculations, I told the sheriff to check the third wing dam downstream."

"Did he find him?"

"A course he did. I reads the river, boys. And I never miss."

Calvin rope started Baby Wildcat and watched as the fisherman motored upriver with his lanterns lit. It was a short trip to the big boat as the sun dipped behind the trees. His stomach growled as Calvin ambled into Leroy's amazing galley. When he slid open the latch on ice box, packages wrapped in brown paper cascaded over the floor. He picked them up and peeked into a few. Wow, what a delicious supper selection! He felt like the cartoon character, Andy Gump piling his sandwich so tall he could hardly handle it. Carefully Calvin climbed the ladder to the bridge balancing two triple-decker ham, salami, and cheese sandwiches.

After delivering his feast, he quickly backtracked down the ladder to the head. Calvin loosened a board on the left side of the porcelain throne to reveal Leroy's special stash: three bottles of imported whiskey and two bottles of cognac. After relieving himself in the head he picked out a full bottle and climbed back to the top deck. Sunsets on the river excel in rich golds and pinks. At dusk dark clouds drifted in from the west as he relaxed in a comfy chair.

Soon Calvin stumbled to the forward cabin and sprawled out on the bed in a drunken stupor. Within minutes a giant crash jolted him right off the bunk. Dazed he crawled to the porthole as the boat tipped wildly. A violent thunderstorm roared down the river. Lightening bolts lit up the sky like fireworks. They struck points on the bluffs creating uncanny shadows. The boat lurched to port with a driving gale from the starboard. As Calvin staggered onto the deck, shallow water around the sandbar slammed against the boat on all sides. Suddenly a sheet of water knocked him back inside. Calvin scrambled for a life jacket from the ship's locker since his downstream journey could happen at any time. Climbing to the bridge, he grabbed the wheel ready to steer. The rain pounded violently against the windshield. He tried to remain vigilant, but the whiskey made him sleepy. Clinging to the wheel he dozed.

In the morning Calvin checked his position against the shore. The Georgia Lee moved downstream several yards. All the slack was out of the anchor line, but luckily the boat stood firmly grounded on the sandbar. As he watched the tree limbs and corn stalks floating past in the swift current, a loud thump whacked the upstream side of the boat. The jolt sent him tumbling across the deck. He crawled to the railing and peered over the side.

In the light of day Calvin squinted down the side of the boat. A small canoe bobbed in choppy water. In the boat sat a beautiful, chestnut-haired woman, and a lop-eared brown dog. They looked amazingly dry sitting under a woolen blanket. The woman smiled and waved.

"Good morning." Calvin waved with his right hand as he slicked back his unruly hair with the other.

"Bonjour my friend," called the woman. "We have lost our way in the storm. Where are we?"

"Lady, you're on the Mississippi River near Alton."

"If this is the Mississippi River I'm in trouble."

"No you're not! I'm the best damn captain on the river and I'm here to help. I'm particularly good at assisting beautiful women. Come aboard and we'll figure out a plan. I have some pastries and coffee in the galley."

"I'm starved. Breakfast would be wonderful. Merci. I am Anne Marie. This is Jean Claude."

"I'm Calvin Johnson, Captain Cal Johnson to the people on the river that know me. Welcome aboard."

Calvin tied her canoe to the cleat of the Georgia Lee, downstream from his outboard. Anne Marie boosted her dog over the rail into Calvin's arms, and then pulled herself up easily. "Where's the galley Captain?"

"Follow me."

Anne Marie made coffee while Calvin fed her dog a ham and cheese sandwich from the ice box. They drank coffee from Leroy's fancy china and devoured the entire box of pastries.

"How did you stay dry in all that rain?"

"Jean Claude and I were lucky. The water just rolled off the blanket. Calvin, you seem young to have such a grand boat."

"I wish this was my boat. I'm watching the Georgia Lee until the tow shows up to take her back to St. Louis."

"Are you really a riverboat captain?"

"I will be soon. I'm working on the license. What's your story?"

"My story started Tuesday as I painted river scenes on Illinois River. I'm very talented you know. Drifting down from Beardstown I planned to meet a man about a job at the River Pub in Grafton, but about noon a squall came up. I had to paddle out of the fury to a place called Otter Creek where I beached the canoe. Exhausted, Jean Claude and I fell asleep under the blanket. Storms continued and high water must have floated us off. This morning we ended up alongside this beautiful boat. That's my story. Now tell me Calvin, how do we get back to Grafton?"

"I don't know."

"What do you mean?"

"I can't go anywhere. I'm being paid to sit the Georgia Lee." A steamboat whistle blasted as the swing span opened on the railroad bridge at Alton. "Hot damn! You're in luck Anne Marie. It looks like the Belle of Calhoun is stopping at the Alton landing."

"Will the Belle of Calhoun take us back Grafton?"

"She just might. Every week the boat comes down with a load of passengers and freight. It turns around at Alton to head back up the Illinois River. I know the captain. It won't be hard to convince him to take you back to Grafton."

"That would be wonderful, Calvin."

"Alton is the turn around point, so the Belle will be there for at least half a day. We don't have to hurry. Let's finish the coffee, and then celebrate with some imported cognac."

"That sounds wonderful. Would you like to see my watercolors of the river? Oui?"

"Sure." The cognac relaxed Calvin. Anne Marie showed him the canvas from the canoe. "Boy, you painted a lot of grass and water. Where are the people?"

"Would you like to be my subject Calvin?" She giggled as she took her paints out of her bag and cleaned her brushes.

"What do you have in mind Anne Marie?"

"I feel like painting the boat, the Georgia Lee, on the sandbar with you, mon chère, scrubbing the deck."

"Hot damn! I'm ready." Without a second thought Calvin hopped over the rail, and fell clumsily ten feet into the shallow water. "I'm okay, nothing's broken." Standing up he staggered through the water, slicking back his hair with his wet hand. "Where do you want me to stand?"

"Over there," she pointed to a flat area. Anne Marie threw him a scrub brush, and then climbed gracefully down the ladder at the stern, balancing her easel, canvas, and paints in her hands. She splashed barefoot through the water to the hard sand. "Be fluid. Move. And Calvin, take off your clothes."

"What?"

"Take off your clothes. You'll look more natural with the river naked."

"Hot Damn!" Calvin pulled off his shirt and started rubbing Georgia Lee's stern with the brush. "This is the first time I've ever been a model for a painting."

"Everything must come off, Calvin. You must look natural with your surroundings."

"I won't feel natural."

"Try it."

"Okay," he sighed. Reluctantly Calvin pulled off his pants and threw them over the rail. "This is the only time I've ever scrubbed a boat naked." He grabbed the brush and splashed the boat. "I don't feel natural, Anne Marie. I feel weird."

"You look just fine. Don't look so worried. No one will recognize you. This is an eight by twelve canvas."

"Okay. Where do you want me to stand? Is this like taking a photograph?"

"This is a watercolor, Calvin. Relax and rub the Georgia Lee in every crevasse. And do it adoringly like you would if she were a beautiful woman."

Calvin splashed around the boat, sinking into the wet sand. He lost his footing swimming out to fondle her stern. Simultaneously he whacked his head on the ladder and lost the brush in the current. "I'm finished here," Calvin called as he awkwardly climbed up the ladder.

Anne Marie looked up from her work as the Belle of Calhoun's whistle sounded. "Is the big boat ready to leave?"

"Yes. We'd better get over to the landing." Calvin pulled on his pants, and then jumped into Baby Wildcat to tie on the canoe.

Anne Marie cleaned her brushes in the river and climbed the ladder. She grabbed her bag and shoved Jean Claude into Calvin's boat. "This has been a wonderful afternoon. Thank you."

"I liked it too."

"You were a good sport." Anne Marie slid over the rail and into the front seat.

"Hang on," shouted Calvin over the rackety noise of the old outboard.

Anne Marie giggled as Calvin zigzagged his boat, with her canoe attached to the stern, across the river to the landing at Alton. Spray flew everywhere.

"This is fun," shouted Anne Marie over the drone of the engine.

On a sandbar near the landing they waved to people sunning themselves. Men and boys skinny-dipped around some half-submerged trees. Groups of laughing girls stood up to their necks in the river as their clothes hung over nearby driftwood on the shore.

"Ahoy, Captain Jim," Calvin called through Leroy's megaphone as his boat approached the bridge of the Belle of Calhoun.

A tall, grey-haired man in a navy blue uniform waved from the bridge. "Calvin Johnson, is that you? I haven't seen you in years. How the hell are you?"

"I'm fine. I need a favor. Do you have room for two more to Grafton? It seems Anne Marie and her dog got caught in the storm and missed their destination."

"There's plenty of room. We'd be proud to take the little lady and her possessions to Grafton, Calvin. No charge."

Say hello to your dad for me. I can still remember diving for pearls with Walter on those vacations in Kampsville."

"I'll tell dad I saw you. Thanks."

Baby Wildcat clunked against the side of the steamer as two strong, colored roustabouts helped Anne Marie and Jean Claude onto the boat. The biggest fellow levered the canoe onto the deck by himself.

"Have a good trip," Calvin called and waved.

"Thank you for everything. Au revoir."

Calvin kept Baby Wildcat away from the turbulence as the Belle of Calhoun set a course upriver. As he headed back to the Georgia Lee he recognized the tow from Mound City kicking up sand around the big boat. The tow line strained. Ole Bill's engines roared as the Georgia Lee bobbed up and down, and then floated free.

"Ahoy, Ollie."

"Where the hell you been, Calvin?"

"I've been helping a lady."

"I could have used help myself. Grab this tow line."

"Captain, I can get Georgia Lee back quicker and easier."

"Are you sure Calvin? I'm going to be in hot water if anything happens to this damn boat."

"I'm sure."

"Then do it. It's a nuisance towing this boat anyways. Here's a couple of Double Eagles for your trouble." Captain Drake tossed two shiny gold coins into the bottom of Calvin's runabout.

"Can I spend these things?"

"You bet you. Those twenty dollar coins spend just like paper money."

"Hot damn! I'll just tie Wildcat to the cleat and be on my way."

"Good luck. Make sure Georgia Lee gets back to Mound City in one piece," called Captain Drake as the tow circled the cruiser and headed downstream.

"See you in St. Louis."

Calvin jingled the gold coins and slipped them in his pocket next to the fifty dollars. Getting paid twice for the same job wasn't too shabby. On the bridge he adjusted Leroy's jaunty captain's hat and started the powerful engines. Lastly Calvin adjusted Wildcat's heavy tow line off the stern of the cruiser. As he pulled the anchor the hemp rope scattered across the polished wooden deck in a symmetrical pattern.

Calvin lit the running lamps and his stogie as he pushed the throttle forward. Georgia Lee gracefully planned down the middle of the river toward St. Louis and Baby Wildcat skittered happily behind on the long tow line.

Baby Wildcat III

CHAPTER 2

POWERBOAT REGATTA

The St. Louis levee exploded with excitement on a crisp Saturday morning in 1928. The Midwest Powerboat Association invited beautiful, fast boats from all over the country to Front Street for the powerboat regatta. Racing between the Eads and Free bridges brought hundreds of spectators.

Calvin exited with the chattering crowd down the long platform of the Granite City to St. Louis streetcar. He walked along the wharf mesmerized by the dozens of fancy powerboats. His aging folding Kodak camera hung around his neck, ready to snap pictures. He needed this breath of fresh air after a terrible week.

After three years at Knox College Calvin quit. He couldn't keep getting excited over a liberal arts education in the middle of rural Illinois just to please his father. After all, Calvin Johnson loved engines and getting his hands dirty. He wasn't cutout to be a school teacher. After hitch-hiking home from college Calvin needed a job, so he signed on making graniteware at the National Enameling and Stamping Company in Granite City. Working in the N.E.S.C.O. plant paid well, but the tasks were repetitious and boring.

On Friday Calvin walked out and never looked back. He took the streetcar to St. Louis. At a speakeasy on Commercial Alley he met a down-east Yankee boat builder. Will Chambers and Calvin Johnson were two peas in a pod.

"I left Long Island to escape my family, Cal. My father was set on me being banker like him. I couldn't imagine being in an office all day. I wanted to work outside."

"I can understand that. My father wants me to be a teacher like him."

"When I moved to St. Louis my cousin, Joe, and his big Italian family took me in. We pooled our money together and opened a boat-building shop on Chestnut Street. We construct runabouts made by the cedar-strip method."

"I've seen your boats at the Mound City Boatyard. They're beautiful. I'm looking to start a business too. I could use a partner."

"I'm busy with boat building, but what do you have in mind?"

"How about a water taxi business? They could use one on Laclede's landing. I'm good with motors and you make boats. It could be a money maker."

"Look Cal, we need a big boat for something like that. I make small boats. And we need capital. I've used all my money to finance the boat building business."

"Will, we can make this happen. I got my sights on this gorgeous Chris Craft with six seats for a water taxi. I saw it on Lake Missaukee in Michigan. And I've got a source for wood in Granite City to build a dock on landing. I could do it this summer."

"That's a big dream."

"We can do it. My father knows an officer at Boatman's Bank. Getting a loan from the bank shouldn't be hard."

"Boy, are you a big dreamer."

"You gotta take risks to make money."

"I like the sound of Will Chambers, millionaire. I'm available."

"Great. Let's go to Boatman's next week."

Will smiled and lifted his glass. "Here's to the Johnson and Chambers water taxi business."

"How does 'Have boat, will travel' sound for a slogan?"

"Let's drink to it."

Thinking about the new business opportunity on the horizon, Calvin skipped down the levee toward the boat races. Hot damn! His life was finally on the right path.

The bands played and the drums sounded as the powerboat regatta organized on the levee. As Calvin walked he noticed the marine ways at Mound City was putting a steamboat in its cradle. The worm gears and cogwheels grinded as the boat moved out of the river. The steamboat, Betsy Ann, looked mountain high as she climbed up to the top of the bank. He took a picture with his camera and moved down the levee to a boat with the converted Star 151 automobile engine. It was a poor man's hydroplane modified to crank out about fifty horsepower. Hispano-Suizas were in many race boats. They were incredibly fast and expensive. A Hisso in its original crate costs two hundred dollars. He saw the Curtiss water-cooled airplane engines on some of the boats. These O.X.-5 engines were manufactured for the Curtiss Jenny airplane during World War I, only ninety horsepower, but very reliable and exciting to watch.

Calvin continued to walk down the levee, snapping pictures of fancy racing boats anchored a few feet off the bank or on trailers. The polished copper water jackets on a three-cylinder, two-cycle Bud caught his eye. He knew they were the slowest of the 151s, but their sweet sound, like a well-oiled sewing machine made up for all their shortcomings.

Near Laclede's landing he stopped in his tracks. She was gorgeous, standing demurely in the sun. He circled the glossy black hydroplane. She was an exquisite beauty about twenty-two feet long with a beam of about five and a half feet. She had sharp curving bow and a deep notch amidships. Her three-bladed brass propeller flashed like jewelry in the sun. Baby Zim was the name painted on the trailer.

A giant of a man with a big bushy red mustache stepped up next to Calvin as he admired the hydroplane.

Calvin smiled. "With that silver-bellied Stetson and those fine snakeskin boots, you don't look like you're from around here."

"No, I'm from Texas, son. You know anything about running boats?" he said putting his arm around Calvin's shoulder.

"Sure I know about running boats and engines too. Is Baby Zim yours?"

"You bet."

"You got a Curtiss O.X.-5 or a Hispano-Suiza?"

"It's a Hisso, of course."

"A Hisso! Hot damn! That V-8 power plant can hop up to two hundred and forty horsepower. Is the gear ratio one to one-and-a-half?"

"You bet. That Hisso is one sweet airplane motor. My assistant's in the calaboose in a town between here and Little Rock. You want a job for a day, son?"

"Sure, I'll take the job."

"Don't just stand there. Get in and clean her up. We'll be racing in an hour."

"Yes, sir!"

The cowboy disappeared into the crowd before Calvin could thank him, so he grabbed some cotton rags and got busy swabbing out the bilge. He used the greasy cotton material to remove dust and fingerprints from the mahogany interior. In short order, the bilge looked like new and the mahogany decks gleamed like the hood of a brand-new Model-T. Calvin slipped into the seat behind the engine and fantasized about driving her right down the river. As Calvin closed his eyes to let his imagination take over the cowboy appeared at eye level with two buckets of brew.

"Wake up. I got us a couple of cold ones from the Blind Pig."

Calvin hopped to the ground. He grabbed the frosty bucket and drank it down.

"That's a fine job," the cowboy said as he took a long drink, wiping the foam from his mustache on his sleeve.

"Thanks for the job."

"You're doing me a big favor, son. I'm Johnny Zimmer from Houston, Texas."

"I'm Cal Johnson. That's an exquisite boat," he said extending his hand. Zimmer shook it hard. "Mr. Zimmer that boat looks like a winner to me."

"Call me Johnny and yes, Cal, Baby Zim is a winner. She's a World Champion in her class. Come on, kiddo. Now that you got her looking real pretty. Let's put her in the water and see how she goes."

"Hot damn!"

Zimmer waved Calvin into the truck. Then he backed the trailer and hydroplane down the cobblestones and into the river.

"Handle the lines, Cal, while I park the truck. I might be awhile. I'm changing my snakeskins. They don't take kindly to water."

Calvin rolled up his pants to the knee and jumped out of the truck. Sloshing through the water he grabbed the lines.

His boots filled with water as Baby Zim bobbed up and down. He hung on tight as the current pulled the stern downstream.

Finally Zimmer splashed back to the boat in old rubber boots. He leaped over the side and started the engine. Over the roar and smoke he yelled. "Cal, get the hell in and prepare for the ride of your life."

Grabbing the lines Calvin leaped over the gunwales like a jack rabbit. His pants dripped and his boots squeaked and leaked as he slid across the mahogany decks to the seat behind the driver.

"You want me to mop up my mess."

"It's only water, kiddo. Hold on, we're moving downstream."

Calvin fell back into his seat as the boat accelerated. They cleared the wharf and took three fast laps around the course. Calvin's heart beat so loud in his chest he could hear it in his ears. "Hot damn! How fast are we going?"

"About sixty-five," Zimmer shouted back.

"Hot damn!"

"Hey, Cal. While I'm in the boat, I'd like you to stand by the trailer and my tools to assure their security."

"Yes, sir."

"How about one more lap? Baby should be able to do seventy with a little coaxing."

Calvin just nodded as Baby Zim sped around the course one more time. The boat's wake rocked dozens of large cruisers anchored in the river across from the St. Louis wharf.

"Look at all those boats ready to watch the race."

"That big white Richardson belongs to Leroy McMillan. I met him at the yacht club. He's quite a Jim dandy, all dressed up in his fancy-pants outfit."

"I heard he isn't much of a navigator. He beached Georgia Lee on a sandbar. Don't you think McMillan looks like Napoleon standing on his forward deck?"

They both laughed as Baby Zim roared under the bridge and headed for the landing. Zimmer shut down the boat near the bank. Calvin jumped over the side into the river to steady the boat so the prop didn't get dinged on the cobblestones.

"Stand by the trailer, Cal. I'll see you soon."

"Sure thing." Calvin pushed the hydroplane out passed the cobblestones, and watched the glossy hydroplane disappear in a cloud of smoke.

Calvin skipped back to the trailer with a smile on his face. His life was changing for the better. Sitting on the fender, he kicked off his wet boots. A roar overhead made him look up. The Jenny airplane circled Eads Bridge, and then tipped its wings to the crowd. Jenny Scrambling was a popular diversion between boat races. The planes were acrobatic and chased each other along the river. Most Jennys used ninety horsepower O.X.-5 engines, but today it looked like a Hisso-powered Jenny slipped into the airplane competition. Watching a one-hundred-and-fifty horsepower Hisso powered Jenny was like watching a cheetah running after a deer. Calvin cheered with the crowd as this special Jenny stole the air show.

"Gol damn! You're guarding that trailer like it's the U.S. Treasury," said a wiry old man attired in a blue uniform with gold trim. He stood partly hidden by Baby Zim's fender. His magnificent foghorn voice made up for his short stature.

"Yes, sir. Johnny Zimmer from Texas enlisted my services for the regatta. Wow! I've never heard a voice like yours."

"My voice is my moniker, young man. I can stand on Market Street and give an order that'll be heard all the way to Eads Bridge. Allow me to introduce myself. I'm Captain George Appleby."

"It's a pleasure to meet you, Captain. I'm Calvin Johnson. Cal is what I like to be called. Do you have a steamboat on the levee?"

"Not right now, young man. However, I am thinking of organizing a cruise to Muscle Shoals on the Tennessee River. The shoals are a most extraordinary feature of a remarkable waterway. Ever been there, son?"

"No. I run my boat on the Mississippi."

"Well, son, at Muscle Shoals the river tries to become a lake, but makes the mistake of running downhill at the same time. It broadens and shallows so the depth changes from two or three feet to a few inches. The river drops tremendously, over one hundred and thirty feet in just thirty-seven miles."

"Can you run a steamboat to such a shallow place?"

"Well, probably not. Come to think about it, there's easier ways to make a buck. Son, do you know that I've been paid more to not run a boat on the Mississippi than to run one?"

"How did you do that?"

Appleby smiled slyly. "I'm a businessman. I've been renting and buying second hand steamboats for forty years. In one deal I got into competition with Eagle packets between St. Louis and Peoria. I cut my rates, ignored insurance premiums, and put off depreciation problems. My spiffy appearance as well as my excellent salesmanship brought me all the business I could handle."

"Hot damn! How long did you do that?"

"Less than a season. Eagle bought me out and paid me a salary to boot. They had me sign a paper to guarantee I wouldn't run another boat in competition with Eagle. In my heyday Cal, I was worth almost a million dollars. I spent it on high living and fancy women between St. Louis and New Orleans. If I could do it all over again, you know what I'd do?"

"You'd change how you did business?"

"I wouldn't change a thing, except maybe try my hand at racing."

"Hot damn! I love racing."

"Cal, you look like an intelligent lad. Have you ever heard of the steamboat race called the Trial of Speed? It was the ultimate race that stirred the world. It started in New Orleans and ended right here in St. Louis."

"Tell me about it."

"I'd love to. Sit down. How about a Virginia Cheroots, my boy?"

"Thanks." Calvin took one of his fancy cigarettes. Captain Appleby lit them with his silver Ronson pocket lighter. They both sat on the fender of the trailer as he told his story.

"The year was 1870. The headline read: *Robt. E. Lee and Natchez Steamboats Race from New Orleans to St. Louis.* Wagers were heavy. Bets were made throughout the country and Europe. The riverboat pilots were famous and experienced."

"Who were the pilots?"

"Captain Leon Leathers was on the Natchez and Captain William Cannon on the Robt. E. Lee. Competition all the way up the river between the boats was fierce. The pilots tried some strategic maneuvers. Captain Cannon lightened his boat for what he thought would be an advantage."

"How do you lighten a steamboat?"

"Cannon removed all the windows and doors and the walls from the cabins on the hurricane decks. He felt it gave him the advantage since the Natchez was an older boat, more heavily loaded with passengers and freight. Despite the changes, the boats steamed along only minutes apart until Cairo, Illinois. That's when heavy fog settled in."

"A fog can slow you down."

"You bet it can. Captain Leathers played it safe. He anchored the Natchez and waited for more than five hours until the fog lifted. On the other hand, Captain Cannon was a risk taker. He pushed on through in the fog and the Robt. E. Lee arrived in St. Louis first, in three days, eighteen hours, and fourteen minutes. The Natchez made it too, but three hours and forty-four minutes later."

"A riverboat captain needs luck."

"Yes, Cal. Luck is an important component in any business."

"I'd like to be a riverboat captain myself. I just completed the paperwork for my motorboat operator's license for vessels up to sixty-five feet."

"That's very interesting. Look Cal." Appleby pointed to the boats out in the river, circling the buoys. "Oh, look. It's time for my favorite race."

"The Free for All is my favorite too. Did you know Buster D. is one of the fastest boats on the river? I've checked out the power plant myself at Mound City. It has an eight cylinder, four-hundred horsepower, air cooled Liberty."

"That big Liberty would be perfect for rum running in the Caribbean."

"Around here it could run hooch from Mosenthein Island to St. Louis."

Captain Appleby laughed. "Cal, you seem to be a peppy lad. If you're serious about being a riverboat captain, you might be interested in working for a friend of mine named Billy Killebrew. He has a steamboat acquisition in the works and he's looking for a young man to train on the helm. Why don't you meet us about six at the Rock House?"

"Thank you. I will," Calvin answered as the big Liberty engine on the Buster D. got hot and very noisy. Calvin covered his ears as the boat took off. The boat driver didn't let up on the gas. The big Liberty engine clanged and knocked until the boat crossed the finish line in a cloud of black smoke. As cheers went up Calvin jumped up and then looked around for Captain Appleby. The old man was gone, but he left a note on a scrap of paper on the trailer fender. It said, "Rock House, Six o'clock. Be there Cal". Calvin stuffed it into his pants pocket. As the smoke subsided, an air-horn whistle blasted from the river.

"Hey Cal!"

Calvin waved to Johnny Zimmer as he circled the race boat, Baby Zim in the river.

"Hey Cal! Come on. Get in. I need a riding mechanic, muy pronto."

"I'll be right there." Calvin grabbed his boots and scurried to pull them on.

"Drop the boots. Come on. I'm on a schedule."

Calvin threw his boots under the trailer and splashed out into the river barefooted. Flinging himself over the gunwales he landed in the seat behind Zimmer. He felt his neck snap back as hydroplane took off at full bore. They were charging for the starting line near the west stone pier of the Eads Bridge.

Looking up from the boat at the bridge, Calvin marveled at the mile long riveted steel trusses. Eads was the first railroad bridge to cross the Mississippi at St. Louis. The bridge was unique. Beneath the pedestrian and streetcar bridge stood a double railroad track that ran into the tunnel under Washington Avenue to the Mill Creek. Soon Baby Zim and the other boats bobbed at the red start buoy.

"Hang on, kiddo. It's time for the gun."

BANG!

It was a near perfect flying start at the gun. Baby Zim, half out of the water forward, bounced and splashed. The big Texan stood up and crouched over the steering wheel like a jockey urging his race horse on. Dixie Darling, a gleaming white Hacker, emerged from the smoke like a ghost from a cemetery. The spectators cheered as the big white racer slid through the fleet of boats into the lead. Calvin held on to the gunwales for dear life. The noise, spray, and engine smoke befuddled his senses.

Baby Zim, like a panther chasing its prey, raced wide with her bow in the air. Causing more than a flutter of excitement, the hydroplane crossed into the Hacker's wake. Johnny Zimmer veered the boat sharply across the chop, and then veered back again. The flying spray drenched the boat. Calvin hung on until his knuckles turned white.

Finally Baby Zim straightened her course as the Texan pushed the throttle all the way forward. All eight cylinders thumped and howled. They flew on top of the water and danced into the lead. Dixie Darling disappeared into the smoke behind them. Half drowned from the spray Calvin wiped his eyes and continued to hang on. Baby Zim took the gun in a wild salute of whistles and shouts echoing from people on the bank. She crossed two boat lengths ahead of the competition.

The flashy Texan posed for a series of pictures for the Post Dispatch photographer. With his folding Kodak

Calvin took his own pictures to remember this special day. Zimmer basked in the glory of the win, while Calvin stood next to him trying to look important.

"Let's load the boat, Cal. I've got a date at the Mayfair for a Texas-style extravaganza."

"Yes, sir."

Johnny Zimmer backed the truck and trailer down the cobblestone levee. Calvin sloshed into the water and handed him the bow line. As he hauled Baby Zim onto the trailer, Calvin tugged the anchor line out of the muddy river bottom. Everything went smoothly as they brought the boat back to the landing.

"Wipe her down, son and take care of things here. Enjoy the rest of the day. I'll see you in a couple of hours after the party with the oilmen at the Mayfair. Everything's Jake!"

"You can count on me. I'll be right here. Yeah! Everything's Jake!"

Calvin took a breath and pulled the wet note out his pocket. "Rock House, Six o'clock. Be there, Cal". Checking his watch he still had a couple of hours, so pulled a blanket out of the truck and spread it out next to the trailer. With a smile, Calvin stretched out to watch the finale.

A voice called from behind. "Bon jour Calvin."

Calvin turned around to see a lovely face smiling down. She sat down on the blanket, untied her chestnut hair, and kicked off her shoes. "Anne Marie. What a surprise!"

"Is this lovely boat yours?"

"No. It belongs to a rich oilman from Texas."

"How do you find such beautiful boats?"

"The same way beautiful women know how to find me. What are you doing here?"

"I've been working downtown for a few weeks. My cousin Armand has a fur store on Locust Street. I couldn't resist walking down to the big party on the levee."

A Jenny airplane roared overhead as Calvin shouted, "Let's watch the finale. It's the Match Race. It's between a boat and an airplane."

Anne Marie cuddled up next to him on the blanket. "An airplane seems to have an unfair advantage in a boat race."

"Don't underestimate the Miss St. Louis. That boat can do more than sixty miles per hour. It's a worthwhile competitor against the Jenny. The plane will have to do better than sixty to stay in the air. A daredevil named Charles Lindbergh is the pilot."

They covered their ears as the airplane buzzed low over the crowd.

"Does Charles Lindbergh always fly underneath the arches of the Eads Bridge?"

"Only when he's showing off."

The plane buzzed and swooped under and over the Eads and Free Bridges. Lindbergh lost time. The airplane wasn't as maneuverable as the nimble Miss St. Louis. The plane emerged from the first lap under the Free Bridge at an altitude of twenty five feet, within feet of the cruisers anchored across the river.

"Look Calvin, isn't that the Georgia Lee from the sandbar?"

"Yes it is. And that's Captain Leroy McMillan standing on the forward deck in full dress attire."

"Oh, No! The airplane brushed the boat! Someone's in the water!"

"Ha! Ha! Ha! I hope Leroy can swim."

They both laughed as McMillan clumsily treaded water with his white pants and blue flannel blazer. Finally a passenger on the boat threw him a life ring. Lindbergh gave Leroy a happy wing tilt as the Jenny crossed the finish line ahead of the boat. The crowd cheered.

Anne Marie put on her patent leather shoes. "My fun is over. It's time to get back to work."

"Are you sure you have to go?"

"Yes. There are still many hours of sorting and marking on the coats. If you have time, stop by Armand's Furs on Locust and Tenth Streets. I sell in the front." Anne Marie waved and quickly disappeared into the crowd.

"Hello kiddo," called a voice from behind the fender.

Calvin waved to the Texan. "Your boat's ready to go."

"I'm kind of spifflicated," slurred Zimmer. "I got a room at the Mayfair to sleep off this whiskey. I'll be heading home tomorrow."

"Did you watch the Match Race? Lindbergh did some pretty fancy flying."

"Pretty risky flying if you ask me. But I think Leroy McMillan will be remembering the day for a long time."

"Yes, sir."

Zimmer handed Calvin a handful of Double Eagles. "I won these shiny beauties in a poker game today. They should be more than enough for your time."

Calvin cupped his hands to hold all the coins. "Thanks."

Johnny Zimmer waved from the truck as he and Baby Zim bumped across the cobblestone levee to the Mayfair Hotel on St. Charles Street.

CHAPTER 3

THE OLD ROCK HOUSE

With two pocketfuls of Double Eagles and more memories than Calvin could fit into a day he headed to the Rock House to meet Captain Appleby.

Scores of parked cars wound down from the river-facing Front Street. Commercial Alley stood behind it. The elevated railroad lines ran parallel to the river. When the river flooded Front Street, people used the back entrances on Commercial Alley to do business. The limestone bluff along the river afforded an opening in the sandy levee that became an east and west gap called Market Street.

The first floor of the nineteenth century brick buildings on Commercial Alley between Chestnut and Market Streets housed the offices of the steamboat agents. Inexpensive fares in the 1850s created many competitive boats. Over six hundred steamboats arrived daily. Grandpa Coolidge as well as Calvin's mother, Helen, loved riding boats. Fares between St. Louis and New Orleans cost $15 for cabin passengers and $3 for deck passage. The St. Louis to St. Paul run was $21. Grandpa said it was almost as cheap to ride a steamboat as to stay home.

On the way to the Rock House Calvin walked past Little Bohemia which occupied the lower level of one of the old brick buildings on Commercial Alley. The speakeasy was a favorite St. Louis gathering place. It belonged to a colorful artist named Salo Radulovich. He wove his batiks in the front, while in the back he ran the club. Calvin couldn't resist a peek in the door.

"Hello, Salo."

Salo was on a ladder dusting batiks on the front wall. "Good evening, Calvin."

"How are you? Every time I see your batiks I think I'm in the St. Louis Art Museum."

"Thank you, Calvin. I love working with the deep greens and blues. They remind me of my native Serbia." Salo climbed down and handed Calvin the duster. "Would you like to keep the artwork clean for me?"

"No Salo. I can barely keep my own clothes clean. I don't see your beautiful daughter. Is she here?"

"Christina is out of town with her mother."

"Do you think she might like to catch Josephine Baker's show at the Rock House when she gets back?"

"I thought you knew that Josephine left town for a new job in New York City. She joined the cast of Shuffle Along."

"That's do bad for St. Louis. She'll be missed."

"During the holidays Belva and I took a train to New York. We bought tickets to Josephine's Negro Revue. She was quite sensual with her globe performance."

"Globe performance? What do you mean, Salo?"

"Think about this. The club darkens. The jazz music plays. This immense globe covered with flowers lowers from the ceiling. The globe opens. Josephine stands tall on a mirror with nothing on except a raffia shirt. She smiles and dances the Charleston. Then she waves to the audience and re-enters the globe. It closes and she is hoisted back to the ceiling."

"Hot damn! If I had the money I'd take the next train to New York City."

"Josephine Baker is a world class performer."

"Who took Josephine's place at the club?"

"A girl named Ann Richardson. She is six feet tall and as graceful as a panther in her satin, ankle length gowns."

"Does she sing or dance?"

"Ann sings like an angel, but she draws an audience because of her other specialties."

"What specialties, Salo?"

"Among other things she can pick up tips from the tables with her shapely thighs."

"What happens if I glue a fin to the table top?"

"Believe me, that won't slow her down."

"When is Christina coming back Salo?"

"Next week."

"Hello, Salo. Hello Cal."

Salo turned around and waved toward Will Chambers who sat down at a table near the door. "How's your boat building coming?"

"Fine, thank you. My boats are selling very well, Salo. It's the water taxi business that can't seem to get off the ground."

Calvin waved and smiled sheepishly. "I guess I forgot about the meeting at Boatman's. I'm sorry."

"They refused the loan."

"What happened? A water taxi is a great investment."

"The bank officers were hard-boiled realists. They said my boat business didn't have enough equity. If you would have bothered to show up and had a job we might have had a better chance to get a loan."

"Will, I'm really sorry. I forgot. I've had a lot of things on my mind. My prospects might be changing. I'm meeting with a man about a job tonight. Couldn't we try to file new loan papers next week?"

Will shook his head in disgust. "I don't know. You've got to be serious."

Bells rang. Bells from the Cathedral. Six o'clock.

"I am serious Will, but I've got to go. It's time for me to see a man about a job. Tell Christina I was looking for her Salo. I'll talk to you later Will."

Calvin ran down Commercial Alley passed a popular speakeasy. The Blue Lantern was a gathering place for would-be poets and philosophers. Soft-glowing lanterns lit up the interior of the club. As the weather warmed up, customers brought the beat-up tables and chairs out of the hot-brick building and into the street. Poetry readings, cool jazz, and cold brew highlighted the sultry summer nights.

At Front Street a group of rowdy roustabouts pushed their way passed him. Calvin jumped off the curb to stay out of their way. Roustabouts were a major part of river life. These strong men rolled casks, kegs, and boxes ashore. At work on the boats they carried burlap bags of tomatoes and potatoes, crates of cockerels, baskets of eggs, and other commodities. This evening the roustabouts were off duty and little drunk. They pushed and shoved. Calvin dodged them by staying next to the gangplanks of the Streckfus and Eagle steamboats.

Scores of people waited on the levee for steamers. In the 1850's steamboats were stacked three deep and a mile long, but not today. Now barges, not steamers, took over river commerce. They more easily unloaded onto nearby rail cars. In 1928 St. Louis epitomized the center of the country's industry with shoe and street car factories, retail stores, and hardwood lumber markets.

As Calvin continued his run to the Rock House a headline in the St. Louis Post Dispatch newspaper stood out on the top of a stack of papers at a corner newsstand. He stopped. It said the last paddlewheel packet company, the Diamond Jo Line that operated boats between St Louis and St. Paul, sold out to Streckfus. Streckfus was converting the three Diamond Jo's steamers into excursion boats with large dance floors. Streckfus planned on keeping one boat on the St. Louis wharf, while others would tramp up and down the Mississippi stopping at smaller river towns in the summer. The Excursion Queen St. Paul was scheduled for dance marathon from St. Louis to Venice, Illinois.

Calvin ran hard the last two blocks until he spotted the Rock House. The brick building stood under the elevated railway line at Chestnut and First Streets. The first floor housed Gus' Greek Restaurant, while a night club, black-run for white customers, occupied the second floor. Ann Richardson's name and exotic photographs appeared on the Rock House marquee. It was almost six thirty when Calvin stumbled through the door of the Gus' Restaurant.

"Where are your customers Gus? There was a crowd on the levee today."

"Visitors don't come down here Calvin."

"You got pork chops for supper?"

Gus threw his hands in the air. "This is no first class place. Pork chops, no sell," stammered Gus in broken English. "Got pig tails, pig jowls, pig ears, pig snouts, and pig feet."

Being ignorant of the delicacies of the pig, Calvin selected the last part of the pig he could remember from Gus' list. "How about a plate of pig's feet with cornbread? And bring me a frosty bucket. Anybody looking for me?"

"Nobody's been here just you."

Calvin sat down at a table near the door. He hoped Captain Appleby's invitation was the real McCoy. His mind wandered. As he looked out the window he imagined the great steamboats days and the Rock House in St. Louis history.

In the early 1830's the Rock House was Manuel Lisa's warehouse outfitting hunters and traders for expeditions on the rivers. Returning voyagers with canoes loaded with deer and beaver pelts sold them to Manuel Lisa and his business partner, Pierre Chouteau, who exported them to the noblemen of Europe.

Thirty years later the Rock House housed offices of steamboat agents, who set cargo for dozens of steamers lining up two and three deep along the levee from Chouteau to Ashley Streets. Those were the days of the elegant and beautiful steamboats like the Robt. E. Lee, the Natchez, the Great Republic, and the J.M. White.

The J. M. White was the cat's pajamas! The boat was the fastest paddle wheeler on the river. It had elaborate steamboat gothic carpentry, fancy lettering, and tall chimneys with ornamental feathers on top. The grand saloon of the boat held rows of elegant staterooms, stained-glass windows, and a ceiling supported by ornate columns and connecting arches in lacelike patterns. The J.M. had unmatched elegance with carpeted decks and illuminated crystal chandeliers equipped with lamps. Richly upholstered and hand-carved furniture, rosewood paneling, a grand piano, and a silver water cooler with silver drinking cups completed the opulence of this one-of-a-kind steamboat.

By the early twenties the levee was paved with cobblestones and railroads running down the center. Steamboats were still the heart and soul of St. Louis. They carried explorers, fur traders, wilderness hunters, soldiers, emigrant families, circuses, theatrical companies, tourists, raftmen, and card sharks. They towed or carried salt, sugar cane, hogsheads of sugar and molasses, tobacco, cotton, rice, corn, wheat, potatoes, mussel shells, coal, logs, barrel staves, railroad ties, mine props, sulphur, potash, and sisal. By 1928 only a dozen steamers landed daily including the Eagle packets and boats from the Streckfus and Lee lines.

The sound of the magnificent foghorn voice brought Calvin's daydream to a screeching halt. "Gus, how about a couple of plates of roasted pig's feet with your mouth-watering cornbread."

Calvin looked around to see Captain Appleby and a tall, squinty-eyed man in a wrinkled pinstripe suit standing at the door. They walked over to Calvin's table.

"Good evening, Captain."

"Good evening, Calvin. May we join you?"

"Sure."

Glancing at the camera on the table, the squinty-eyed man sat down next to Calvin. "Do any photography for money?"

"Yes. I've sold a few photographs."

"Do you live around there?"

"Granite City."

"I live on the east side too. The Killebrews own the land at the eastern end of Horseshoe Lake. My Daddy and his brother operate the Horseshoe Tavern."

"Calvin, I'd like you to meet Billy Killebrew," said Appleby pulling up a chair. "He's putting together a new business venture."

"I'm pleased to meet you, Mr. Killebrew." Calvin extended his hand, but Killebrew ignored him.

Killebrew looked Calvin in the eye. "Captain Appleby tells me you know a lot about boats."

"Yes, sir. I just filed papers for my motorboat operator's license for a vessel up to sixty-five feet. I'm starting a water-taxi business on the wharf, but being a riverboat captain is what I'd really like to do."

"Being a riverboat captain is a noble profession, but to be successful, a man needs a mentor and experience. I'm buying an excursion steamer. I'm looking for a young man to train as captain. Are you interested?"

Calvin's mouth dropped open. "Tell me more."

Race Boat Baby Zim

CHAPTER 4

GREAT STEAMBOAT VENTURE

The burly man walked briskly down Front Street. Billy Killebrew was known around town as a small-time politician and a big-time promoter of unscrupulous practices. Billy gravitated toward deals that lined his pockets with cash at the expense of others. His office was in a row building on Commercial Alley.

Billy lit up a cigar. He scanned the waterfront for Mike Muldoon. Between a coal barge and the Excursion Queen St. Paul he spotted the old man snoozing on a piece of comfortable-looking driftwood with his fishing pole in hand. The cork at the end of his line was making circles in the water.

"Good morning, Captain Mike. Catch any big ones?"

The old man awoke with a start and jerked the line straight out of the water. "Gol damn! That's the second time today I lost a big cat."

"I guess you heard the gossip going around town?"

"If you're talking about the Cincinnati Packet Company's going belly-up. I sure did. George Appleby told me."

"They closed their doors for good last week. But I'm thinking it might be good opportunity for us."

"What kind of a scheme you got in mind?"

"It's not a scheme, Mike. It's an opportunity."

"Look Billy, Appleby told me the best boats were bought by Streckfus. They're rebuilding the Cincinnati into a plush steamer for the St. Louis riverfront. What kind of opportunities are you talking about?"

"Wasn't there another older steamboat up for grabs?"

"Yes, but I wouldn't get involved with the Hubbard. It's a tired old boat with a tarnish reputation."

"If I can get it cheap, it might be the right boat for an excursion steamer business."

"Forget it. A twenty year old steamboat's got too many ghosts. Look Billy, you don't want to be locking horns with Streckfus. J. S. has no intention of giving up his monopoly of all that lucrative steamer business."

"Captain Mike, I'm not going to compete with Streckfus. I was thinking more of a steamboat venture on the Missouri River. That river is wide open for excursion boats with new names and altered logs."

"If you're serious, son, you better get it done. The Reconstruction Financial Corporation is selling the Hubbard to the highest bidder this Friday."

"I plan to be there. Captain Mike, how would you like to get involved?"

"What can I do?"

"Today I filled out the paperwork for the Killebrew Navigation Company at the law office. I need one more investor. How would you like be in the excursion boat business?"

"Billy, the Hubbard's got a lot of unanswered questions hanging over it. Besides, I'm almost eighty years old. I don't have cash for investing or the energy for working full time."

"Don't sell yourself short. I'm not looking for money from you. Do you still have your master pilot's license for the Missouri River?"

"Reckon I do."

"To get a bank loan to make this excursion business a reality, I need the expertise of a seasoned river man. Mike, that license of yours would make it a lot easier to complete the paperwork."

"Billy, I haven't been on a boat in years, except for fishing with Old Rudy in his rowboat."

"Don't worry, you won't actually be piloting. I recruited a young guy for that job. He's got boat experience and he's working on a motorboat operator's license. I know that after lessons from you, he'll be able to handle the boat."

"Is he serious about learning to be a riverboat captain?"

"He said he'd welcome the hard work."

"I might be interested. Do I know this young fella?"

"No. His name is Calvin Johnson. He's not working right now, but he knows boats and engines and makes no bones about having his sights set on being a riverboat captain. I know with a little help from this energetic young man we can fulfill our dreams of riches."

It was sunny Monday morning in May. Pink redbuds and daffodil bulbs brightened the road as Calvin crossed the McKinley Bridge from Granite City to St. Louis. This morning he packed his valise for the trip to the steamboat. He stopped first at Boatman's Bank on Broadway where he withdrew his savings account. After stuffing the cash into his pocket he cranked up his Ford. Whistling a catchy tune Calvin Johnson started out on an adventure of a lifetime.

The wharf traffic bustled with cars and people as he drove to Billy Killebrew's downtown office. His trailered outboard bumped along behind the Ford. It took a couple of times around the block before Calvin found a place to park big enough for his car with a boat trailer behind it.

Walking down the street Calvin nervously slicked back his hair as he searched for Killebrew's office. Finally he found 20A Commercial Alley. Glancing up the outside iron staircase made his heart pound. His life was finally changing for the better. Hot Damn! With his travel bag clutched in his sweaty hand Calvin leaped the steps two at a time and knocked on the door.

"Come in," called a husky, but feminine voice.

Calvin's smile faded as he opened the door.

Light streamed in the front window illuminating the stark interior with frayed wallpaper. A huge spider stood between Calvin and the dusty drape. He brushed it down and stepped on it. The room was musty with the smell of stale cigar smoke. A dingy photograph of Horseshoe Lake with the Killebrew's Tavern in the background stood on the wall. Guys from the tavern posed in suits and ties holding stringers of big fish. They looked overdressed for the occasion.

Finally the middle-aged woman with heavy owl-like glasses looked up from her typewriter. The name plate with 'Mrs. Myrtle R. Goodwall' stood out prominently on her desk. She stood up and towered over Calvin. "What can I do for you?"

Calvin slowly looked up into the chest this tall, gaunt woman with a sharp nose and the voice of a deckhand. "I'm Calvin Johnson. I'm here to see Mr. Killebrew."

"Are you the guy that Billy's got watching the old steamboat in Jeffersonville?"

"I'm going to Jeffersonville to learn the excursion boat business."

"That's a bit of a stretch. Billy's in the back. Go ahead." She pointed at the curtain and continued working at the desk.

"Thanks."

Clutching his valise in one hand, Calvin parted the curtains. Billy Killebrew sat at his desk reading the newspaper. It was a messy place with letters and papers everywhere. The drapes were closed to hubbub traffic of the streets, but allowed dim daylight to filter into the room. The same unflattering photograph of the Horseshoe Tavern hung on the wall behind him.

"Hello, Mr. Killebrew."

Killebrew looked up from his desk. "You should have left the bag in your car, Johnson. Sit down."

"Yes, sir." Calvin tripped over an enormous brass spittoon and fell in the chair next to Killebrew's desk. He slid his valise under his feet. "Thank you for the job. I'm looking forward to the trip to Jeffersonville and learning the steamboat business."

"Yes Cal, I'm counting on you to handle things in Jeffersonville until I've got financing for the boat secured. Here's a twenty to get you started. I'll wire you money periodically. How's that sound to you?"

"Sounds good. Thank you, Mr. Killebrew."

"When my investors are finalized, I'll contact you. We'll have the Hubbard outfitted with new engines and the furnishings of an elegant Missouri River excursion steamer."

"Where's the boat?"

"It's anchored just east of the Howard Shipyard. Maybe we'll negotiate with the shipyards to refurbish the steamer for us?"

"Good idea! The Howard Shipyards have outfitted the finest packets in the world."

"Yes. They have quite a reputation. Since you brought your travel bag, I'm assuming you're ready to go?"

"Yes, sir. I can leave right away."

"Great. Remember, this is an opportunity of a lifetime."

"I know. You can count on me."

"Keep in touch. Update me on the boat."

"Yes, sir. Thank you, sir. I'll update you on the progress weekly."

"Weekly is definitely too often. I'll tell you what Cal. I'll contact you. I'll send you a telegram when the financial arrangements are completed. It might be awhile."

"That will be fine, Mr. Killebrew. I'm looking forward to driving to Jeffersonville. It should be a grand adventure."

"Adventure is an interesting way to look at it. One man's adventure is another man's nightmare." He laughed. "Good luck Cal."

"I'll be waiting for your telegram." Billy reopened his newspaper and brusquely waved Calvin out. "Thank you, sir." Calvin grabbed his bag, waved at Mrs. Goodwall and skipped the steps two at a time to the street.

With sweaty palms and a smile on his face Calvin stuffed his bag in the back of his jalopy. He checked the trailer tires and the ropes holding the boat on the trailer. As he cranked up the Ford, Calvin heard a familiar sexy voice behind his ear.

"Bonjour Calvin. How are you doing today? Do you have time to spend with an old friend?"

"I'm great Anne Marie."

"Do you have time for an old friend?"

"I love spending time with you, but I'm in a hurry. I'm leaving town for a new job."

"Can I go with you? My bag and paints are ready to go at the store."

"I'm heading to a steamboat in Jeffersonville. Do you want to go all the way to Indiana?"

"Yes, Indiana sounds fine to me. I really must get out of this town. I am fed up with Armand and the fur business."

"Okay. Get your things. I'll meet you in twenty minutes in front of the Blue Lantern."

"Thank you, Calvin. I'll be there."

After Calvin gassed up his jalopy he rumbled over the cobblestones to the club. Waiting for Anne Marie his mind wandered.

In his daydream he sat back in his custom-made Italian leather chair in the pilot house of the elegant John W. Hubbard. Adjusting his new captain's cap with shiny gold braid, Calvin Johnson gazed out the windows to the river.

"If luxury and comfort are what they want, then that is what I'll give them. My steamboat's as fine as the J. M. White: ornate, commodious, and sumptuous. The Hubbard sets a standard never equaled on the Missouri River with sterling silver flatware, china decorated with hand-painted boats, and Irish linen napkins. It has wooden parquet floors, hand carved molding and embellishments on the walls and ceiling, stain glass windows and skylights, wall-to-wall carpeting, and smartly upholstered furniture. The John W. Hubbard is an excursion boat everyone will remember."

"Bonjour Calvin." Anne Marie tapped on his jalopy door.

His daydream evaporated as reality set in. "Hello, Anne Marie."

"I'll put my things in the back. It looks like there's plenty of room for Jean Claude between us."

"Are you positive that you want to go all the way to Indiana?"

"Yes, any place would be better than Armand's smelly fur store. Come Jean Claude. We are going to a wonderful place called Indiana." The dog jumped in the front seat next to Calvin. She plopped in the front next to the dog and grabbed the road map. "Thank you again, Calvin. You are always ready to help a lady in distress."

"Did you tell the people at the fur company that you're leaving?"

"No. Armand will know I am gone when he looks in the cash register."

"You took money from the cash register?"

"Oui. Only my salary. I am a hard worker." Anne Marie stuffed a roll of bills in her corset.

"Fine. I'm taking the route over the Free Bridge through East St. Louis."

"I am good at reading maps. I will be your navigator. Jean Claude is always a good rider," remarked Anne Marie as she spread the map out in her lap. "Let's not doddle Calvin. Armand will soon realize this week's receipts are gone." The dog barked approvingly.

The old Ford chugged over the Free Bridge and bumped through the smoky industrial areas of East St. Louis. Highway 50 headed out of town to the Illinois farm country. Jean Claude dozed with his head in Anne Marie's lap while Anne Marie dozed with her head on Calvin's shoulder.

Without a gas gauge, Calvin decided to fill up at a Standard Gas Station in Salem near the Wabash River. As he pumped gas, Anne Marie woke up.

"Are we in Indiana already?"

"No. This is the farm land of Illinois. How about eating lunch on the banks of the Wabash River? I have a basket of goodies in the back."

"Wonderful! Jean Claude and I need to stretch. Do you have enough food?"

"Sure. Come on." Calvin grabbed the basket and ran down the hill toward the river. Anne Marie and her dog followed him. On a big piece of driftwood Calvin unpacked the bologna sandwiches and two Coca-Colas that his mother packed for him. They ate silently admiring the plum, crabapple, and persimmon trees entangled with grapevines on the river bottom land. The trees were budding. The flowers were beautiful and fragrant.

"I read in a book that at the Wabash River the forests march west to meet the prairies marching east. Come on Calvin." Anne Marie grabbed Calvin's hand and pulled him along the river path. They walked through the bottomland lined with groves of pecan trees. Up on the hill early flowering apple trees filled the horizon.

A grizzly old man stepped out from behind a pecan tree. "What are you doing on my land?"

Calvin and Anne Marie stopped. The old man pointed a shot gun at Calvin's head.

"We just stopped for lunch."

"These are lovely apple trees," added Anne Marie. She picked up Jean Claude who was whimpering softly.

The man put his gun on the ground. "That orchard belongs to me. Apple trees are an easy way to farm. No planting seed. No plowing fields. I just have to spray for bugs and rebuild the mud road to the ferry to bring the apple crop to market."

"We've got to get back to the road. It's getting late. I really enjoyed hearing about farming apples, but I've got a job in Jeffersonville, Indiana."

With arms folded, the old man squinted at Calvin. "Is that your Ford and boat trailer sitting in the river?"

"That's not where I left them."

Calvin turned and bolted toward the water. Anne Marie and her dog followed. At the bank he saw his beloved Baby Wildcat floating in the river. The rear tires of the Ford were halfway mired in mud.

"You'll be needing some help," remarked the farmer. "Why don't you walk back to the house with me? I'll get my truck and a tow chain."

"Thanks. I'm Calvin Johnson. I guess my brakes weren't up to the job. And this is my friend, Anne Marie, and her dog."

"I'm Ed Fox. Calvin, I had a problem like yours last year at the ferry landing at Riverton. Almost drown my Oldsmobile Touring Car. It's a long story. I'll tell you as we walk. The house is about a half mile up the road."

"Thanks again."

As they walked Ed talked and talked and talked. "We were coming back from church in the Touring Car. The back seat was loaded with apples and a crate of chickens. My daughters were perched cross-legged on the top of the chicken crate as we crept down the hill. At the ferry my brakes let go. Helga, my wife, screamed. 'Brace yourself, girls. I can't stop', I called. At the last possible moment I made a hard turn, straight into the river."

"Was anyone hurt?" asked Anne Marie.

"My girls hardly noticed. They never stopped talking. They take after me, I guess. Helga, on the other hand, gave me the eagle eye with her cold silence. Luckily my Oldsmobile came to rest in only a foot of water. I walked back to the house to get my helper, Henry. He got the Touring Car going and we all went home for Sunday dinner."

It was a short walk up the gravel road to Ed's place. The driver's door of a well-used farm truck was open next to the house. Inside the truck was a burly, bare-chested, sandy haired man about Calvin's age. He wore patched overalls and no shoes. Stretched out on the front seat of the truck under a newspaper he snored loudly.

Anne Marie and Calvin looked at Ed.

"Who's he?" Calvin asked.

Ed grabbed the newspaper. "Henry, you lout! Wake up! Did you finish my fence?"

"Not yet. Not yet!" Henry answered springing up with wide eyes.

"What about spraying my trees?"

"Not yet! Not yet!"

"I pay you to work Henry. What have you been doing all day?"

With a serious look on his face Henry said. "Been doing some koosen around."

"Henry, I'm tired of your alibis. I know what your koosen around means."

"You know what it means?"

"It means being all dressed up ready to work, and then sitting on your tail all day and sleeping. That's what it means! Make yourself useful, Henry. This here is Calvin Johnson. Calvin has a car and trailer in the river. Put a chain on the truck and go help him get out."

"Yes, sir," answered Henry as he smiled at Anne Marie. She waved. Jean Claude growled.

"Anne Marie and her dog can stay here with my girls. Hurry back for supper. I shot a dozen pheasants this week. Helga cooked them up with pecan stuffing and apple sauce. My daughter Bess made an apple pie."

"That sounds like a meal from a fancy restaurant. We'll be back in a jiffy to enjoy that spread."

"Come on Calvin," snarled Henry. "Get in the truck." We're going to the river. What happened to your car anyway?"

"I guess my brake wasn't set."

"Is Anne Marie your wife?"

"No. She's a friend. I've got a job in Jeffersonville. She needed a change of scenery, so she came with me. Did Ed really shoot a dozen pheasants?"

"He likes to think so. We hunt together, but I do most of the shooting. I'm a crack shot. Ed picks out a bird in a string of birds flying overhead. I shoot down the one he picks. I never miss. By the way Calvin, Anne Marie is a very beautiful woman."

"Yes she is."

"I like women with big breasts and long legs."

Calvin frowned and leaped out when they reached the river. "Henry, I'll put on the chain and you do the pulling." He tried to direct Henry, but for the most part Henry ignored him. The big fellow put on the chain himself and pulled out the car and trailer to the gravel road his way.

"You'll have to leave it here with the brake on overnight."

"I have a job waiting for me in Jeffersonville, Indiana."

"It's too wet. You'll have trouble starting it. Relax. There's always tomorrow."

"I guess you're right. Thanks, Henry. You need some help fixing the fence?"

"Nope. It's time for supper. I got plenty of time for doing work tomorrow."

Henry and Calvin drove the truck to the red brick house at the end of the gravel road. Jean Claude was sprawled out on the porch, chewing on a bone. Inside the door sat Ed Fox in his overstuffed green chair with a washtub full of pecans in front of him.

"Sit down, boys. We'll have some fresh pecans while Helga and the girls put supper on the table. Don't just stand there Calvin, sit down next to Heidelberg. He don't bite."

"Sure Ed."

Calvin reluctantly sat on the divan next to a long-legged yellow mutt that farted and snored. Henry plopped into the old rocker and fooled with the radio on the table. Ed took care in cracking the nuts. In a crystal bowl Ed placed the perfect pecan halves. The broken pieces he put in a paper bag.

"Have some nuts," said Ed.

Calvin grabbed a handful of pecans. When he sat back his seat was taken. Heidelberg stretched out across the entire divan, so Calvin stood up to munch on the nuts.

"Time to eat," announced Helga as the girls put the plates of food on the dining room table.

"Boy, dinner smells great." Calvin walked over to an open chair next to Anne Marie.

In a flash Henry slid passed him into the chair. "I'll sit here."

Calvin looked perplexed and sat in the last open chair on the other side of the table between two of Ed's homely daughters. Mouthwatering aromas filled the air. The spread looked like Thanksgiving and Christmas all rolled into one. Roasted pheasant, pecan stuffing, apple sauce, freshly shelled peas, bread and butter, and the most gorgeous apple pie filled the table. Everyone ate without much conversation.

"This pie must have been made with perfect apples," added Calvin as he moved his belt a notch bigger.

"We never get to eat the perfect apples," snapped Ed's most opinionated daughter, Bess. "The perfect apples are always harvested first. Perfect apples are always placed on the bottom of the bushel in special protected baskets. Daddy always sells the perfect apples."

"I don't understand you, Bess," said Ed. "These not-so-perfect apples are the ones sent to the cider mill to make delicious cider. After all, the apples with the bad spots are free. These are the apples that make the best apple butter, apple sauce, and apples pies for us."

"We deserve the best too, Daddy." Bess got up and stomped away into the kitchen.

Henry and Anne Marie disappeared after supper for a walk along the river while Calvin listened to the radio with Ed. About eight o'clock Anne Marie bunked with the girls on the featherbed upstairs while Calvin slept on a pallet on the living room floor next to Jean Claude.

Being exhausted and eating too much food caused Calvin's imagination to race. He looked up at the ceiling dreaming of tomorrow's road trip. In his dream the truck ahead skidded off the icy, snowy road. He watched as the boat and trailer jackknife into the ditch. Naturally, Calvin stopped. As he approached the truck a short, heavy-set man with a curly white beard climbed out of the cab.

"Got a rope?" asked the jolly gent.

"Sure."

"Can I use your car?"

"Sure. Can I take pictures with my folding Kodak camera?"

"Sure."

The jolly gent, with the curly white beard, did a magnificent job of pulling his trailer out of the ditch while Calvin took pictures.

"These are photographs for the East St. Louis Journal," Calvin called as the jolly gent cranked up his truck and jumped in.

The man with the white beard waved and pushed over the wrapped boxes that filled his truck. As the snow covered his windshield the jolly gent called, "Merry Christmas to all and to all a good night."

"Merry Christmas to all and to all a good night," echoed Calvin.

"What are you talking about Calvin?" asked Henry as he shook him. "It's not Christmas and it's not night."

"What? Is it snowing?" Calvin rubbed his eyes.

"It's morning and it's not snowing. It's spring Calvin. We haven't had a snow for months. Your Ford's dried out. I cranked her up and she's running fine. I got your car and trailer pointed to the highway. It's all ready to go."

"Thanks, Henry." Calvin slipped on his boots and slicked back his unruly hair.

"Bonjour Calvin." Anne Marie stood next to him. She had her paints and easel in her hands. "I'm going to paint apple trees by the river until Helga needs me in the kitchen."

"The car's cranked up and ready to go, Anne Marie."

"I'm not."

"But I've got a job Jeffersonville. We've been here too long already."

"You go Calvin. Jean Claude and I are staying here."

"Are you sure that's what you want to do?"

"Yes. Ed is paying me to teach his daughters to paint. I think it will be a fine opportunity for me. Thank you for the ride. Good luck on your new job."

"I'll be at the John W. Hubbard steamboat near the Howard Shipyards if you get tired of painting."

"Au revoir," she whispered as she gave him a peck on the cheek.

Anne Marie waved as Calvin walked with Henry to the Ford. Henry opened the door and put his bag on the seat. "Have a good trip."

"Where's Ed? I'd like to say good-bye."

"Ed's working. This is a farm, Calvin. Everybody works, except me of course. I'll be koosen around."

"I can't be koosen around. I've got a job on a steamboat in Jeffersonville, Indiana. Thank everyone for their fine hospitality."

Calvin got in the Ford, slicked his hair with a little spit, and then turned east toward Indiana. He pressed the gas petal to the floor to make up some time. The jalopy rolled along effortlessly until Vincennes, Indiana. This gas station was his last stop before Jeffersonville.

Railroad tracks joined him alongside the road. The white sandstone buildings in the towns replaced the red brick of St. Louis. In a couple of hours the sign for town of New Albany came into view. New Albany, Indiana was the last town above the Falls of the Ohio River. Jeffersonville was the first town below the rapids. The metropolis of Louisville, Kentucky stood across the river. At the Jeffersonville road sign Calvin pulled off. He headed up Spring Street to the river. Crossing the railroad tracks he drove seven more blocks until he spotted a paved landing for ferry boats and a Shell Gas Station. He pulled in. A dark haired, dark eyed man in greasy overalls was leaning against the pump reading the Jeffersonville Evening News.

"Good morning." Calvin walked over to him, leaving his jalopy running.

"What do you want?"

"How do I get to the Howard Shipyards?"

The man looked up. "Who the hell are you?"

"I'm Cal Johnson. Captain Cal Johnson." He knew this wasn't exactly the truth but he did have trailered outboard and an official motorboat operator's license. Calvin didn't have a master pilot's papers, but this guy at the Shell Gas Station didn't have to know that.

"Well, Captain Cal Johnson go back a couple blocks. That's Market Street. It turns into the Utica Pike. Take Market Street about two miles. You can't miss the Shipyards because it takes up four city blocks between the Pike and the river. I'm Gus Shapiro. I own this gas station."

"Thanks, Gus."

"What's your business in Port Fulton?"

"Port Fulton? Where's Port Fulton?"

"It's where you're heading Captain."

"I thought I was going to Jeffersonville."

"Not on the river side of the Pike. When you pass the Howard place, you're in Port Fulton."

"Then I guess I'm going to Port Fulton."

"You got a job at the yard?"

"No. I'm watching a steamboat anchored on the river. It's called the John W. Hubbard. We're getting financing to make her an excursion steamer."

"I know that old steamboat. The hull is bad and her engines are shot. It'll take a bundle of money to make that boat run. You got a bundle of money?"

"Not exactly, but my boss and I are optimistic about the Hubbard's future. How do I find the boat?"

"Captain Cal, let me give you some pointers, seeing you're new to Port Fulton. Port Fultonites aren't optimistic and they don't take kindly to strangers. If you're going to the river, you'll pass the Howard's place. Don't stop. Go another three blocks to the grocery store on Main Street."

"Will they help me find the steamboat?"

"No. Usually the guys at Ruddell's are sitting around on chairs under the awning. They can be hostile to newcomers. Go another half block more to Murphy's garage. He's a friendly guy. He'll help you. You can't miss Pat's place. Out front he's got his race car, a tow truck, and a gizmo built on a converted Model-T Ford chassis."

"Thanks."

"And Calvin, tell him you talked to Gus Shapiro. Pat knows everything that's going on in Clark County and maybe in all of southern Indiana."

"Thanks again."

Calvin waved to Gus, and then drove down Market Street to Port Fulton. At High Street he recognized the massive iron gates leading to the Howard's brick mansion. The surface of carriage road glimmered with shiny river gravel, pebbles of white, quartz, brown, and pieces of red jasper. Across the street from the mansion stood a brick building with a bell tower and beyond it was the shipyard office.

Continuing, Calvin saw Ruddell's Grocery Store on Main Street. It was early, but, like Gus said, there were four men under the awning playing cards. All of them stopped and stared as his Ford rumbled down the cobblestones. It seemed like December, not May, since the cottonwood pods let fly cottony tufts. They drifted in the air and lodged in rough spots on the street like a light fall of snow.

Finally Calvin spotted a yellow painted frame cottage with a bunch of vehicles and automotive machinery along one side. On the other side of the road he caught a glimpse of a pilot house and the stacks of a steamboat peeking through the cottonwood, water maple, and horse chestnut trees. He waved to the man on the porch of the yellow house. The tall fellow in worn bib overalls and a broad smile waved back.

"Hello, I'm Cal Johnson?"

"Hello Cal. I'm Pat Murphy. Are you lost?"

"Gus Shapiro from the gas station told me you could help me find the John W. Hubbard steamboat. Are those the stacks?"

"Yes, but I don't recommend driving down to it. We've had high water and the landing is soft."

"Can I leave my car and trailer here? I'll walk."

"Sure. Take that path down Green Hill. It goes directly to the steamer. And Cal, before you go aboard, make yourself known."

"Why?"

"There's a watchman on board named Tom Green. He's from Towhead Island, over on the Kentucky side. He doesn't trust strangers and he's quick on the trigger. Make sure he knows who you are and why you're there before you go aboard. Or, you might get a load of buckshot."

"I wouldn't want that. Thanks."

Calvin grabbed his bag from the back of the Ford. Whistling a happy tune he slid down the path on Green Hill through the cottonwoods, beeches, and catalpas to the steamboat.

CHAPTER 5

TOM GREEN AND THE RED TABLECLOTH

It didn't take long for Calvin to realize his slick-soled cowboy boots worked poorly for walking down the muddy, slippery path to the river. Halfway down Green Hill, he slid on the soft, squishy mud and landed hard on a rock. Sitting on the path Calvin looked up in awe of the tall stacks of the John W. Hubbard towering majestically toward the clouds.

To Calvin Johnson all wooden steamboats were treasures of the river. He marveled at the stacks painted glossy black with no ornamentation and the deck and roof darkened with faded shades of blue. A scuffed red stripe, painted on the white hull, ran parallel to the waterline. The Hubbard had three magnificent decks with a pilot house that stood above them all. An ornate porch with peeling white paint circled the passenger deck. The huge paddlewheel reflected majestically in the water. In big bold black letters, two feet tall on the stern was the name John W. Hubbard. He could already see that she'd make a beautiful Missouri River excursion boat, all gleaming in the sun, painted glossy white with gold trim and a fresh red stripe.

Calvin studied the boat. The steamer was hundred feet with about seven foot of freeboard at the bow. That's five feet more than the standard for riverboats. One sprawling gangplank off the bow extended to the shore. A sky piercing jackstaff with yard arms rose tall from her stem. Most steamboats had a shallower draft with two wooden gangplanks hanging over the forecastle.

The mud was like quicksand as Calvin struggled to the gangplank. On the bow, under the middle deck, he spotted a burly man with a scraggly beard in a metal chair. The man wore a weather-beaten brown felt hat, tilted down to cover his eyes. He snored loudly as he caught the rays of the late afternoon sun. A shotgun propped against the rail was close at hand. An aged hound dog snoozed next to him.

"Ahoy, there."

The man tilted back his hat and slowly picked up his gun.

"Hello. I'd like permission to come aboard."

"Who the hell are you?" He pointed the barrel of his gun right between Calvin's eyes.

"I'm Calvin Johnson from St. Louis."

"I heared they was sending a guy from St. Louis. You must be that new captain for the boat. Sure, come on aboard, but take off those boots. I don't like unnecessary cleaning. And don't you mind Ole Roy here. He don't bother most folks."

At the gangplank Calvin sucked himself out of his socks and boots which were buried in five inches of muck. Then he hopped barefooted up the rickety gangplank. The man stood up from his chair and put down his shotgun. He smiled at Calvin and extended his hand for a friendly handshake.

"They call me Tom Green."

"I'm Cal. Captain Cal Johnson."

"My name's Tom but it's not really Green. Everybody calls me Tom Green cause I live in that green houseboat on the near side of Towhead Island."

"Well, I'm glad to meet you, Tom. I see you try to keep a clean boat. That's a good idea."

"I'm a man who's not looking for more work, if you know what I mean."

"Sure, I know what you mean."

"And right off Captain, I want you to know that there's no connection between me and that towboat around here they call the Tom Greene."

"I don't know much about the boats on the Ohio."

"I'm glad to see you've come to take over here. I need to get back to my fish business on Towhead. I've been using the Hubbard's yawl to get me home weekends, but I'll leave the boat for you. Today my woman will row over to pick me up." Tom picked up an old red tablecloth wadded up under his chair. "Come on Captain." Light-footedly he climbed the ladder to the top deck. Calvin followed. Tom shook out the tablecloth and waved in the air like a matador in a bullfight.

"That's a fine waving technique, Tom."

"Ivy knows my signal. She'll be over from Towhead real soon," he answered as he hopped down the ladder. "I won't go over what's on the boat. You can check that yourself. A few things are missing, like the ship's compass, bronze trim from the staterooms and the silverware. Those shanty boaters caught me off guard one night. I guess they planned on looting the boat, but I scared the shit out of them, if you know what I mean. The guys jumped overboard into their boat with all the silverware, but not before I winged one of them."

"You shot a guy!"

"No, I just winged one of them. They had it coming. They was up to no good. You look a bit whitish Captain."

"I'm just tired Tom."

"Then I guess you'll want to check out the captain's cabin for sleeping. It's the room right in front of the crew quarters. Ivy made it up with fresh sheets and pillowcases. She washed them herself when she heared you was coming."

"Thanks."

"Engine don't work. Seized up before I got here. The locker's in the engine room at the stern. It holds the night lights. There's no kerosene for filling the lanterns right now. And the hull leaks, more than a little, if you know what I mean."

"Not exactly. What do you mean?"

"I mean this old wooden boat's got a bad leaking problem. You'll have to pump about ten minutes an hour, or if you put it off for four hours, you'll have to pump forty minutes or more. Hand pump's not real effective, if you know what I mean. Just in case you can't keep up with the water, use this here red tablecloth to flag down the steamer Tom Greene. She passes by in the late afternoon, coming back from Cincinnati. The captain's real neighborly. She'll loan you a pump with a steam siphon if you ask."

"Thanks. I really appreciate your help."

"Here comes Ivy now." Tom waved to a red-headed woman wearing men's bib overalls in a wooden yawl. Ivy rowed to the port side and threw a rope. Tom Green tied the rope to the cleat.

"It must be a long row all the way from the Kentucky side."

"Not for Ivy. She's experienced, if you know what I mean. By the way Captain, do you have a gun?"

"Yes, I do. I have a Colt 1851 Navy in my bag."

Tom Green squinted his beady eyes. "Sounds fancy. Get it out. Keep it handy and loaded."

"What kind of trouble can I expect? You think those shanty boaters will show up again?"

"You damn right them shanty boaters will show up again. They'll come out from behind the island to check you out. They'll rob you blind if you're not careful. Shoot first and ask questions later, if you know what I mean."

"I guess I know what you mean."

"After a few shots Captain, they won't bother you no more? By the way, this old boat's has strange things going on. I guess you heared?"

"Heard what?"

"This here boat's got ghosts. I seen one a couple of times. Probably cause of the killings and gold disappearing."

Steamboat John W. Hubbard

"Is that why the owners sold the boat?"

"Don't know about that. Ghosts don't bother nothing. But the kids from the orphanage are another thing. They keep coming here so I've been letting them dive off the front deck and swim. For the ones that likes to fish, I let them use the starboard deck. There are catalpa worms in the trees along the bank that make good bait."

"You've been helpful. Good luck on your business."

"Thanks Captain, but you're the one who'll be needing luck. If you got any questions I ain't already answered, just wave this red tablecloth. I'll come over and do what I can." The hound trotted over to the bow of the boat. "Get in Roy," Tom said to the hound as he handed his shotgun down to Ivy. "See you around, Captain." As he headed out of sight he called, "And have fun with them ghosts, if you know what I mean."

Calvin was perplexed. This time he really didn't know what Tom Green meant. When he took this job, nobody in St. Louis mentioned ghosts or murders or shanty boaters. Calvin waved as Tom's woman rowed toward Towhead Island.

CHAPTER 6

THE FIRST DAYS OF CAPTAIN CALVIN JOHNSON

After Ivy and Tom rowed off, Calvin grabbed his bag and decided check out the boat for himself. The middle deck was enclosed, slab-sided and crudely ornate. Inside Calvin found quarters for passengers: gentlemen's cabins, ladies' cabins, a bar, dining room, and some tiny staterooms. Sheets covered most of the berths. Under the beds he found dusty life preservers. Most rooms contained porcelain wash bowls, slop buckets, and little framed mirrors from the dime store. Squinting into a framed mirror Calvin gasped, his face looked contorted like a circus freak. Quickly he put down the mirror. The ladder next to him took him up one more level.

Aft of the tall, Neptune-crowned stacks stood a long, narrow house called a texas. The captain's quarters was there. On the advice of Tom Green, Calvin threw his valise on the bed and took over the forward cabin. The captain's cabin measured ten- by-twelve feet with a double bed already made up with sheets and a pillow. A small dresser, an overstuffed, leather chair, and a desk completed the room.

One more ladder brought him to the wheelhouse on the hurricane deck. It seemed cozy with a wooden pit wheel, engine bell pulls, speaking tubes, a comfortable armchair, a wood stove, and a tarnished brass spittoon. The panoramic view from the pilot house was breathtaking. Willows, poplars, sycamores, and water beeches crowned the shore as far as Calvin could see. Mud turtles, awakened by the spring sunshine, slumbered on logs. Fish leaped from the water, and an occasional yellow butterfly drifted across the bow. The sticky muddy shore started drying out under the warm south wind. He could see the trees leafing out in a variety of colors from yellow to deep blue green. The silence was broken by the shrill of a kingfisher in the catalpa and hum of locusts in the thickets. A blue heron flapped across the river with its gaunt neck tucked in and its legs stretched out behind. Soon Captain Calvin Johnson made his way back to the texas. There was something magical about his steamboat.

In the captain's cabin Calvin opened his bag on the dresser, carefully removing the gun nestled between his clean socks and underwear. The Colt 1851 Navy revolver inherited from his great grandfather was special. Checking the chambers, he added two more bullets. Pappy Coolidge always believed in keeping his gun loaded and ready, and so did Calvin. Pappy would approve of this steamboat venture even Calvin's father did not. Wouldn't it be great to use Pappy's Colt! Calvin playfully spun around and aimed the gun. "Bang! Bang!"

"Don't shoot! I comes to pay you a visit." Standing in the doorway was a tall, colored kid with frizzy hair and crooked teeth.

Calvin aimed the gun at him. "Are you a shanty boater?"

His eyes got wide, "No, sir."

Calvin put the gun on the dresser "Well, I wasn't expecting guests. How long have you been standing there?"

"I follows you around the boat. You looked pretty silly in that mirror."

"What do you want?"

"Kids from the home walks down here all the time. Mr. Tom always lets us swim and fish if we wants."

"You must be from the orphanage."

"Yes, sir. I'm Mud King. Will you be needin' some help around here? I'm strong and I learns fast."

"I'm sure I will. I'm Cal Johnson. Captain Cal Johnson.

"I'm willin' to work hard, Captain." Mud smiled with his silly crooked grin. "That's a fine gun."

"It was my Pappy's. George Calvin Coolidge, my great grandfather, bought the gun to take on the Western Engineer steamboat. He was part of the government expedition sending an army and scientists up the Missouri to the Yellowstone River. Pappy Coolidge enlisted as a botanist to catalog the plant life of the West."

"That gun don't look big enough to hunt with."

"Pappy kept this gun for his own protection. After all, the Western Engineer was only the second steamboat to travel up the Missouri River."

"It was nice talkin' to you Captain, but I gotta be gettin' back to the orphanage. It's my turn to make supper for the boys. When you be needin' help, stop by the home on Jefferson Street."

Calvin watched as Mud jogged down the gangplank toward town. He slid Pappy's gun under his pillow, and then plopped back into the worn leather chair. Closing his eyes he imagined the John W. Hubbard as a finer steamer than the Grey Eagle or the Bald Eagle in St. Louis. He could already see the elegant, refurbished Hubbard docked next to the Robt. E. Lee on the St. Charles levee. If he tried real hard could smell the sumptuous trays of food being served in the Hubbard's magnificent dining room.

His stomach growled. His last food was yesterday. Calvin pulled himself up and slid down the ladder to the galley on the main deck. A bag of rice lay on a shelf. Next to it stood cans of hominy, spinach, and potted meat. And no drinking water anywhere. Even for a weary traveler, a visit to the grocery store seemed inevitable.

The four block walk to the Ruddell's Grocery Store was exhausting. A cow bell clanged as Calvin opened the door. It was dark and cool inside like a basement. Three men laughed and played cards at a table in the back. They got quiet when he walked passed them to the counter.

"Good afternoon. Nice place you got here."

"Yup," answered the man behind the counter. "What do you need, stranger?"

"I'm not a stranger. I'm Cal Johnson from the steamboat John W. Hubbard. I need a jug for drinking water and four cans of beans."

"I'm the owner of the store, Clyde Ruddell. I got some cans of beans right here and one of them one gallon crockery jugs in back that's intended for corn liquor. Is that good for you?"

"That's good for me."

"It'll cost you twenty five cents."

Calvin laid a quarter on the counter and stuffed the cans of beans in his jacket pockets. "Where can I get drinkable water around here?"

"The town fathers boxed up a spring in the hills years ago. They piped the water directly to the homes of Port Fulton for a fee."

"I live on a boat."

"Well, for those who can't afford the water rent, or for those who lives on boats, there's always them free corner pump hydrants for water."

"Where's the closest one?"

"You can get all the pure spring waters you want across the street. Nobody in town is more then a block away from a public hydrant. Do you need anything else?"

"What about kerosene?"

"I don't sell kerosene. You need a special can for it."

"Where can I get some?"

"Pat Murphy's the only one in town that sells kerosene. He'll have a can for you."

"Thanks." Calvin waved and walked out the door. Across the street he filled his jug at the hydrant, and then slowly headed back to the boat.

Back in the galley Calvin stacked up the cans of beans on the table. With a rusty can opener he opened one. He peeked in the top cabinets for a spoon. China was neatly stacked under a fine layer of dust. The ship's bar had some silverware and a steamer trunk covered with a couple of useable tablecloths. He jiggled the lock, but it didn't open, so he pushed the trunk to the back of the cabinet. Calvin grabbed a spoon and highball glass. He wished for some of Leroy's fine whiskey to pep up this pure spring water. After eating Calvin was tired, but decided to check out the Hubbard's power plant before he went to bed.

Steamboat machinery was confined to the rear end of the main deck, back next to the paddlewheel. It was a mess of cogs, gauges, and pulleys that stayed idle when the engines were down. The engine room looked clean and so did the coal bunker. The array of fire doors in the furnace room looked ominous. Seven yawning holes delivered the coal when the Hubbard was steamed up. Calvin looked down at several inches of water that collected in the bottom of the hull. A gasoline powered pump to dry out the bilges would make this job easier. Calvin made a mental note to find a pump in the morning.

As Calvin dragged his tired body up the ladder to his bunk in captain's cabin, stacks of papers on the desk in the Purser's Office caught his eye. He walked inside. Covered with cobwebs, he found what appeared to be the ship's history. He sat down and lit a lantern. Propping up his feet on a home-made footrest under the desk, he blew off inches of dust. Calvin smiled. Indeed, the book of papers revealed the life of the John W. Hubbard.

The John W. Hubbard was built in 1902 at the Avondale Shipyards in New Orleans. The boat's original name was Miss Lillian Burke. The Miss Lillian was designed to be a packet between New Orleans, Louisiana and Mobile, Alabama. The wooden boat was built with a very high bow to withstand the open water in Mobile Bay and Lake Ponchartrain. Lillian Burke had seven feet of freeboard. It was two hundred feet long with a forty foot beam and three decks. The pilot house, at eye level, stood forty-five feet above the water. The engines were two compound, with a high pressure cylinder, thirteen inches in diameter; and a low pressure cylinder, twenty-six inches. It was rated for two hundred and twenty pounds of steam and had an eight foot stroke turning a paddle wheel. Two boilers supplied steam.

In 1922 the Miss Lillian Burke was purchased by the Cincinnati Packet Company and renamed by Commodore Wyatt Andrew Laidlaw for his maternal grandfather John W. Hubbard. Logs indicated that during prohibition times the steamboat hauled malt nutrine, an invigorating sedative tonic from John W. Hubbard's Petersburg, Kentucky plant, opposite Lawrenceburg, Indiana to Cincinnati.

In 1924 the steamboat John W. Hubbard ran between Cincinnati, Ohio and Pittsburgh, Pennsylvania, sometimes hosting high stakes poker games. The Hubbard was confiscated by the state of Ohio in June, 1925.

In the summer of 1925 the state of Ohio ran the Hubbard as a relief boat from Cincinnati, Ohio to Louisville, Kentucky. Hubbard's engines failed in Cincinnati in

September, 1925. The boat was towed to Jeffersonville, Indiana in 1927.

As Calvin closed the book his eyes grew heavy. The turmoil of the day caught up with him. He shuffled back to the captain's cabin wondered where Tom Green's ghosts fit in to the steamer history. Calvin poured another glass of water from the jug and drank it. Pushing the worn leather chair across the room to the window, he flopped down and sat back, his body and mind exhausted. He closed his eyes. He could barely hear the melodious chanting of the tree frogs.

CRASH! BANG! CRASH!

He sat up and listened for more sounds.

"What you doin' that fer?" A voice shouted from the lower deck.

"You want us to get our heads shot off? Shut up your face Bubba."

"Ifin I don't tie up your boat we'll be swimmin' back to Towhead."

Calvin popped out of the chair, his eyes as big as cantaloupes. He scrambled for Pappy's revolver under the pillow. With his finger cocking the hammer, he approached the ladder to the passenger deck. He stopped and listened.

"Catfish, my foot's stuck. Shine the light over here. What did you say we're lookin' fer?"

"Gold. Bags of gold."

Calvin listened intently. Nobody ever mentioned gold to him. He looked down the ladder. A lantern illuminated the lower deck just enough for him to see shadows moving around. He took aim with Pappy's Colt at the lantern light, but idea of starting a fire made him reconsider. Instead, Calvin shot straight up into the air.

A hair-raising scream and a thump emanated from below. "Don't shoot! Don't shoot!"

"What are you doing on my boat?"

"We didn't know anybody was here, did we Bubba?" called a raspy voice.

"Don't move! Stop right where you are!"

Carelessly Calvin leaped down the ladder with revolver in hand. Both men scrambled down the side deck to the stern. One man hopped overboard into a boat tied to the cleat. The second man untied the line, and flung himself over the side too. Splash! Calvin fired another shot in the air. He rushed to the railing just in time to see the small boat floating downstream in the moonlight.

"Bubba don't leave me," yelled Catfish as he swam after the boat. The big man rowed hard with the current. Catfish caught the side of the boat. He tried to get in, but the boat capsized. Both men surfaced and hung onto the boat. In the light of the moon Calvin heard the bickering and splashing moving farther and farther away as the current floated the men downstream.

"Jumpin' overboard in the dark is down right unsafe," sputtered Bubba.

"Ifin you thinks that's bad, try swimmin' with this bum wing."

"I ain't ever goin' along with another of your stupid ideas. This here gold's a figment of your imagination."

"Bubba, what's imagination?"

"Keep kickin' Catfish. Keep kickin'."

CHAPTER 7

FROGGY WOODSON AND THE SUGGESTION BOAT

Last night's shanty boater encounter caused a small mess on the steamboat. There was mud on the deck and broken glass. Everything else looked hunky dory.

After coffee and a cold can of beans Calvin inspected the hull from the inside. To his dismay he found a foot of river water in the bottom. Tom Green didn't mention using Portland cement to fill the holes, but Calvin found a half-used container sitting out. Cement might be just the ticket to slow down the water.

First Calvin pumped by hand. Then he planted two handfuls of cement on every leak. It hardened quickly, but didn't last. Soon a fountain spurted through the middle. There's got to be a more permanent solution.

"Hello! Hey There! Anybody around this here boat?"

"Hang on. I'm coming." Calvin hopped out of the bilges and headed to the bow. At the end of the gangplank there stood an odd little man with a croaky voice. He carried a big brown box.

He gave a friendly wave. "Hello there."

"Who are you?"

A happy-looking fellow with clumpy red hair and bulging eyes set down his box on the deck. "That tone don't sound friendly. Why are you so cranky on this beautiful sunny morning?"

"Well, I've got a problem I can't fix. And it's making me cranky."

"Well, Mr. Cranky, I'm Froggy Woodson, retired ace carpenter from the Howard Shipyards. I'm here to offer my expert advice."

"I'm Cal Johnson, Captain Cal Johnson. This old wooden steamboat is slowing sinking. Do you have any solutions?"

"I sure do. In fact, I brought you just the thing to help your leaky bottom." Froggy pointed to the long-handled box brimming to the top with sawdust on the deck.

"I have a foot of water in the bilges. How is a box of sawdust going to help?"

"Sawdust can be real helpful in leak prevention and you can get as much as you want for free. Tom always asked me to bring him a box when I stopped by the mill. I figure you'd be needing it too."

"I've pumped the hull and used up most of the Portland cement. I can't see how a box of sawdust will do me any good."

"It's all in how you use it, Captain. I'll demonstrate. Come on over to the rail. First, you scoot this here long-handled box over the bow of the boat. Do you see how the current and water pressure sucks the sawdust? The sawdust sticks in the holes and cracks and swells up. The leak stops. It's not a permanent solution, you understand, but it'll stop the steamboat from sinking."

"I'll try anything until I get a gas pump. I do appreciate your help. I'm sorry I got crabby with you, Froggy."

"Think nothing of it. This boat's got a lot of problems. By the way Captain, have you seen any spooks yet?"

"What?"

"Spooks, you know ghosts?"

"On this boat?"

"Yeah, on this boat, Captain. Last week Tom said he saw two ghosts on the deck in the moonlight. One was a tall guy with a curly mustache and the other one was a little guy with a big, floppy hat."

"Tom said something about ghosts, and killings, and gold. I thought he was kidding."

"No, Tom Green's from the Kentucky side, but he's a pretty straight shooter. Speaking of shooting, down at the garage we heard that you had some visitors last night."

"I did have a couple of guys prowling around. I scared them off. They said they were looking for gold."

"Gold? How interesting?"

"What do you mean?"

"Do you know the history of this here boat?"

"I read the logs."

"Well, the real history of this here boat won't be in the logs. First of all, it's got a shady past. It used to run brew and big stakes poker games on the Ohio."

"The logs mentioned running whiskey and gambling."

"I'll bet it didn't say anything about the Mexicans gamblers who got murdered for their gold coins."

"Are you sure you've got the right boat? When my boss hired me he didn't say anything about ghosts or gold."

"Well, Captain maybe your boss didn't know the truth. Mark Twain and I never let the truth get in the way of a good story."

"Look Froggy, I've got to keep this boat afloat. Where I can buy a good second-hand gasoline pump?"

"I got one at my place that will be just the ticket. I used it a couple of times for sour mash. I'll sell it cheap."

"Perfect! Where's your place?"

"I'm your closest neighbor Captain. My house and my boat ramp are between the steamboat and the shipyards. You can't miss it. It's the only place with a couple of half-built motor launches in the yard. Come on over after supper. I'll sell you the pump plus I'll tell you the true story about them Hubbard spooks. In the mean time use this here sawdust for your pesky leaks." Froggy handed Calvin the box and walked down the landing. "So long, Captain."

"See you later, Froggy. Thanks, again."

After Froggy left, Calvin pitched the box of sawdust over the stern and hoped for the best. Climbing to the texas deck he watched the panorama of the Ohio and thought about his next move.

Unlike the muddy Mississippi, the Ohio was called the Green River. Its name came from the green color of the underground streams which flowed into it and the springs which rose in its bed. The Green River practically never froze solid, but fogs caused major problems for steamboats.

About six o'clock, Calvin ate a cold supper of canned hominy, potted meat, and spring water. He was a little homesick and thought about Christina. She was his best girl during high school. When Calvin left town for Knox College in Illinois she wrote and visited often. It wasn't until Christina enrolled at the Washington University Art School last year that things changed. Calvin didn't have much in common with her new artsy-fartsy friends.

From the galley drawer he pulled out a tablet of paper, a bottle of ink, and a pen.

Dear Christina,

I have a new and exciting job on a steamboat anchored near Jeffersonville, Indiana on the beautiful Ohio River. My boss and his financial backers are turning the John W. Hubbard into a fancy Missouri River excursion steamer and I'm going to be the pilot. I've met some new people, but I miss you. This job could be the financial opportunity that will change my life. How about taking a train to Indiana for the Fourth of July? I'm including cash for your ticket. We need to talk about our future.

Love and Kisses,

Your riverboat captain,

Calvin

Calvin put Christina's letter in an envelope with his last five bucks, addressed it, and left it on the galley table. It might be a couple of days until he got to the post office.

On his way to Froggy's place he walked on the grass and out of the muck. Soon Calvin spotted a small, white frame house with peeling dark green shutters and shingled roof. It faced the Utica Pike in front, with the backyard running down to the river. One strangely constructed boat on a trestle rested next to the rear of the house. As he walked around the house he noticed another boat in a trestle between the front yard and the Pike. Next to the second boat frame, Calvin noticed Froggy and two men sitting on stools. They laughed and passed around a jug.

Froggy waved. "Howdy, Captain. We was just enjoying the cool of the evening and some fine corn liquor. Come and join us."

"Don't mind if I do." Calvin sat on the boat frame and took a swig from the jug. He swallowed hard. Tears filled his eyes. "Hot damn!"

Froggy laughed. "Captain, this is Elmer and Jake."

"It's nice meeting you. This stuff has quite a kick."

"This mountain dew's aged five days." Jake blurted out as he scratched his bare-calloused feet.

"Mountain dew is bound to improve taste of the water I get from the hydrants. Can I get some from you guys?"

"Maybe. When we gets to know you better," grunted Elmer. He grabbed the jug from Calvin and took a gulp, and then stepped behind the trestle to pee.

"Froggy, why are you working on two boats at a time?"

"It's a long story Captain."

"We got all night."

"I guess we do. Well, it all started with a dream, Captain. I always wanted to build my own motor launch. When I retired from the shipyards last year I had lots of time on my hands, so I decided to build my dream boat."

"But there are two boats. One's sitting in grass knee-high and the other one is barely planked."

"I told you it was a long story Captain. Have another swig of this excellent brew and listen. This is a damn good story."

Calvin smiled and took another drink.

"After I retired, I set up this trestle in the front yard to build my dream launch. I was in no particular hurry. My friends from the shipyard, the so-called experts, constantly stopped by the house with ideas for my launch. Some of the guys worked with nothing but six-by-twelve timbers. How was I to know that they knowed nothing about constructing an eighteen foot double-ender. I didn't want to hurt nobody's feelings so I took their ideas in the construction of my boat. That was a mistake. Soon my dream boat became a big mess!"

Jake stood up, adjusted his bib overalls and then put his arm around Froggy's shoulder. "That's when we helped Froggy haul that first boat behind the house."

"Yes, sir. Jake and Elmer did me a big favor."

"Tared aseein' him unhappy," said Elmer.

"With that chapter of my life behind the house, Elmer and Jake helped me build a new trestle in the front yard for a new motor launch. I'm calling this boat, My Way, because I'm doing it all my way. If any of them so-called experts from the shipyards have suggestions on boat building, I tell them to step to the backyard. You're more than welcome to include any idea you have in that boat. This boat in the front yard I'm building my way."

"That's a remarkable story, but I came here for a pump. Remember? The Hubbard's bilges still have a leaking problem. Do you have a pump for me?"

"Sure, Captain. Elmer, go get that pump in the kitchen we been using for brew."

"Okay, Froggy."

Elmer walked back with a small gasoline pump in his left hand. His right hand was wrapped up with a rag. It dripped blood on the ground next to Calvin. "Here you are, Captain."

"What happened to your hand?"

"Just gots my finger caught in the screen door."

"Clean it up so you don't get an infection."

"I did. I stuck it in some brew before I wrapped it up with a rag. Stings some."

"Good I guess. What do I owe you, Froggy?"

"Since it's been used exclusively for mash, how about fifty cents?"

"Sold." Calvin handed over two quarters from his pants pocket. "This pump will make my job a lot easier. Thanks."

"You got time to hear the real story about your boat?"

"Sure Froggy."

"I'm surprised you ain't heard about the biggest damn poker game on the Ohio." Elmer remarked as he pulled burrs out of his long, tangled hair. He crunched them between his teeth and spit them across the yard.

"It was the biggest heist of all time," added Jake swigging the jug.

"This is the true story of the John W. Hubbard and I'll be happy to tell it." Froggy pointed to four rusty metal lawn chairs. "Let's sit on the porch. The mosquitoes are coming up from the river. Besides we might need another jug from the house." The men trotted up the steps to the porch and sat like four monkeys in a row. Froggy passed around the jug. "The Hubbard's problems started in 1924."

"She ran between Louisville and Cinny. The boat was a floating poker game," interrupted Jake.

"Froggy tells the story betteren you Jake, so shut up your face."

"Thank you, Elmer." He patted Elmer on the shoulder. "It was a Saturday in May of 1924. Two fancy dressed Mexicans showed up for the poker game with a bag of gold coins. One guy was named Paco and the other guy I think was Felix."

"The Double Eagle gold coins they carried came from an Army payroll heist out West," interrupted Jake.

"I can tell this here story," snapped Froggy.

"Sure."

"Well, despite the warnings posted all over the boat, about not playing cards with strangers, these Mexicans sat down with two gamblers from around Moorsville, Indiana. They played seven card stud. No limit."

"The guys were John Dillinger and Charlie Marky," interrupted Jake. "And my cousin, Oscar Peabody, the sheriff of Monroe County, was hired to keep the game honest."

Froggy stared hard at Jake. "The gamblers played all weekend and into Monday night. The Mexicans began losing their gold. Dillinger and Marky lost money too. Meals and drinks were served at the table. Nobody slept."

"I heard these guys smoked fifty packs of cigarettes, five boxes of Mexican cigars, and ran up a bar bill of over $900," added Jake.

"Look Jake, I'm telling this story."

"Sorry, Froggy. I got carried away."

"Well, the Hubbard arrived at the Cinny landing Monday night. She sounded her whistles and was ready to tie up between the steamers, Sara Conway and the Udora Adams."

"That's when the fire started," exclaimed Elmer.

"The boilers of the Belle of Ohio exploded. This was a big problem since the levee was packed with boats. The steward of the paddle wheeler Sara Conway was airing bedding on the hurricane deck when sparks and embers from the Belle ignited some mattresses.

"What does this fire have to do with the Hubbard?"

"Well Calvin, the Hubbard's lines were nearly tied to the cleats next to the Sara Conway. Strong winds carried the flames to both boats. But since the Hubbard's lines weren't secured, she backed off and steamed free. The Sara Conway wasn't so lucky; she quickly burned to the water line. In the commotion, the two Mexicans at the poker table got shot and wound up dead. Their gold coins vanished."

"My Uncle Buck saw John Dillinger and his friend rowing upriver in one of the Hubbard's yawls," remarked Jake. "Oscar Peabody wound up going to jail for killing the Mexicans because they were killed with bullets from his gun."

Froggy took another swig of brew. "But Sheriff Peabody wasn't the guilty one. That gangster, Dillinger, probably killed the Mexicans and took all their money."

"Yeah. I seen Dillinger's pitcher in the papers," added Elmer.

"With all this bad publicity the Hubbard's business went to other boats. It didn't take long for the steamboat to go bankrupt."

"That's interesting, Froggy. It gives me a lot to think about."

"Do you want me to stop by next week with more sawdust?"

"You can stop by if you want to, Froggy, but this pump should take care of the leaks. I got a long day tomorrow. I'd better be heading back."

Calvin waved to the guys as he stumbled down the path back to the Hubbard. He saw the towboat Duffy returning with the last load from the sand dredge. The showboats Calliope and Penelope at the Louisville landing, across from Jeffersonville, lit up and filled the river with music. A golden glow reflected in the river from the clouds as the sun disappeared behind the trees. The story of Froggy's boats made Calvin think about running his own boat, Baby Wildcat III. As far as he knew she stood in the high grass on the trailer in Pat Murphy's yard. Tomorrow might be a good day to pay Pat Murphy a call.

CHAPTER 8

CIRCUS WAGON

The sun, breaking through the clouds, painted a path of gold in the river. With the coming of the first streaks of blue and hazy violet to the east, it was like life born anew. The yellows and oranges danced on the horizon as the last visages of fog mysteriously floated over Towhead Island. This feeling was the nearest thing to religion that a riverman could experience.

Calvin sat back on the front deck of the Hubbard and drank his coffee. He watched a million diamonds gleaming in the churning wake of a stern-wheeler heading upriver. One more cup of coffee and it was time to climb Green Hill to Murphy's place to check on Wildcat. He heard the voice of the packet, a chime whistle. Its deep-voiced sound announced its arrival at the nearby dock. It seemed steamboat whistles were prosaic noise, heard only by those listening for them.

At Pat's place Calvin noticed Baby Wildcat III exactly where he left her. She was sitting peacefully on the trailer in the tall grass next to his garage. Clanking and swearing from inside the garage reverberated in the silent morning air. Calvin peered cautiously through the door.

"Good morning, Pat. Sounds like you might need some help."

"You got an Ouija board, Cal?"

"What?"

"This car has problems only a clairvoyant can solve."

"I'm not clairvoyant that I know of." He walked around the car. "Hot damn! What a grand Pierce Arrow!"

"It had a leak," Pat answered sliding out on an old pine board from under the car. "I hope it's fixed. Keeping this beauty running is complicated."

"I wish the car were mine. Who owns it?"

"It belongs to banker named Byron Van DeMeer up on Millionaire's Row. He wants it running for a business trip to Cincinnati this morning. I don't know why he doesn't use his National or his Packard limousine. I've got both of them running perfectly."

"I'll bet it's because this Pierce Arrow is his favorite. What a beauty?" Calvin slid across the seat to get a feel of the wheel.

"I'm glad to see you, but isn't it pretty early for a visit?"

"Froggy got me thinking about boats yesterday. I wanted to see Baby Wildcat." Calvin fondly caressed the leather upholstery on the Pierce and then walked over to the work bench where Pat was sorting tools.

"I heard shanty boaters surprised you on the boat the other night."

"How did you find out?"

"Everybody knows your business in Port Fulton."

"That's what Froggy said. Tom Green told me shanty boaters could be a problem on the boat. What do you think?"

"First of all Cal, shanty boaters aren't bad. Most live on home-made boats around Towhead where they don't pay rent. The men fish or do jobs in town to support their families."

"I think the two guys that climbed aboard were robbers. A guy called Catfish said he was looking for gold."

"I know him. That scoundrel Catfish is always in trouble."

"Well, I surprised him and his friend with some shots from my revolver. The last I saw they were swimming their hinnies downstream."

"Don't judge shanty boaters by Catfish McCoy. Most don't rob kitchen gardens and hen roosts. They mind their own business. Toad Plunket lives on a boat near Towhead. He helps me out sometime by cleaning the garage. His family fishes and plants their own patch of sweet corn and potatoes on the bottoms. They peddle their fish and crops in town."

"Toad Plunket sounds like an ordinary guy."

"Shanty boaters are peaceable, but a different breed. Life in the city is just too complex for them."

"Speaking of complex things, what is that device sitting next to my boat?"

"That's a gizmo. Two cylinders of the motor operate the other two. It acts like an air compressor to drive the sawmill for cutting wood."

"What a clever use for a Model-T chassis!" Calvin pointed to the big, covered object next to Pat in the garage. "What's under this cover? A bigger gizmo?"

"Not exactly. Go ahead. Pull back the cover."

Eagerly Calvin peeled back the tarp. "Hot Damn!" He walked around the car and lifted the hood. "That's not an ordinary Ford."

"No, she's a special edition, equipped with a sixteen valve Frontenac cylinder head."

"Hot damn! Hot Damn! And hot damn! I'll bet she's harder to catch than a wild cheetah."

"You bet. This wild cheetah and I held the dirt track racing record in Indiana two years in a row. Of course, that was before Minnie and the three kids."

The police siren got louder. Calvin walked to the front of the garage and followed an official vehicle with a big gold star that stopped at the street. "Here comes the sheriff, Pat."

Pat walked to the street to meet the sheriff. Calvin followed.

"Hello boys."

"Good morning, Sheriff."

"Pat, I got a job for you. I found Byron Van DeMeer's Packard Twin-Six on Clarksville Road. It was abandoned."

"What happened?"

"I don't know. It wasn't damaged. I guess the limousine ran out of gas. I want you to tow it back to your garage. Gas it up. Check it over. Then tell Van DeMeer where his car is. I'd take care of this myself, but I've got to pick up the Chief and get up to New Albany by noon."

"I'll take care of it. By the way is the party still on for Friday night?"

"No. The party's off. Johnny's kitchen caught fire. It'll take him awhile to fix it."

"What terrible luck!"

The sheriff squinted at Calvin with a funny look. "Who are you?"

"I'm Captain Cal Johnson of the steamboat John W. Hubbard, Sheriff. It's moored on the other side of Green Hill." Calvin extended his hand, but the sheriff ignored him.

"Homer, I've got an idea," added Pat. "What about using Cal's boat for a party?"

"Maybe." The sheriff looked Calvin straight in the eye. "Are you up for a party on Friday night Captain?"

"Sure, why not?"

"Then we'll see you on Friday night. Take care of the car Pat. I've got to pick up Johnny for our trip to New Albany."

"There's going to be a full moon on Friday. Maybe there'll be some of them Hubbard ghosts partying with us," chuckled Pat.

"Ghosts are a lot of baloney." The sheriff got in his patrol car and slammed the door. He sped off in a trail of dust with his lights flashing.

"Let's get the tow car," said Pat as they walked back to the garage.

"Froggy mentioned spooks on the steamboat too. What do you know about them?"

"Like Homer said, ghosts are a lot of baloney. Personally, I think Tom Green made up the ghost sightings to keep people away from the boat. I'll need you to steer the Packard while I tow her in. I think I'll check with Van DeMeer in person first just in case there's more to the story."

"I'm ready."

They took the tow car downtown to a part of Jeffersonville where the bankers and industrialists built their fine mansions overlooking the river. Every house sat gracefully in the wooded setting. Flowering bushes and beautifully landscaped lawns filled the neighborhood.

"I've seen museums that weren't as big as some of these homes."

"Every mansion is unique. They're owned by some of the richest men in Indiana. Port Fulton people call this place Millionaire's Row."

Pat stopped his truck at Number 4 Capital Assets Drive. It was a columned, plantation-like, gleaming white mansion with magnificent old magnolia trees lining the walkway to the house. "Come on, Cal. We're walking the rest of the way."

"It's a long walk. Why don't we just drive down Van DeMeer's magnificent driveway to the door?"

"We're the help, Cal. Only guests can drive to the door. We walk. I don't want the old man mad at me."

"Horse feathers."

Calvin kept up the fast pace behind Pat as they headed down the driveway to knock on Van DeMeer's mahogany front door.

The butler peeked out. "Mr. Van DeMeer is not available. Please come back later."

"Stand back Wilson," interrupted a gruff voice. The old man pushed open the door. He stood bare-footed in his blue silk pajamas, wiping his watering eyes on his sleeve. "Hello Patrick."

"Good morning, Mr. Van DeMeer. The sheriff told me your Packard ran out of gas on Clarksville Road. He asked me to tow it back."

"Homer found my car?" Van DeMeer asked choking back tears.

"He sure did. I'll check it over and then tow the car back here."

"Patrick, I never want to see that damn automobile again. Drive that Packard into the river!"

"It's a beautiful car. I really can't do that!"

"Yes, you can! I'm instructing you to do it. It's my car." He clutched his heart and staggered.

"Relax Mr. Van DeMeer." Pat helped the old man inside to a nearby chair. "Sit down. Calm yourself or you'll have another heart attack."

"This has been a terrible night for me. Lily's gone. My darling daughter, Lily, eloped with Eli."

"Eli, your chauffeur!"

"Yes, that black devil! Three days ago he drove Lily to Louisville for a shopping trip. This morning she called me from Las Vegas. Lily married Eli Jones! What am I going to tell her mother? Until now Lily has been a perfect daughter. She's talented, bright, and she's always listened to me. Lily was accepted to Vassar College in the fall. Now she's ruined her life."

"Take it easy, Mr. Van DeMeer. Don't get your blood pressure up. Relax. I'll take care of the Packard."

"Do you have my Pierce running?"

"As a matter of fact, I do. I'll bring it over after I get the Packard."

"I can't wait. I have a business meeting in Cincinnati this morning. I'll send my driver, Clyde, to pick up the Pierce. And Patrick, I'm serious. Don't bring that Packard back to my garage."

"You really want me to drive it into the river?"

"Yes."

"That seems a waste of a fine limousine."

"Then you take the car, Patrick."

"Are you sure?"

"Yes, I'm sure. I don't have any use for it."

"I guess I could make a tow car out of it."

"Do whatever you want. I'll have Clyde drop off the title when he picks up my Pierce. I never want to see that Packard again. Please leave. I must get to Cincinnati by noon."

"Don't worry Mr. Van DeMeer. I'll take care of everything. Come on, Cal." They walked briskly down the driveway to the tow car.

"Boy, are you lucky. You got yourself a swell Packard Twin-Six. Hot damn!"

"Yeah, she's one fancy black limousine with a bad reputation. Get in the truck. We've got a job to do."

As they approached Clarksville Road the big, black car stood off the pavement in the weeds with the trunk lid propped up. They walked down to it. Pat checked it out.

"It won't start, but otherwise it looks okay to me. We'll tow it back to my garage and gas it up."

Pat backed down the truck while Calvin hooked the bumper with a chain and a lock. Calvin steered as Pat towed the black beauty slowly down the Utica Pike. At the house Pat took off the chains.

Calvin smiled as he crawled inside the luxurious automobile. "A person can get spoiled by this aromatic leather interior. Do you know this car has a bar? I opened this cabinet door and found whiskey and two crystal glasses." He waved the bottle and glasses.

"That doesn't look like moonshine."

"Nope. It has a fancy label from Ireland. I guess this liquor is yours too."

"You talked me into it. Let's check out Byron's vintage Irish whiskey in these fine crystal glasses on my vintage Irish stoop."

They laughed as they drank.

"Do you think Minnie will mind us drinking so early?"

"Probably if she was home, but Minnie's at her mother's house in Artic Springs picking beans for canning. She won't be back until tomorrow."

"Hot damn!"

While they celebrated on the porch stoop, Calvin noticed a small, wiry man milling around the limousine. He walked around and around the Packard. He measured the car with a tape measure, stared in the windows, and made some notes on a piece of paper.

Calvin pointed to the stranger. "Do you know that queer little guy?"

Pat squinted into the sunlight. "Sure, that's Benny Barton. Hey, Benny, you like my new limo? It's a gift from Byron Van DeMeer."

Benny waved and walked to the porch. "Patrick Murphy, that car is the bee's knees! Is she for sale?"

"Might be. I didn't know you were looking for a fine Packard limousine. Sit down, Benny. Try some vintage Irish whiskey."

"No liquor for me, I've got a gig tonight." The jolly, fellow sat down on the stoop. Benny Barton looked like a colorful leprechaun. He wore red corduroy knickers with an orange polka dotted bow tie with purple and white striped vest.

"Cal, this is Benny Barton. Benny is making his mark as the band leader of the hillbilly band known as the River Bottom Ramblers."

"Top of the morning, Benny, or maybe its afternoon. I'm Captain Cal Johnson of the steamboat John W. Hubbard. Is your band playing around town?"

"We got jobs all over southern Indiana and Louisville too. What about that gorgeous car, Patrick? Will you sell it? Please. Please."

"Sure, I'll sell it to you. But Benny, that car gets four miles to the gallon. Do you think you can afford to run it?"

"It's not just for me. It's for the band. We'll buy it together. The car's big enough for all the guys to ride in. With a rack on the roof, we could carry our instruments. Gentlemen, with the acquisition of this fine automobile the River Bottom Ramblers will be the cat's pajamas!"

"You do know this is Byron Van DeMeer's Packard, don't you? He told me he never wanted to see this car again. If he sees this limousine anywhere in Clark County there will be dire consequences for me."

Benny smiled and rubbed his whiskery chin. "Don't worry, everything's copasetic Patrick. Believe me, when I get through with the restoration, Mr. Van DeMeer will never recognize his old car."

Later that month Calvin recognized Benny and the car in town. He could hardly believe the transformation. The black paint was replaced by bright red and gold. The luggage rack on the roof, a gilded filigree, created a circus-like quality. The four metal disks spiral-painted red and black set the car apart from all others. Two of the disks were attached to the front wheels and were held in place by lug nuts. The spirals constantly unwound giving the front wheels of the car the effect of motion. On the back wheels, Benny hung the disks over the wheels. He drilled holes and attached sheet-metal clips to hold them in place. The clips were attached to the underside of the fenders. When the car rolled down the street there was the illusion of the front wheels unwinding while the back wheels stood still. The gold lettering along the side of the car read: River Bottom Ramblers of Port Fulton, Indiana.

Benny honked the reverberating and bellowing horn. "Hello there Captain Cal. Isn't the Circus Wagon the berries?"

Calvin removed his fingers from his ears. "Van De-Meer certainly won't recognize this car as his old Packard."

"Hotsy-Totsy! Hotssy-Totsseee!" Benny shouted as he screeched the tires in a quick take-off toward the Utica Pike.

CHAPTER 9

WHITE LIGHTNING

Froggy's second-hand pump worked like a charm. Every twelve hours Calvin pumped for thirty minutes and the bilges remained dry.

With the extra time on his hands Calvin wrote Christina a letter daily, and then made a game of checking the boat for the gold coins. Sneezing and wheezing Calvin scrounged through the dirt and dust on the Hubbard. Insects and rodents, dead and alive, lay quietly in dark crevices. As for finding gold, he always came up empty-handed.

One day he thumbed through some yellowing papers in the galley drawer. It looked like a home-made cookbook. The first recipe sounded interesting. How to Make Mule: 50 pounds cornmeal, 10 pounds bran, 200 pounds sugar, 12 ounces yeast, and 200 gallons of water.

Where would a person get two hundred gallons of clean water around here? Probably the same place Captain Fluent got his water for the turtle soup. Calvin stuffed the yellowing papers back in the drawer and wondered why making mule didn't include a mule in the ingredients.

Sunday was just another day in the life of the captain of the Hubbard. Calvin yawned, slipped on his boots and pumped the bilges, and then headed to Pat's place. As he walked into the garage he noticed a black telephone on a wall in the back.

"Hot Damn! You got your own telephone. Can I use it to call St. Louis?"

"No Cal. This is for local business calls only. If you want to call long distance you'll have to use the pay telephone at Schimpff's Confectionary."

"Too bad. Having a close telephone to call my boss would have been great. Do you need any help, Pat?"

"Sure, slide over that oil can and hand me the tools I ask for."

"I noticed Minnie on the steps of the house handling bushel baskets of beans. What's she up to?"

"Minnie and Evelyn got one of them cooking projects going today. They're canning. It's hot and it's tedious. I try to stay out of the way so I don't have to help."

"Good idea. I've been meaning to ask you. Is there anything I should be doing to get ready for the party?"

Pat kept working. "Don't worry about the party. Details just sort of take care of themselves. How about handing me that monkey wrench?"

"How many people should I expect?"

"All you need to know about Friday is we're going to have food, music and white lightning. Guests will bring everything you need."

"What's white lightning? Is it the same as hooch?"

"You're full of questions today, Cal. White lightning, hooch, brew, mountain dew, moonshine, white mule is all the same. Some people say moonshine's made at night and white lightning during the day, and white mule's the stuff that made so far back in the hills that it takes a mule to haul it out. There are variations, but the recipe's simple. Its corn, sugar, yeast, and water. Around here, the right proportions of ingredients and the cook make the batch."

"I saw a paper in the Hubbard's galley called How to Make Mule. Do you think somebody made moonshine on the boat?"

"Probably not. It's too dangerous. More likely one of the Hubbard's crew had an operation on the bottoms."

"I'd like to have a jug of that white lightening for the party. Can you help me out?"

"Sure. After it gets dark, I'll take you to the source."

"Great. Can I help you clean those engine parts?"

"You bet." They worked in the garage all afternoon. "It's five. Let's get something to eat, and then we'll take a ride."

"Sounds copasetic."

The men washed up in water bucket in the garage. Pat opened the screen door to the house. Calvin followed.

"Minnie, we're gonna eat, then we got business in the hills tonight."

Minnie and Evelyn looked up from the big pots on the wood stove. Minnie frowned at Pat and put her hands on her hips. "Business, ha! You mean you're agoin' up to the still, don't you?"

"Sure. Cal wants to get some of Johnny's brew. What's for supper?"

"I got some greens and bacon grease acookin' on the stove. Why don't you and Calvin get yourselves a plate?"

"Thanks, dear. You'll love Minnie's fixings, Cal. Nineteen different greens. It really fills you up." Pat served up two plates and set them down at the end of kitchen table.

Calvin pulled up a chair and reluctantly tasted a mouthful of the strong smelling green stuff. "I like the bacon flavor. Are there really nineteen different greens in this concoction? I bet you can't name them all Minnie?"

Minnie turned from canning and looked directly at him. "What are you bettin' Calvin?"

"Uh. Well. How about you get a boat ride if you win?"

"That's fine, but I'll run your boat. That little outboard called Baby Wildcat III is down-right cute."

"Can you run a boat?"

"She's as good as you," interrupted Pat, putting his plate in the sink.

"Minnie's gotta win first. Okay Minnie, tell me all nineteen ingredients. I win if you look any up."

"I've got them all memorized. I use the same greens every time. There's bear's lettuce, crowfoot, cow's glory, creese, dandelion, dock, goose's tooth, elder leaves, lady's thumb, lamb's quarters, plantain, pepper-and-salt, poke, puccoon leaves, shone, sissle, speckledick, wild turnip, and touch of woolen breeches. I got time for that boat ride tomorrow. Is that good for you, Calvin?"

"Fine. See you tomorrow." Calvin pushed the greens around the plate and then put his dish in the sink.

"Let's go, Cal." They walked out the door and down the porch steps. "Minnie, we'll be back in a couple of hours. Don't wait up. I should have warned you," added Pat. "Don't ever challenge Minnie, because you'll loose every time."

Pat cranked up the truck. The men climbed in as the sun set in the west.

"Aren't those weeds we ate?"

"Greens, weeds, all that green stuff is edible with bacon grease. Come on, it's best get to the still before dark."

"Why before dark?"

"It's better that way. Take my word for it."

Pat drove out of town on the Utica Pike. It was about ten miles until the truck approached the gravel road by a gnarly oak. Pat turned off his headlights as they turned onto the road, and then he drove slowly for another mile. The sun set as Pat parked behind the old red barn. Pat pulled between a National and a Model-T and got out.

"Keep up Calvin. We've got a long walk."

"I'm right behind you."

Pat walked briskly up the hill on the trampled grass path. The path was uneven with rocks and stumps. Calvin stumbled along behind Pat.

"We didn't have any trouble getting here before dark. I think. . . " Suddenly from out of the bushes a rifle fell in front of Calvin's face.

"Whoa there fella!" A beady eyed man with a floppy hat pulled down over his ears pushed the barrel of his rifle right between Calvin's eyes. He swallowed hard as a warm liquid ran down his legs.

Pat turned around. "Evening, Bobby Lee. It's all right. He's my guest, Calvin Johnson from the steamboat."

The rifleman grunted. He promptly retracted his gun and stepped back into the shadow of the bushes.

"Have a good evening, Bobby Lee," called Pat. "We still got a ways to go Calvin. Come on."

"I hope nobody realizes I peed in my pants."

"It's dark. Don't worry about that. Stay close and be quiet."

Calvin followed Pat like a shadow until they came to a big cottonwood tree. Under the tree two men sat on a bench. They drank from jugs and laughed. Their coon dogs howled loudly.

"Good evening, fellas," Pat called and waved.

"Howdy, Pat. Sit a spell," called a tall, skinny man with a buck-tooth smile. He held a skinny, but lively coon dog on a short lead.

"We're here to see, Johnny. We'll visit later."

"Who are they?" Calvin mumbled.

"That's Buck Snort and Tommy Lee Brush. It's Tommy's twin brother, Bobby Lee that we met on the path."

In the open near the spring they walked into a bunch of moonshine-collecting paraphernalia.

"Pat, those boilers look like old copper wash buckets. There must be six of them. Is white lightening that clear stuff dripping out?"

"Yes, but the less conversation from you, the better," mumbled Pat. "Evening, Johnny."

Calvin eyed the devices. "I wonder how your still works." The burly man with a full growth of black beard tending the fire squinted at Calvin and frowned.

"Johnny, this is Cal Johnson from the steamboat," added Pat.

"Well, Cal Johnson from the steamboat, you got curiosity about my operation?"

"Yes, I've never seen anything like this."

"This set up makes the finest white lightning in Indiana. My secret recipe is in the tub. Then the lid is welded on and the worm, or this coiled copper pipe, is fitted into the top. I cook it on this hot charcoal fire. When the mash quits bubbling, the steam is caught in this barrel filled with water called the thump. The steam is cooled by water from Turkey Spring. It runs through a long copper pipe called the flakestand. Condensed liquid drips from the flakestand into jugs where it's aged for at least three hours. Did you understand that Captain?"

"Not exactly."

"Good. That means you won't be making whiskey anytime soon. I don't like competition. This batch's has a subtle nutty flavor with a hint of oak." Johnny handed each of them a half filled cup of the brew from a cracked brown jug.

"Tasty brew." Pat took a swig and motioned for Calvin to take a drink.

"It doesn't look sanitary to me."

"Everything's antiseptic at two-hundred proof. You wanted white lightening Calvin. Drink it."

"I'll rather sip straight gasoline."

"Look Cal, act like you like it. Johnny is serious about his brew. I like it."

"It tastes like turpentine."

"Swallow it," instructed Pat. "Then we'll go over to the bucket by the tree and cut the batch fifty-fifty. That way it's still got a kick, but it won't kill you. Johnny, I like the nutty flavor."

Swallowing the white lightning made Calvin's eyes water and his stomach feel queasy. "The hint of oak must be the tree bark."

"What did you say Johnson?"

"Uh, the hint of oak gives the brew a lot of spark."

Johnny motioned them toward the bucket under the sycamore tree. "Spring water's over there if it's got too much spark for you, Johnson. Tommy and Buck and their dogs are up on the hill."

"We saw the boys on the way in." Pat poured water from the ladle in the bucket into their cups.

Calvin tried it, and then grabbed the ladle to add more water. "This stuff is hard to get down."

"If you can't handle it, don't drink it," whispered Pat. "Just hold the cup and smile. We'll walk up to see Buck and Tommy, and then we'll leave." As they stumbled up the hill they heard the dogs howling. "Good evening, fellows. This is my friend Cal. He's watching the steamboat tied up by the shipyard." Calvin waved and smiled.

"Howdy Cal. Drinkin' likker up here in the woods is relaxin', don't you think?" Tommy refilled his cup.

"Yeah, I'm beginning to like it," Calvin mumbled as he and Pat sat down on two stumps. "Does it make everyone feel hot and nauseous?"

"Maybe."

"You know, we wouldn't have to make so much, ifin people didn't drink so much," chuckled Buck through his protruding teeth.

"I'm glad you boys could sit a spell," said Tommy. "You just missed Sheridan. He porked down a whole cup a likker like it was water, and then he lit up like a honky tonk on Saturday night."

"Where did he go?" asked Pat. "We didn't see him on the way in."

"He's layin' under the cottonwood by the crick," laughed Buck. "Pat, did you hear what happened to Doc Renski?"

"Nothing bad I hope."

Buck Snort sat back under the tree. "Nope. He ain't been hurt yet."

Tommy continued the story. "Doc stopped by to borrow back them water jugs he loaned to Sheridan. He left thinkin' them jugs was empty, but they wasn't. At night time when Doc mixed up the Mrs. tonic with water from the jug, she laughed and said she felt betteren usual. In fact, instead of restin' she took off to town in Doc's new Model-T Ford with nothing on except her Sunday hat."

Buck laughed so hard he fell off the bench. "She was havin' so much fun she drived his car right off'n the dock and into five foot of water."

Calvin's mouth fell open. "Did she drown?"

"No. Mattie Renski did just fine," answered Tommy. "She climbed out of the car and swam to shore."

"Doc Renski was surprised since Mattie never swimmed before."

"Pat I don't feel well," moaned Calvin.

Pat grabbed Calvin's arm. "We gotta go fellas. We'll see you Friday on the steamboat."

Tommy offered them another cup. "Come on, stick around. This run puts on a fine jag."

Calvin nodded no.

"Cal, grab a jug and stick a corn cob in the top and we'll go."

"I'm feeling bad. Can you grab mine?"

Pat grabbed two jugs and Calvin's arm. "Thanks. We're going back to town."

"I don't want to gyp these guys. How do I pay for this stuff?"

"Believe me, nobody gets gypped. They collect later."

Pat and Calvin retracted their steps down the hill. The moon lit up the path to the barn. In the shadows along one side Calvin stumbled and fell on top of the first of a series of long pine boxes.

"Are you okay?"

"I don't have my sea legs. Gee Pat don't these boxes look like caskets?"

"They are caskets. Tommy and Buck make them."

"Are there bodies inside?"

"Hell, no. They're filled with shine."

"That's a strange way to move the stuff."

"Calvin, think about it. Nobody's going to open a casket. People generally let the dead be. Come on. Follow me."

Once in the truck, the men traveled back up the gravel road. This time Pat turned the headlights off. When they reached the gnarly oak at the Utica Pike, he turned on his headlights and headed away from town.

"Isn't Jeffersonville the other way?"

"We're going back to town the long way, Cal."

In about a mile they passed a car parked along side the road. The moonlight reflected off the star on the side. Pat slowed down and flashed his lights. The car signaled back by flashing its lights.

"Pat, wasn't that's the deputy's car?"

"Yes."

"Is he trying to spot the still?"

"I think he knows where it is."

"What's going to happen to us if we get caught red-handed with this brew? Do you think he's going to call the sheriff? Nuts! I feel terrible. I don't want to go to jail!"

"We're not going to jail."

"How do you know? The deputy just saw us."

"The deputy's not going to be calling anybody. Cal, the police chief was running the still."

"Johnny is the police chief. If everybody knows about the operation, why is the deputy sitting alongside the road with his lights out?"

"The Deputy is the look-out. If an unauthorized person comes down the road in the wrong direction he calls the barn on the police radio. When the stranger arrives there won't be anything up on the hill except coon hunters and their dogs."

"Now I get it."

"It's about time."

"Pat, my head is buzzing like there's a hive of bees swarming inside. When I close my eyes I see six-hundred million torch-light processions charging, ten abreast, and when I open my eyes the moonlight blinds me and everything is dancing around."

"You're feeling the effects of the white lightening. You've got a jag on."

"I'm not sure I like this feeling. Pat, this stuff tastes terrible. How can I make it drinkable?"

"Here's my tip. Cut the brew again with water like we did at the still, or slip a few caramels in it and let it stand for awhile. It's not Jack Daniels by any stretch of the imagination, but for prohibition brew, it's real tasty."

CHAPTER 10

FOUR FAMILIES ON THE RIVERSIDE OF THE PIKE

Pat and Minnie Murphy lived on Front Street, the first street over Green Hill from the river. Minnie Murphy was the quiet type who came from the hills. Her country cooking did not impress Calvin, but her physical prowess made him sit up and take notice. She could swing an axe and cut stove wood with the best of the men, or crank up a Model-T and drive it away. Minnie's specialty seemed to be rope-starting outboard engines and boating driving.

"Good mornin', Calvin. Guess you come to ride with me to the Louisville wharf. That's good because you can watch the boat while I shop at the Five and Ten Store. I need to buy thread for darnin'."

"I'll back the trailer in the water for you Cal."

"Sure Pat. I'll handle the lines."

"You want me to pull that rope to start it Calvin?" asked Minnie.

"Not until I get Baby Wildcat heading upriver. Remember there's no neutral. When the engine turns over the boat takes off in whatever direction she's headed."

After Pat backed the trailer into the river, Calvin held the boat in knee-deep water while Minnie pulled up her dress and slid over the stern. Minnie confidently eased herself next to the engine and straightened her skirt. Effortlessly she slipped the rope around the starter pulley.

"Are you ready Calvin?"

"Sure. Keep the choke on and give a pull. I got us pointed into the river."

Minnie pulled once and the engine purred. "Hop in, Calvin. We're agoin' to Louisville."

Three more families lived next to the Murphys and Froggy Woodson on the riverside of the Pike.

Sitting catty corner from the path stood a tar-paper shack with a rough-sewn wooden porch. This was the Gibson place. The windows were without glass and curtains. A discarded orange crate served as a step to the rickety porch. Mr. Gibson was called Hoot after a popular movie star, Hoot Gibson. But Hoot Gibson of Port Fulton wasn't a big star. Once upon a time Hoot Gibson lived high on the hog with big money he made as a welder at the Howard Shipyards. He lavished his money on liquor, guns, and fancy cowboy clothes, while his family barely got by. Hoot fantasized about being in western movies like Pride of the Range with Tom Mix and Harry Carey. He even wore a gun in his belt or in his boot like the movie star did.

When the war ended, jobs were cut at the shipyard. By that time Hoot's was an alcoholic and delusional. When he was laid off, he lost his reason living. Hoot picked fights and shot at people who disagreed with him. For days he disappeared on drinking binges while his wife, Johnnie Sue, and his six kids hardly had enough money to buy food.

The unsupervised Gibson boys caused their share of trouble in Port Fulton. Tommy, Harry, and Little Hooter were named after Hoot Gibson's western heroes. The boys ranged in age from eight to ten. Mostly they excelled at cheating, stealing, and hustling. Encounters with the law were many, but somehow they managed to stay out of jail. Tom Mix Gibson was the oldest and most thoughtful of the litter. Tom was ten, about the same age as Oscar Murphy, Pat's youngest son. Tom and Baby (Oscar's nickname) played together. The middle Gibson, Harry, had a lisp, was a little slow mentally, and did any job Little Hooter could think up. Without doubt, eight year old Little Hooter was the brains of the group. His schemes brought in money and kept his family from starving. Little Hooter's weakness was smoking. He smoked cigar and cigarette butts as well as dry grass in Sears Roebuck catalog papers.

After the boat trip to Louisville with Minnie, Calvin's clothes were drenched and his nerves frazzled. As Baby Wildcat left the Jeffersonville landing they struggled through the wash of the packet Revonah. Minnie made a quick stop at the Louisville dock which nearly capsized the boat. On the return trip Minnie cut boldly through the wake of the City of Memphis. Gallons of water flew over the bow.

Calvin waved to Minnie. He was relieved the trip was over as he slowly walked to the Hubbard to change clothes. In the galley the growing stack of mail covered one end of the table. Every time Froggy stopped by the post office he grabbed the boat's mail which consisted of bills, legal notices, and letters to people Calvin didn't know. One of these days he'd have to tackle the mail, but not today.

After changing to dry clothes, Calvin filled a cup of coffee. He climbed to the pilot house, and sat back in the well-worn pilot's chair to watch the sternwheeler Southland move majestically upriver. The sun, breaking through the clouds, painted a path of gold across the Ohio. The rollers spent themselves behind the boat in lacelike splendor. Calvin finally began to relax from the chaos of Louisville.

The Ohio was a beautiful river. Within its full tide, the river was a mile wide, tawny green, winding around bold headlands and through lush bottom lands on a course a thousand miles long. Calvin watched scores of birds wheeling over treetops, flying through the branches, squalling on limbs with wings outspread to the sunshine. Some birds drank at the river's edge, jostling and hissing at each other. His eyes were closing when he heard some odd staccato sounds. He perked up. The sputtering and coughing emanated from the stern.

COFF! COFF! COFF!

Calvin wondered if Froggy's spooks were awake in the daylight. Calvin listened again.

COFF! COFF! COFF!

Could this be more shanty boaters? Calvin followed the noise to the stern.

COFF! COFF! COFF! COFF! COFF! COFF!

Crossing over to the starboard side Calvin peered behind a pile of boxes. A skinny, bare-foot, shirtless kid with a mangy head of sandy blond hair that looked like it had been cut with a soup bowl stared up at him with soulful eyes. The boy sucked a cigar butt into his mouth and swallowed it. He coughed again.

COFF! COFF! COFF!

"Don't I know you kid?"

"Yep."

"Aren't you Little Hooter?"

The freckled face boy nodded with a smile that showed his missing front teeth. "Yep. Hi yah, Captin'." In front of Little Hooter lay all the butts from the ash trays. They were methodically organized in order of size. He quickly stuffed the used stogies in his pants pocket.

"Are you a smoking addict? Give me those things?" Little Hooter's lip curled up as he reluctantly handed them over. Calvin tossed the butts overboard. "What are you doing here?"

"I seen you leavin' fer Louisville today, so I thinks I'd check out the boat fer smokes." As he talked Little Hooter eyed a long cigar in Calvin's shirt pocket.

"You should know smoking other people's cigars isn't sanitary."

"But they're free."

"Smoking's not good for you. You're a kid. Hoot would you like to try something new? It might downright eliminate your smoking."

"I like smokin'. Can I have that cigar in your pocket?"

"No, I've got something better. Last week I bought a box of premium, two for a nickel, Italian stogies over in Louisville. Wanna try one?"

"You just said I shouldn't be smokin'. What's the catch?"

"No catch. Follow me. The box is in my cabin."

"Sure, Captin'."

Little Hooter followed Calvin up the ladder to his cabin. Calvin pulled a red cigar box out of the desk drawer and opened it. He flashed it under Little Hooter's nose. The aroma of strong tobacco permeated the air. Little Hooter took a long sniff and smiled.

"These stogies are potent. However, since you're a connoisseur of good strong smokes, you'll probably like them." Calvin smiled slyly as he handed one to Hooter.

Hooter took it, and then made himself comfortable in Calvin's leather chair. He bit off the tip of the stogie like a professional. From his pants pocket he pulled out a pack of matches and lit up. Hooter sat back and inhaled, and then puffed a series of concentric smoke rings.

"Good, Captin'. By the way what's a connesewer?"

"A connoisseur is an expert."

"I guess I'm an expert in many things."

"Do you like those smokes?"

"They taste pretty good, but smells like burnin' garbage. Are you goin' to smoke with me?"

"Not right now. My stomach's feeling a little funny from my boat trip to Louisville. Go ahead enjoy it."

"Thanks Captin'." Hoot puffed.

Calvin's eyes followed the smoke rings as they hovered like apparitions against the ceiling. "You seem like an intelligent kid. Why don't I see you playing outside with other boys?"

"I'm smart and a connesewer like you said, but other kids don't like to come around me. They don't like my smokin' and not washin' regular like. But mostly I has a bad habit that keeps them away."

"What kind of habit?"

"I shits in the path. My brothers go in the grass, but that's too fer."

"Too far for what?"

"Too fer from the river. Them black flies bites my ass in the high grass, so I poops closer to water. Then I can dive in the river and get rid of them damn flies. Don't that make sense?"

Calvin laughed out loud. "Yeah Hooter, that does make sense."

"You better watch where you walk on Green Hill. I'm gonna vamoose." In a flash Little Hooter grabbed the box of cigars off Calvin's desk. Then he hopped over the railing and shimmed down the side of the boat.

Calvin shouted. "Are you sure you can smoke all those?"

"Sure. Thanks Captin'." Hooter skittered up Green Hill watching where he stepped.

Walking back to the galley, Calvin hoped smoking those potent Italian stogies would teach him a lesson. Then again, he might enjoy them. Calvin poured some coffee. His eyes caught a glimpse of fancy pink envelope in the middle of the stack of mail on the table. He pulled the letter out and whiffed the pink envelope for Christina's flowery fragrance. He sat down with a letter opener and a smile when his ambiance was shattered.

"Help! Help Captin'!"

Calvin looked up to see a tow-headed boy with bowl-like haircut. He wore tattered bib-overalls and no shoes.

"Captin' you gotta come quick."

"Aren't you another one of those Gibson kids? What are you doing on my boat?"

"Yes, sir. I'm Tommy. My mama is havin' a baby and Doc Renski needs you to come over and help. Come on. Come on right now."

"Tommy, Doc's got the wrong person. I know absolutely nothing about babies. I fix engines and watch old steamboats. Are you sure he wants me?"

"Yep, I already tried to get Miss Murphy and Miss Harris. They ain't home. Doc says to heat up some water. Bring it with you."

"Okay." Calvin grabbed the kettle of hot water off the stove. Tommy ran down the gangplank. Calvin followed behind him at a slow trot.

Huffing and puffing Calvin hiked up the path on Green Hill. He thought about Little Hooter's confession and tried to watch where he stepped. Finally Calvin caught his breath at the house. Tommy scampered ahead while Calvin stepped from the ground to the orange crate step to the porch. A burlap curtain made out of flour sacks covered the front entry. Holding the kettle ahead Calvin pulled the curtain aside. A table made of boards, a cast-iron stove and two broken chairs sparsely furnished the room. The little Gibsons lined up on the floor, sitting Indian fashion. They waved.

Calvin put the kettle on the stove. "What happened to your door?"

"We bornd it fer firewood," answered one of the three little Gibson girls. Except for size, the girls looked alike with their pigtails and freckled faces. They watched with wide eyes and open mouths as Dr. Renski appeared from the bedroom. In his arms was the seventh little Gibson wrapped in a flour sack.

"I brought the water Doc."

"You're late, Johnson. Hopalong Gibson was born ten minutes ago. Don't look so disappointed. And don't let that hot water go to waste. Make us some tea. There's some Earl Grey in my case."

Next to the Gibsons' tar paper shack on the riverside of the Pike sat the unpainted, four-room house of Fod Smith. Fod was the nickname for Father. Fod had twelve sons.

According to Pat Murphy, the Smiths were a remarkable, generally law-abiding family. The oldest boys were twins. Hutch worked at a boat store in Louisville while Butch drove a cab in town. The other Smith boys joined the U.S. Navy. They were stationed in Guam operating a coal-loading facility for the government. Being a proud father, Fod plastered his kitchen with photographs of the young sailors and with newspaper clips of the gooney birds of Guam they kept as pets. The youngest sailor named Happ practiced the skills he learned at home. Unfortunately he got caught with a still on the boat. He was sentenced to a year in the brig for distributing moonshine to the Polynesians. When Fod's wife Edna ran off with a one-legged Fuller Brush salesman three years ago Fod became a recluse. He lived for his monthly government pension check. When the check arrived, Fod drank away his troubles.

Living on the porch at the Smith house was a cross-eyed German Shepherd dog named Rex. These police dogs became popular pets in Port Fulton. The movie, The Rum Runners, in 1923 started the craze. Froggy told Calvin that Fod watched the movie eleven times in a Louisville show because he fell in love with Fearless, the canine star. Fod renamed his dog Rex, Fearless Rex.

Normally Fearless Rex slept on the stoop of the porch. However, when Fod drank in town, the dog's mission was to take care of him. No matter where Fod wandered, no one dared touch the old man because Fearless Rex growled at his side. The only exceptions were taxi drivers.

Sometimes Calvin noticed Fod laying in the gutter Market Street. Fearless Rex sat down next to him. They waited patiently to be picked up by Fod's oldest son who drove for the Jeffersonville Taxi Company. Butch kept his taxicab at the Flatiron Building. He had an understanding with the drivers that if anyone found Fod passed out in town that they would call the taxi company. A taxicab came, no questions asked, and took Fod and Fearless Rex home. That was all right with the dog. No one else touched the old man.

Butch and Hutch were identical twins and the smartest boys in the family. Butch drove for the Jeffersonville Taxi Company while Hutch worked as a boat polisher for Soupy Sikennette's Boat Store in Louisville. Butch was a fun-loving practical joker who drove a cab like he was on a race track. Years ago Butch Smith and Pat Murphy raced on the dirt tracks of southern Indiana. Butch won more races than he lost.

Living next door to Fod Smith, separated by a tall fence, was the Harris Family. The house was a well-kept, white-painted cottage that Buddy Harris built himself. There were three bright rooms. The kitchen had running water and new screens. Buddy bought the furniture second hand or he made it himself with wood Froggy scrounged from the

Howard Shipyards cabinet shop. Evelyn and three daughters, as well as Evelyn's mother, kept the house neat and tidy.

Buddy Harris worked on the tender, Greenbrier. It was a regular job that paid ten dollars a week. The Greenbrier brought oil, globes, and wicks to the government lights along the Ohio River. Riverboat pilots steered by the lights, which were lanterns set upon white tripods in trees or on the bank, with white Greek crosses behind them for daymarks. By night the captain at the wheel held a jackstaff on one of these government lights to keep the boat on track and out of danger.

Buddy's job on the Greenbriar was a grueling one month on and one month off. For years Buddy tried to get a job in town. He applied in the cabinet operation at the Howard Shipyards where he could use his carpentry skills, but lay-offs at the shipyard closed the shop. When Evelyn Harris lost her job at the clothing factory, things got harder for the family.

One afternoon Calvin walked past the Harris cottage. Evelyn sat on the porch darning socks.

"Good afternoon, Evelyn. How are you?"

"Not very good Calvin. Did you hear the Depot shut down the shirt factory?"

"Froggy told me. Did you work there?"

"Yes I made flannel shirts and breeches. When the shirt department installed electric cutting knives and employed three shifts of cutters, they issued garments for completion at home. I worked at home for three years. It was a very fine job, paid by the piece. When the department closed it caused a hardship on many families."

"Sounds like you've got a lot of fine sewing experience. I need a favor Evelyn. I'd pay you for it."

"What can I do for you?"

"Could you make me a boat cover? My outboard, Baby Wildcat, sits around in the grass and a cover would keep out the leaves for the winter."

"Calvin, I'd be perfectly willing, but my sewing machine is broke. We can't afford to fix it."

"I'm pretty good with mechanical things, let me look at it. I might be able to fix it. Would you make me a cover if I repaired your machine?"

"Sure. That would be wonderful. Having a working sewing machine will help me bring in money for the family".

"Where's your machine?"

"In the bureau. I'll show you."

Calvin followed Evelyn Harris to a back room and examined the old Singer. "Looks like it's got a piece missing. Pat's got some old machines and stuff behind the garage. I'll see if he has the part that will work."

"That would be a God-sent. Thanks Calvin."

The next day Calvin scrounged the piles of junk at Pat's for a part for Evelyn's sewing machine. There is was. A cog sat in the corner that could replace the broken piece. "Pat, what you do want for this?"

"Take it. You've been a big help this week. See you tonight. The party starts at sundown."

"I'm looking forward to it."

At the Harris house that afternoon Calvin fixed the sewing machine. "This will work fine Evelyn."

"I really do appreciate your fixing it. Bring me some fabric I'll make you a cover at no cost."

"Thanks, but I'll pay you for the job."

"Thanks again, Calvin. Having this machine working is truly a God-sent. I can get some jobs to bring in money."

"I'm glad I could help."

Evelyn threaded the machine and chattered like a giddy school girl as she pulled material out of a drawer. "Calvin, I know what I'm going to buy me with the first money I get from sewing. Right off, I'm going to buy some dishes. Not fancy ones like you see the magazines, but just a few so the whole family can to eat supper together."

"You don't have enough dishes for your family to eat together?"

"No Calvin. The girls eat first, then Mama and me, and Buddy when he's not on the boat."

"Evelyn, you don't need to buy dishes. Use money you make for something else. I have a steamboat full of dishes gathering dust. It's a shame for me to have all that china in the galley, when your family eats in shifts. When I bring the canvas for my boat cover, I'll bring you enough china to fill your kitchen cabinet."

"That would be a wonderful thing, Calvin. Thank you. I'll make you an especially fine boat cover for free."

The fourth family on the riverside of the Pike was next to the landing. Captain Ham Duffy and Mrs. Duffy owned one of the prettiest brick houses in Port Fulton. It had a porch on three sides with railings of fancy ironwork that looked like black lace from a distance. Gorgeous flower beds lined the front of the house with rose bushes along the porch. Fruit trees and calycanthus bushes grew along the walkway. Fancy stone steps lead to a massive wooden door that had once been part of the steamer Bonnie Belle. The front porch had a swing right in the middle of it where Mrs. Duffy sat and knitted and looked out at the river. Captain Duffy's real last name wasn't Duffy, but everyone called him that because he was the captain of the steamboat Duffy.

CHAPTER 11

HOMEBREW PARTY ON THE HUBBARD

The steamboat Duffy operated out of Louisville for the Duffy Sand and Gravel Company. Calvin watched the steamer pass the Hubbard every day like clockwork. The Duffy was built in 1893 and carried about fourteen gross tons. It was a strangely prophetic boat about fifty-five feet long with a beam of fourteen feet and two propellers instead of a paddle wheel. In the morning it chugged upstream with empty barges. At sundown the steamer returned with the barges loaded with sand and gravel. Captain Ham Duffy lived on the river most of the time. His wife, Dora, saw him only when there was something important going on, or he needed laundry washed. Ham rowed ashore on the ship's yawl while the engineer and first mate stood watch in the pilot's house.

"Ahoy, Captain Duffy," Calvin called as the yawl approached the landing.

"Ahoy, Captain Johnson. You're just the man I wanted to see." The Captain beached the yawl next to the Hubbard. "When's the fun starting on the Hubbard tonight?"

"At sundown."

"Great. That'll give me enough time to eat with Dora and change my clothes. See you later."

After gulping down a cold supper, Calvin dragged out barrels, chairs, and lanterns onto the lower deck of the Hubbard. Calvin pulled out his jug of white lightning and shoved it under his chair. He hoped that cutting the brew with spring water and aging it with caramels made the drink more palatable.

The sky, the wooded hills, and the river, combined in peace at the end of the day. As the twilight invaded the river, Calvin caught sight of a line of people walking over Green Hill and down the path. Each of them carried a lantern. Laughter, whooping, and music filled the air. Three fiddlers danced at the front and played such jigging numbers as Arkansas Traveler, Boating up Sandy, Money Musk, Sourwood Mountain, Turkey in the Straw, and Weevily Wheat. Men carried pints, half-pints, and jugs. A heavy-set man with a luxuriant black beard walked along the bank balancing a tremendous mound of potato salad on a platter over his head. Two men danced up the gangplank shouldering cheeses, breads, and sausages.

At the end of the line stumbled a man dressed like a cowboy with a ten-gallon hat. He carried two jugs of brew, one in each hand. When he stepped on the deck he yelled and slid the jugs down the deck. "Whoopee! This is gonna be a damn fine party." He grabbed the revolver from his belt, twirled it around his finger like a gunslinger, and then promptly shot out two lanterns next to Calvin's head.

The Chief put down his platter of potato salad and shoved the cowboy into a chair. "Ain't you got a lick of sense, Hoot? Put that damn gun back in your pants or I'll hog tie you and drag you to jail."

"Gol damn Chief, I'm just havin' a good time. Shootin' up stuff is what cowboys do. Remember Tom Mix in Deadwood Coach and Harry Carey in that two reel classic Straight Shooting? They blew the whole town away." Hoot staggered to his feet and shot again, but this time he blasted a hole in Calvin's jug. "Sorry, but shooten up stuff is what cowboys do. This stuff ain't half bad," added Hoot as he dropped to his knees and lapped up the brew.

The Chief stepped on Hoot's back with one foot and grabbed his gun. "Homer, cuff him! This guy is a menace."

The sheriff snapped handcuffs on him and shoved him toward the gangplank. "I'll be back as soon as I lock up this here cowboy."

"You can't scare the gizzard out of me!" The sheriff just laughed and dragged him down the gangplank.

"Where can I put this potato salad, Captain?"

"Put it in the galley. It's straight forward through the doors. I put ice in the ice box this afternoon so you can stack all the food in there." Calvin motioned to the other men with the breads, sausages, and cheese.

"Hoot Gibson is harmless. Sometimes he thinks he's a western movie star," added Pat, handing Calvin a half pint with a smile. "Try this Cal. I made it from persimmons. It's been aging in the cellar since last fall."

"Thanks."

The Chief pulled up a chair. "When Hoot Gibson's got a jag on and a loaded pistol he's better off sleeping it off in jail." He smiled at the friendly colored kid from the orphanage standing next to Pat. "Good evening Mud. I'm glad to see you. Aren't you a little young to be drinking?"

"I don't drink alcohol, Chief. Pat gots me a job."

"Mud King's going to be the bartender. Set the jugs up right here," said Pat.

"No diving or swimming tonight," added Calvin.

"No, Captain. I comes to do a job for Mr. Pat. He's payin' me two bits."

"I guess you'll want me to pay you too?"

"Yes sir, Captain. Good help's worth at least two bits. I got an account at the City Bank."

"You got a plan for your money?"

"I'm just savin' it right now, Captain. Might open me a business someday."

"Did you know that Mud's a nickname?" added Pat.

"Yes sir. My full name's Earl M. King, but I likes to be called Mud. Mud like the river mud between my toes."

"Mud's a good kid," said Butch Smith. "I saw him swim across to the Kentucky side and back seven times without touching land." He grabbed a bucket of brew and sat down. As he drank it he took some deep breaths.

"Mud and the other kids from the orphanage come down to the boat. They use the bow for diving and swimming. You look out of breath, Butch. Where have you been?"

"I've been running all over. I got a call about five o'clock to pick up Fod and Fearless Rex on Main Street, but I couldn't find them."

"Fod and that dog of his are sitting on the top deck," added Gus as he climbed down the ladder. "And they're both drinking."

"How did they get here? I better see what's going on." Butch grabbed a sandwich and headed to the hurricane deck.

Dozens of noisy men congregated on the lower deck at the bar on chairs and barrels. Everybody clapped and drank as the fiddlers played. Pat's persimmon brandy gave Calvin a pleasant sensation. He snoozed peacefully in a chair despite the raucous activity.

Sheriff Homer Satterlee charged up the gangplank. "Hoot's in the calaboose."

"This party is great! There ain't no houses close to make complaints so nobody's going to get drugged to jail," said Froggy swigging down an entire half pint without a breath.

Shapiro slapped his knee with a laugh. "You think that's because all the police is right here?"

"Homer, don't look so damn serious. We're just funnin'," said Froggy taking another half pint out of his back pocket.

"You guys better behave yourselves. Remember the cell next to Hoot Gibson is open tonight. When I left him he was sleeping and farting. I didn't search him, so he's probably still carrying bullets for that gun in his boot."

Froggy and Gus laughed and ducked under the bar just as an old man and a German shepherd dog stumbled onto the deck.

"Good evening, fellas. Wanna see a pitcher of my sons standin' around the coal ship in Guam? Charlie here is going to school to be a captain in the U.S. Navy." He pushed the photograph into Calvin's face.

"Great looking boys," Calvin struggled to wake up. He rubbed his eyes and pushed the photo back to Fod. The dog growled and showed his teeth.

Calvin backed away. "Fod, why don't you and your dog sit over here near the rail?"

"Good idea. Fearless Rex and me pees a lot when we're drinkin'."

"You have a great party going here, Captain. But seats are in short supply," remarked Captain Duffy.

"I know exactly where you can get some excellent seating and cheap, Calvin," interrupted Soupy Sikennette.

"Don't you sell boats? What do you know about chairs?"

"Sure, I sell boats. I sell some of the fastest boats on the Ohio River. But that doesn't stop me from checking out the Depot for bargains."

Calvin's head was still spinning so he sat down on a barrel. "Evelyn Harris told me she worked for the factory at the Depot making clothes. She never mentioned the Depot sold chairs."

Soupy sat back. "The Depot goes way back to the Civil War when the Union Army established Camp Joe Holt near Big Eddy of the Ohio Falls. Camp Holt became the General Hospital here in Jeffersonville. The Depot's changed with the times."

"The Depot covers four city blocks, Cal," remarked Pat. "In its heyday the Depot made saddles, metal castings, rubber stamps, hardtack, as well as shirts and clothes."

"You'd never know it today, but Jeffersonville was one of the most prosperous steamboat towns along the Ohio," added Ham Duffy.

Butch interrupted. "The railroads cut into river traffic so a lot of businesses dried up. Today the Depot's a government storage facility."

"When I stopped by," said Soupy. "I spotted some fine mahogany pews being stacked up. A church up north had a fire and cancelled their order. The Clark Barge Company sold them to the Depot. They might be just what you need for seating. The pews were dirt cheap."

"More seating is a great idea, but I'm curious about the Depot. Tell me more about it?"

"For one thing Calvin, it's the biggest employer in Port Fulton, next to the shipyards," Froggy added. "Mostly the Depot stores stuff."

"Last month I bought some ambulance tailgates made out of white oak bound with iron straps," said Butch Smith. "I built an entire driveway out of them."

"I got you all beat. Last year I got the deal of the century at the Depot," smiled Shapiro, sipping from his jug.

"What kind of deal?" Calvin asked.

"Motorcycle parts. I bought Indian motorcycle parts for five dollars a ton!"

"I remember that. Didn't you set up a warehouse in Louisville to sell them?" Pat said.

"Yes, sir. I put an ad in big print in The Louisville Post. It said: *Indian Motorcycles. $25 apiece.* The machines were all disassembled, and then wrapped in wax paper and card board. The catch was these Indian motorcycles weren't new. They were made in 1907."

"Age didn't matter. The sale appealed to the boys in Louisville and around here too," added Soupy.

"It didn't take anytime for customers to pick out the parts necessary to assemble their very own Indian."

"I heard some guys tried to sneak in and steal pistons, connecting rods, and other spare parts."

"That wasn't a problem Pat. As long as they didn't haul away a ton of parts, I was ahead."

Pat chuckled. "Last summer every kid for miles around was riding a genuine hand-made Twin Indian motorcycle. That thirty-nine cubic inch engine produced a whooping four horsepower."

"Some of them motorcycles was real pretty. I laughed about it all the way to the bank."

"Do you know what they're asking for those Civil War cannons? My brother said there were four smooth bore cannons standing in a corner."

"I never noticed any cannons, Buddy."

"Speaking of cannons and the Civil War. You guys wanna hear a good story? It's about the incident that happened around here on Buffington Island," added Homer.

"I'm sure you wanna tell us about it, Sheriff Satterlee," smiled Froggy, drinking down a bucket of brew.

Homer grabbed a bucket of beer from Mud's bar and plunked himself down in the middle of the group. "I like telling stories."

"You're a piss poor storyteller. Don't make it too long," mumbled Froggy.

"What did you say about my stories being long?"

"I said your stories are strong. You know, good stories."

"Well thanks Froggy. The story starts with John Morgan's Confederate Raiders being cornered between a Union gunboat and the pursuing cavalry."

"Are you sure that happened at Buffington?" asked Froggy.

"Sure, I'm sure. After the fight the Raiders surrendered to the bluejackets. Both sides were sweaty and dirty. Since it was a hot day all the soldiers looked longingly at the green, clear, and cool Ohio. Before you could count to ten, the captors and the captives all shucked their clothes and charged into the river."

"That's pretty strange," interrupted Froggy.

Homer ignored Froggy. "The soldiers were all shouting and laughing, and all you could see was them naked asses." Homer laughed and laughed, but everybody else was quiet.

"Speaking of naked asses. Johnny, when are you going to shave off that scraggily beard of yours?" asked Gus.

"Never. This luxuriant beard's gonna be a permanent part of my handsome face."

"We made this bet on a fishing trip. The last guy that shaves has to buy dinner at that fancy Black Bear Restaurant in Louisville," added the Sheriff. "Me and the deputies are waiting on the Chief to buy us dinner."

Johnny stroked his beard. "I ain't buying dinner no matter what, Homer, so you guys better get used to my handsome hairy face."

Mud pulled Calvin by the shirt. "Come quick. Two guys is fightin' on the top deck and I thinks one of them fell overboard. Come on."

"Lead the way Mud." Calvin ran behind Mud as the kid hopped over drunks and around obstacles. They climbed the ladder two steps at a time. On the top deck in the light of the full moon Butch Smith and Buddy Harris sat wet and naked on two barrels. They were laughing, hiccupping, and singing God Bless America. Buddy wore the life ring from the Hubbard around his neck.

"What's going on? Are you guys all right?"

"Don't we look all wight, Captain," slurred Buddy, holding on to the barrel with both hands.

Calvin stopped in front of the men. "What happened to your clothes?"

Buddy adjusted the life ring around his neck and laughed. He passed the jug of moonshine between his legs to Butch. "We can't wemember, wheelie wemember where we put our clothes." They laughed and passed the jug.

"Mud said there was a fight."

"We ain't fightin'. Butch and me are best friends."

" I just dared Buddy to jump over the side and bring back the life ring."

"I did and I won. The moon was wheelie bright. I could have found a dozen life wings out there. I think it's time to pay up, Butch."

"What did I bet anyways?"

"It was a wide in your fancy new taxi cab to Tobacco Landing on Sunday, don't you wemember?"

"Sure I remember that I bet a ride to Tobacco Landing. Can I bring my wife?"

"Sure. You can bring your taxi and your wife. And I'll bring my wife and a wheelie big picnic lunch to the Falls."

"Where's the falls?" Calvin asked.

"I can tell you're not from around here. Can't you Buddy? People around here know the Falls of the Ohio is a famous natural wonder of the world."

"Calvin, the Falls is a wheelie nice trip even for a guy with no sense of wumor," remarked Buddy.

"I'm pretty busy to see a famous natural wonder."

"But it's fun, Captain. First, you go past the shipyard over the old levee area to Spring Street. When you see the Big Four Bridge, go under it, and keep going until you pass the Pennsylvania Railroad Bridge. It's the big rusty one. At the top of the riverbank, you can see the Falls."

"The Falls are wheelie beautiful. They tumble down and stir the river with a big woar. It's a sight to behold. Butch, we'll bring the picnic lunch, the tablecloth, and the dishes. You know my wheelie good friend Captain Cal gave us a whole bunch of wheelie nice dishes from the steamboat. Thanks again wheelie good friend."

Mud handed the crumpled clothes to the men. "Here's your clothes, Mr. Buddy and Mr. Butch."

Buddy and Butch laughed as they struggled to sort their clothes and get dressed.

"I hope you have a great time at the Falls. Let's get back to the party Mud. Everything here seems under control."

Walking back Calvin and Mud noticed that drunks either slept where they drank, or disappeared. Calvin hoped the missing guys didn't fall overboard or drown.

COFF! COFF! COFF!

COFF! COFF! COFF!

"Whoopee! Yeah, yeah, yeah!"

COFF! COFF! COFF!

"What do you thinks is goin' on, Captain?"

"Well, Mud it could be one of the steamboat's ghost, but most likely it's just Little Hooter in my cabin. He's probably picking up butts again. I hope he doesn't set the place on fire."

They followed the coughing sounds right to the captain's cabin. Little Hooter was sitting in the worn leather chair perusing Calvin's book of photographs.

"What's going on Hoot?"

The boy looked up and smiled a silly grin. Then Hooter inhaled and blew smoke rings into the air.

"Hi yah Captin', these are very nice pitchers of neked ladies. This is a great party. I collected a big bag a butts. Can I take these pitchers too?"

"No! Those are my art pictures."

"They looks like neked ladies to me."

Calvin grabbed the book and stuffed it back under his bunk. "Hooter, we can use your help cleaning up."

"Sure, Captin'." He tied the burlap bag of used cigars to a rope around his waist that held up his pants, and then followed them.

They checked the cabins on the top deck. Small and agile Hooter crawled around and spotted men under bunks and tables.

"Some of these guys are sleepin' in funny places," remarked Hoot. He picked up some stray butts and stuffed them in his pockets.

"Captain, there's water all over the deck," said Mud. "Maybe somethin's broke."

"It's not water, Captin'. I checked it out before. Somebody besides me don't use the path."

"Nuts!"

"See yah Captin'." Little Hooter slid over the side and disappeared into the night.

Without power to operate the pumps, there was no running water. Calvin recommended the party-goers pee over the stern, but inebriated as well as fascinated by the porcelain heads, the men used the shiny toilets anyway. Mud and Calvin took turns bucketing water from over the side to clean up the mess.

"Do you believe in them ghost stories about the Hubbard, Captain?" asked Mud while they worked in the moonlight.

"I don't think so, Mud. Even with this full moon, the only spirits around are here in the jugs."

That night was only the beginning of a summer of brew parties on the steamboat. They happened monthly because it took that long to accumulate enough homebrew in prohibition times.

CHAPTER 12

INDIAN CORN REMEDY

Soon after Calvin's arrival in Port Fulton, he noticed an uncanny market for pint and half-pint whiskey bottles. Empty pints were worth a dime apiece, while half-pints brought in the handsome sum of two cents. Calvin listened from his bunk as someone bumped and clanked down the gangplank. One morning the curiosity got the better of him. He pulled on his pants and followed the clanking. Calvin called to the shadow lingering near the ladder. "Hey, what are you doing on my boat?"

Quickly the apparition vanished into the morning fog on the lower deck. Calvin trotted down the deck behind the shadowy figure with a pillow sack full of whisky bottles. The man wore a shabby white lab coat with a floppy hat that fell over his pointed ears. He stuffed his prizes from the sack into the pockets of his coat. Staying right behind him Calvin watched the bottle collector skittering in and out of the early morning fog along Green Hill disappearing and reappearing in the shadows. Calvin followed the fellow up the steps of a neat bungalow facing High Street. The blue painted house was catty-corner from Pat Murphy's garage. Calvin balanced himself on the rickety top step and knocked briskly on the closed door. Bang! Bang!

"Hello in there. Is anybody home?" After a couple of minutes Calvin walked around to the backyard. He found the elf-like bottle collector under a tree.

With his back to Calvin, he sat cross-legged in the grass like a garden gnome in the low morning fog. As the sun barely lit up the sky, Calvin watched as he methodically lined up the bottles in straight rows on the ground. An orange crate and a large dented washtub stood in front of him. A small crock in the center of the tub had ice packed around it. With his wire rim glasses resting on his nose, the old man poured the clear liquid out of the crock and meticulously filled the whiskey bottles. He applied labels to the bottles and corked each bottle. Carefully he placed them into the crate. Calvin quietly stepped up behind him. While squinting to read the labels on the bottles Calvin lost his balance and landed spread eagle next to him. The old man's glasses flew up in the air.

"What happen to my cheaters? Dear God, where did you come from?"

Calvin sheepishly handed him his glasses. "Hello. I'm Captain Cal Johnson. I'm watching that steamboat tied up on the other side of Green Hill."

"Well, you scared the living daylights out of me doing a fancy cartwheel over my head. Not to mention bending up my cheaters." The fellow sized Calvin up. "So you're the Captain of that steamboat over yonder. You met them ghosts yet?"

"You know about the ghosts?"

"Intimately, my friend. Or, should I say, first hand."

"It seems that everybody in Port Fulton knows about the ghosts of John W. Hubbard. Do you know about the gold?"

"Sure. It's contraband, my friend. Gold Double Eagles stolen from our own U.S. Army payroll. Being that you're the captain of that nefarious boat, have you, per chance, found any shiny coins?"

"Are you kidding? If there were any gold coins on the Hubbard they disappeared years ago. Maybe the ghosts took them?"

"Ghosts don't need gold, Captain. Ghosts come around the living because they're inquisitive. They won't hurt you. If you see them, tell them: You're dead, Señors. Vamos. Go away. They will."

"Do you know why I followed you here?"

"Are you a revenuer?"

"No. But I am curious about what you're doing with the bottles you've been carting off my boat."

"Are you sure you ain't a revenuer?"

"I'm not sure what a revenuer is. But I can assure you, I don't work for the government."

"Good. Then I'll tell you that these bottles from your boat have an ultimately good purpose."

"And what might that be?"

"I'm filling the bottles with Doc Park's Indian Corn Remedy, the greatest elixir of all time. I invented it. I am Doc Zebula Park. And for God sake, don't smoke! This stuff could blow the whole town away!"

Calvin tucked the Virginia Cheroots deeper into his pants pocket. "Don't worry, Doc. I won't be smoking."

A familiar voice echoed from behind the cottonwood tree. "I'm smokin' right now, Doc. There ain't nothin' happenin' to me." Little Hooter stepped out of the shadows. "Hi yah, Captin'."

Calvin snatched the smoldering cigar butt away from Little Hooter's fingers and crushed it. "That's not safe!"

"Is that your kid?"

"Heavens no!"

"Doc, we ain't kin. I'm Hoot Hollywood Gibson, but most people calls me Little Hooter. I hears you got somethin' powerful in them bottles."

"Please to meet you Little Hooter. Yes, these bottles are filled with Doc Park's Indian Corn Remedy. It's very powerful stuff, and best of all, it's a moneymaker."

"Them bottles been a moneymaker for me too. I used to sell them to the shine boys for a nickel apiece."

"Little Hooter I'm sorry to have taken your booty. Why don't you and the Captain sit down and stick around. I'll tell you about this lucrative, yet explosive business."

Hoot and Calvin looked at each other, their sense of curiosity overwhelming their sense of imminent danger. Little Hooter smiled and sat on the grass next to Calvin.

"Okay Doc. I give up. Why is your concoction so explosive?"

"It's simple. The main ingredient is five gallons white gasoline, stove gas they call it. Then I add a pint of motor ether, and a half pound of carbon tet."

"That'll make a big boom. Won't it Captin'?"

"It sure will. Doc, I'm surprised you'd divulge your special formula to strangers."

"I don't consider you strangers. We've been talking for almost an hour. Do you want to help me with the business? My modus operendi is simple. I want to bottle up and sell as much of this stuff as I can."

"Can I make a lot of money?"

"Yes, Little Hooter. A person can make a very fine living selling Doc Park's Indian Corn Remedy."

"Doc, how do you gets people to buy your stuff?"

"Don't you have to do some fancy selling?" asked Calvin.

"No. The key to my business success is selection. That is selecting the right mark."

"Is the mark a dumb bunny that'll do the dirty work for you?"

"Crudely put, Little Hooter, but true. The mark has to have painful corns and he can't be too sharp. And he's got to be the convincing kind so the crowd will believe him."

"I'd be lookin' for a gimpy guy."

"You're right. He has to limp. I like to pick a fellow with tight shoes."

"What do you do after you gots the mark?"

"It's easy. First, I coax him onto the tailgate of my truck. I say. Which foot's got the corn? The fellow painfully holds out his foot. Try this and you'll be pain free. As I pour my elixir slowly on the guy's shoe the cooling feeling sets in and the rest is up to the sufferer."

"That's a good strategy Doc. The guy with the corns sells your remedy."

"That he does, Cal. The potion soaks quickly through his shoe. The rapid evaporation of the carbon tet and the ether has a chilling effect on the corn. Friend, I say. Do you feel the pain disappearing? Yes, yes, the man says. Is it cool? Are you getting relief? Oh, yes! Yes! With that convincing confirmation, the crowd applauds and they buy up all my bottles of Doc Park's Indian Corn Remedy. As soon I collect on the last bottle, I move on to the next fair."

"I ain't never been to no fair, but I been to a lot of saloons. Guys move these shells around for money. People say it's 'no fair'."

"You are a very intuitive young man. You might be very good at selling Doc Park's Indian Corn Remedy. It takes showmanship."

"I like you. You're convincing."

"I have to be, Captain. I'm like an actor in a talky or a lawyer in court."

"How long do you works?"

"Usually I work like the dickens all summer long."

"Can you makes enough money sellin' that licksir stuff so you don't have to do nothing else?"

"Yes, I make enough money in the summer to take off the rest of the year. You both seem like energetic, creative fellows. Play the banjo? Juggle? Tap dance?"

"Sometimes I steals."

Calvin gave Hoot a long, dirty look. "Count us out, Doc. Our skills and time are limited."

"Can you do anything to draw a crowd? Perhaps I can teach one of you to be a magician? I'd be glad to take you along."

"I don't have the hand-to-eye dexterity to be a magician, Doc. Besides I've got a lot to learn with this steamboat. Little Hooter, on the other hand, has the physical and mental attributes for many things, but for now he needs to go to grammar school to learn to read and write."

"Captin', nobody makes me go to school. You mean that's where I learns to read and write?"

"That's right Hoot. If you want your own business someday you've got to go to school. Thank you, Doc, but neither patent medicines nor theatrics ever have been my calling. It's time to be getting back to the boat. I've got a bilge to pump."

"I understand. Steamboats are like demanding women. It's been a pleasure meeting you, Captain. And Hooter, school is the best place for a smart lad like you with natural entrepreneurial skills."

Calvin grabbed Little Hooter by the hand and headed to the sidewalk. "So long, Doc."

Hoot waved. "What's hondo-balonel gots to do with makin' money, Captin'?"

"Entrepreneurs are the industrial tycoons and capitalists of the world. They make lots of money."

"If I goes to school and learns to read, do you think I could be one of them tycooners?"

"You never can tell, Hoot."

Little Hooter and Calvin walked across the street to Pat's garage. Looking in the door they saw Pat and Gus Shapiro drinking black coffee and smoking stogies.

"Good morning, Cal. Do you want a cup coffee? Hide your cigars Gus, Little Hooter's here."

"Sure. I can sit awhile. But I've got to pump the boat soon, or I'll have most of the Ohio River in the bilges."

Hooter interrupted. "Did you ever meet Doc Park?"

Pat and Gus looked at each other quizzically.

"Hoot and I just met Doc Zebula Park. He lives in the blue house catty-corner from here. He admitted to carting off the whiskey bottles from the boat.

"Doc's been collectin' them bottles I used to sell to the shine boys."

"Doc's got quite a business going. He even knew about the ghosts and the gold on the Hubbard."

"Doc said the gold eagles gots rolled by the U.S. Army."

"Hoot you got that wrong. He said the gold Double Eagles were stolen from a U.S. Army payroll. How do you think he knew that?" Calvin poured another cup of coffee. "Have you ever heard of a patent medicine called Doc Park's Indian Corn Remedy?"

"He told us how he sold the stuff to dumb people."

"Doc's real friendly. He told us all about his elixir and even asked us to join him on the road."

"Doc wanted to teach me how to do them magic tricks. But the Captin' says I needs to go to school. Nuts!"

"How come I haven't seen Dr. Park around here before?"

"None of us have seen Doc Park walking around in Port Fulton for years," Gus snickered.

"Sit down, Cal," Pat said seriously. "We got something you should hear."

"The Park house has been empty for a long time," added Gus, keeping his stogies out of Little Hooter's reach.

Pat looked Calvin right in the eye. "Dr. Park came from a long line of charlatans, inept magicians, and tricksters. For decades his family peddled a patent medicine consisting of gasoline and cayenne pepper."

"Doc said the recipe was white gas, motor ether, and carbon tet," corrected Little Hooter.

"The exact recipe is unimportant. What is important for you to know is that Dr. Park died in a fire ten years ago at the Clark County Fair. His car exploded when he lit up a fancy Virginia Cheroot with a load of Doc Park's Indian Corn Remedy in the back seat."

"I got shivers all over Captin'."

"Me too, Hoot."

CHAPTER 13

SERGEANT FLOYD

The shipyard bell rang at seven o'clock to start the day.

CLANG! CLANG! CLANG!

The sound echoed throughout Port Fulton. Standing on the top deck of the Hubbard, Calvin watched the colony of busy workers starting projects in the shipyard.

The aromatic sawmill stood between the activity and the river. Groups of men tied up log rafts at the upper end of the shipyard at the river so that the trackway could be used. Men hauled logs with teams of horses. Soon the hum and screech of machinery from the mill filled the air. Men worked among the wood piles, rolling logs with long hooks to the sawmill to be cut into lumber for boat building.

CLANG! CLANG! CLANG!

At twelve o'clock noon the bell rang for work to stop. Workers streamed out into the streets to go home for noonday dinner. Each man carried on his shoulder a stack of discarded wood to use for firewood at home.

Enjoying a ham and cheese sandwich on the top deck of the Hubbard, Calvin noticed the construction of a large boat hull. Froggy knew about happenings in the shipyard, so after lunch Calvin meandered down to his cottage for the lowdown.

"Hello, Froggy."

Froggy put down his whittling. "Howdy Captain."

"What are you making?"

"It's a duck decoy."

"Make any money at it?"

"Sure. My decoys are in demand. Johnny bought six last year. I'm making more to supplement my pension. Need any? Got five right here on the porch. I could sell them all to you. What's your price?"

"No Froggy, I'm not much of a hunter. I was wondering, are there any seagoing boats being built at the shipyards?"

"I doubt it."

"From the top deck of the Hubbard I can see a very big boat being constructed."

"Howard never built no seagoing ships while I was there. In 1923 there was a two-hundred-and-ten-foot packet called Cape Girardeau that slid down the ways. I guess it could have been a seagoing boat. It was constructed for Eagle Packet in St. Louis for carrying freight on the Mississippi."

"The hull I saw at least one-hundred-and-forty-feet with a thirty-foot beam."

"I remember a one-hundred-and-forty-foot steel towboat called Cordova that went down the ways about 1920. She had two sister ships called Demopolis and Montgomery. All three boats had beautiful, compound, reciprocating steam engines about four-hundred horsepower turning propellers as big as a man."

"What about this new boat? Do you think it's a paddle wheeler?"

"I doubt it Captain. Those glorious pineapple tops aren't practical anymore. Dr. Mayo's boat, Minnesota, was the last one we built at the shipyard."

"That big boat intrigues me. How can I see it up close?"

"What do you mean? Ain't no fence around the place? All you do is walk in. People know who you are."

"People know me?"

"Sure, Calvin. People know your business. This is a small town."

"In St. Louis even the smallest factory built a fence and implemented security measures. I was always taught that before you start nosin' around, you'd better get permission."

Froggy put down his wood and knife. "This is Port Fulton. It ain't no big city. Do you want to go right now?"

"Okay. Sure."

"Come on. We'll take a shortcut. I'll introduce you around and you can check out the boat. Is that what you want?"

"Great!"

"Look Calvin, I was the ace carpenter over there. I know everybody. Some of those guys influenced the design of my first boat. Let's go." Froggy took off. Calvin followed behind him trying to keep up with the spry old man.

"Is tramping through all this high grass and weeds the easiest way to get there? Aren't we trespassing?"

Froggy turned around, put his hands in his overall pockets and glared at Calvin. "Yes, this is the easiest way Captain. You're still standing in my backyard and I'm standing directly in the shipyard. We ain't trespassing." Froggy continued walking through the high grass, around timbers, and through a dilapidated shed. Calvin struggled to keep up. Suddenly Froggy stopped and turned around at the old brown building.

"What's up Froggy?"

"Well Captain, I just wanted to show you the cabinet shop. Time was when they made fancy carved steering wheels and stair rails for wooden steamboats here. Only thing they make now is them ordinary steering wheels and signs for the pilot house. When I worked here I carved ornate woodwork and wheels for steamboats. They were beautiful pieces of art that lasted a lifetime. Come on. We still got a ways to go."

Froggy and Calvin walked past a white two-story building built on high ground. Across the front stood a porch with a spindle railing and broad front steps with ornamental banisters leading up from the street.

"This is shipyard office, Captain."

"It looks like a house with flower beds in the front."

"Yeah, Howard's a gardener of sorts. He likes to grow them orange and yellow flowers called marigolds."

"Do you think those purple flowers in beds are weeds?"

"No. They're called heliotropes. Howard likes them flowers too."

Froggy and Calvin walked right through the front gate of the Howard Shipyards. The big boat that Calvin was watching stood in a cradle straight ahead. Froggy visited with the workers who knocked off from their work to gab while Calvin walked around and admired the big boat hull.

"Nobody seems worried about strangers on the premises."

"I've been telling you, Calvin. We're not strangers."

"Good afternoon, guys. It looks like that's going to be a very large boat."

"Sure is. I'm deckin' over the hull," answered a young man with his shoulder length red hair tied back so it didn't interfere with his tools.

Froggy smiled. "Red, she looks a bit fancier than most. Is she a seagoing boat?"

"Nope. She's a one-hundred-and-thirty-eight footer. Beam's thirty-foot, She'll draft about five. The government's callin' her Sergeant Floyd. She's going to be a river boat."

Calvin interrupted. "Wasn't there a man called Charles Floyd on the wheel with the Lewis and Clark Expedition?"

"Yes," added Froggy. "Sergeant Charles Floyd was on the trip. Charlie was a relative of William Clark. He joined the expedition in Louisville before the men came down the Ohio and wintered at Camp Wood River on the Mississippi in 1803."

"I'm impressed, Froggy. You know a lot about American history."

"I don't know about American history, I know about Charlie Floyd because he has roots around here."

"Didn't Sergeant Charles Floyd die on the Lewis and Clark Expedition?"

"Yes. Charlie was the first soldier to die west of the Mississippi River. Hey Red, what's the government's plan for Sergeant Floyd?"

"She's gonna be an inspection boat."

"Inspection boat? Inspecting what?" Calvin inquired.

Red sat back and stared at him. "A play toy for the Corps of Engineers out of Kansas City. You know, towin' and surveyin'."

"I'm kind of disappointed. I was hoping for a grand old paddle wheeler."

"We ain't buildin' shallow drafters no more. The locks and dams on the river nowadays channels the water."

"He's right, Calvin. With the locks and dams and Howard's patent for rudders on towboats, building deep-hulled boats is gonna make the shipyard prosper."

Every day Calvin walked to the shipyard to watch how the building of Sergeant Floyd proceeded. The aromatic smell of cut wood permeated the air. Calvin spotted bright, shiny nails peeking up through the sawdust on the decks. As he paged through the blueprints on the hull of the Floyd he noticed a change to the bow penciled in. On the original blueprint the bow was concave, sharp like a yacht. The change made the bow blunt, fat like a riverboat. Workmen walked up to check the blueprints.

"Are you following the penciled line?"

"Are you the inspector?"

"No, I'm just curious."

"Engineers make changes to the blueprints. I ain't no engineer. I do what the line on them blueprints says."

"Did you know the penciled line will make a big difference when Sergeant Floyd is launched?"

"Look mister, I follow them prints because that's what the engineer wants. Sergeant Floyd slides down the ways Sunday. I trust the engineer. I'll bet she floats real pretty." He walked away.

CLANG! CLANG! CLANG!

It was five o'clock. The carpenters, steelworkers, laborers, riveters, and mechanics packed up their tools and headed home. Calvin tried to stay ahead of the crowd.

By one o'clock on Sunday scores of people gathered at the ways for the official boat launch of Sergeant Floyd. Women from nearby cottages walked under umbrellas. Some wore sunbonnets and pushed their children in prams. Whistles and bells sounded the event.

"Bonjour Calvin." As he turned Calvin spotted Anne Marie waving from the crowd. Jean Claude stood next to her barking approvingly. Slowly they made their way to where Calvin stood at the dock. She gave him a big hug.

Suddenly the sounds of whistles and bells ceased and mechanical noises around them increased. People pointed to the big boat, resting at the top of the ways. The crowd got quiet.

BANG! BANG! BANG!

The hammering continued as the crowd grew larger.

BANG! BANG! BANG!

The noise stopped. The workmen moved from under the boat and rested their hammers on the ground. Only large hemp ropes held the boat.

The crowd came alive. "Go. Go. Go. Go." Jean Claude barked and barked.

"This is like a party," exclaimed Anne Marie. "I can hardly wait for the big splash.

Calvin glanced over at Anne Marie in her lacy yellow sundress and bare legs. As he marveled at how the ways gleamed in the sun, being well-greased with thick black lubricant he thought about how Anne Marie looked pretty good too. Calvin smiled as she took his arm. "It's going to be a great party!"

As the boat reached the top, the chattery crowd quieted down.

WACK!

The foreman cut the final rope with his ax.

At first the boat moved slowly. Then she gathered speed, sliding smoothly and swiftly down the ways.

SPLASH!

Sergeant Floyd hit the water and a cheer exploded from the crowd. The whistles and bells echoed from bank to bank. The big boat moved out into the current of the Ohio. Two skiffs followed the Floyd, retrieving the timbers she had ridden on down the ways. The shipyard tug, Loretta Harper towed her back to the dock.

"That's a beautiful boat. When will it leave?"

"It's not finished yet, Anne Marie. It has to be fitted with engines, interior woodwork, and a ship's whistle before she's ready for the Corps of Engineers. Boy, am I surprised to see you? What happened with the painting lessons at the farm?"

"There are only so many apple trees to paint, Calvin. Besides Henry wanted to get married and I couldn't see myself koosen around with that lazy oaf the rest of my life."

"You made a good decision. I'm really glad to see you."

"I'm really glad to see you too. Why are people in Jeffersonville so crazy about whistles and bells? They are everywhere for this event."

"Bells and whistles are important to rivermen. My friend, Froggy, told me that in Louisville when the courthouse clock stopped, people set their timepieces with the seven o'clock whistle of the steamer Tom Greene."

"What a funny way to set your clock."

"That's not all. Boat captains insist on being buried on the river bank near Spring Street so the passing packets can salute their memory daily."

"Are bells and whistles the way you want to be remembered?"

"No memorials for me. Not yet anyway! Do you and Jean Claude need a place to stay? There's plenty of room on my steamboat."

"We would love to stay with you, but I've got a job lined up on the Golden Palace showboat. It's leaving from Louisville in a few hours."

"Does the Golden Palace need a painter?"

"No, my paints are in my valise. My job on the showboat is acting. I have a part in the current melodrama. If they like my work I'll have the chance to apprentice for the heroine on the next cruise."

"What an exciting opportunity! I'm sure they'll love you. Look me up when you get back, Anne Marie. You can't miss the Hubbard. It's the only steamboat anchored upstream from the Howard Shipyard."

"It's time to catch the ferry to Louisville. Au revoir, Calvin," called Anne Marie as she skittered through the crowd to the landing with Jean Claude barking at her heels.

"Have a great trip." Calvin called as she disappeared out of sight. "I'll miss you."

The following week Froggy and Calvin arrived at the Howard dock to admire Sergeant Floyd. She looked mighty pretty sitting in the water. To preserve the yachty character of the boat, the shipyard painted the hull black. A wide-white boot-top water line stripe gave it a pleasure-boat look. Calvin scratched his head in amazement. Extra displacement forward allowed the boot-top to ride a foot or more higher than the waterline boot-top stripe. The stern submerged by the same amount.

"Froggy, why isn't the boat floating on her designated lines?"

"It's not a problem if you add concrete."

Calvin's mouth dropped open in surprise. "What do you mean?"

"Don't fret about how she looks right now. Believe me, when you stop by tomorrow, it'll be better."

When Calvin checked out the boat the next day he found that Froggy was right. Sergeant Floyd floated jauntily on her designated lines. Noticing two men squabbling on the deck, Calvin stepped back into the shadows to listen to their conversation.

"You did what?" shouted the man in a blue uniform.

"We used concrete sir."

"That solution won't do. I can't pass it. You'll have to pull up the hull, chisel out the concrete, repair the hull, and then repaint the water line."

"That's an expense solution."

"It's the only solution. And it's the only way I'll pass it. Also I noticed heat from the welding blistered the white paint inside the cabin. The interior needs repainting too. Do all the repairs at the same time. Save me another trip."

In about a week Froggy and Calvin walked back over to the shipyard to check on progress. Sergeant Floyd looked magnificent in the water with the stripe in just the right place. An official blue stamp was attached to the front window. They watched workmen lifting the hatches and operating machinery to lower a huge engine onto the boat.

"Good afternoon fellas. Aren't those Fairbanks Morris engines?" asked Froggy.

One of the mechanics looked up. "You bet. The two main engines are direct-reversing diesels."

Calvin admired the big shiny engines. "They're pretty unique."

"You bet. To reverse the boat, engines are cut to an idle. When the engines almost die, the reversing lever shifts the cam shaft."

Calvin's mouth dropped open. "Doesn't that cause a horrendous clatter?"

"You bet it does. It's what the government ordered."

"What's good enough for the government is good for us. Calvin, it's almost five. Want to have supper on my porch? Sun don't hit it, so it's pretty cool. I got a couple of mason jars of brew and some head cheese in the icebox."

"Yeah, let's go. Our opinions aren't appreciated here."

They walked back to Froggy's cottage without saying a word. He brought out the sandwiches and brew. Calvin smoldered silently as they ate on the porch.

"I can see you didn't take lightly to them engine guys."

"That boat has a lot of mistakes."

"Look Calvin. It don't do no good to argue with them professionals."

"Sure."

"Hi yah Captin'," called a hoarse voice next to the porch. "Hi yah Mr. Frog, you gots another one of them sandwiches?"

"Hello Little Hooter. Fixings are in the kitchen. Help yourself."

"What you carrying there?" Calvin asked.

"Books," said Little Hooter as he sprang up the steps and into the house.

Froggy looked at Calvin. "Boy, that's a change!"

Hooter came out of the house with a sandwich in one hand and two books in the other. His pockets bulged with cigar butts.

"Since you're going to school, you should give up smoking. It'll stunt your growth and your mind."

"I can't give up smokin' Captin'. Hooter sat down between the men. He laid his books on the top step and stuffed a sandwich into his mouth.

Calvin fingered his books. "I remember my grammar school days. Arithmetic and the McGuffy Reader weren't my favorites either. How's school going?"

"Arithmetic's not so bad. It helps me with countin' money. Readin' is hard. That McGuffy book don't have no good pitchers of neked ladies."

"My McGuffy Reader didn't have any either."

"You is pretty old Captin'. Can you still remember your school days?" Hoot laughed and pulled out a butt and a match from his faded breeches tied around his waist with a piece of rope. "Did you know next Sunday is the big day for that boat you been watchin' at the shipyard?"

"Little Hooter's right, Calvin. On Sunday Sergeant Floyd is scheduled for a trial run. If she passes, then the Corps will have them a new boat for the Missouri River."

"What does it take to get an invite on the trial run?"

"I wanna go too."

"This is a grown-up event. You'll have to wait at least ten years."

"Nuts!" Hoot stomped down the steps. On the bottom step he blew a series of concentric smoke rings that floated up into their faces.

"What would it take to grab an invitation, Froggy?"

Hooter put down his smoke and listened.

"Don't need one, Calvin."

"What do you mean?"

"The launching of a new boat is a big deal in Port Fulton. Lots of people come for the day. There's always an open house on the boat. There are plates of sandwiches and Schimpff's Confectionary brings over dessert candy. Try them caramel Modjeskas, they're the best."

"I likes the red hots. I steals them sometimes."

"The cinnamon red hots don't hold a candle to them Modjeskas."

"Quit squabbling. Tell me more about how to get a ride on Sergeant Floyd."

"It won't be hard Captain. Since this boat launch is a big deal, people will be tripping in and out of the boat all day. When the trial run is about to start the Corps will ring a bell. That means that all unauthorized personnel go ashore."

"That's when I'll have to leave since I won't have any authorization."

"The bells ringing don't necessarily mean you have to leave, if you can find an inconspicuous place. The aft end of the engine room might be good. It's out of the way. Walk in there and just stay quiet until the boat leaves the dock. The Corps ain't gonna come back to throw you off on an official run."

Like Froggy said, Sunday's open house on Sergeant Floyd was a busy time. Calvin ate and drank with the crowd. When the bell sounded he quietly made his way to the aft end of the engine room. The bell made a jingling sound, then there was deep gong. The different bells signaled to go ahead, or stop, or reverse.

As the ropes were thrown and boat moved upriver, Calvin walked toward the stern to fit in inconspicuously behind the loud-talking official crowd. Before he reached the group a familiar noise caught his attention.

COFF! COFF! COFF!

Calvin peeked behind the three large drums of oil on the starboard side. Little Hooter was stretched out by the rail, smoking a butt with an uninterrupted view of the Ohio. Next to him was a large platter of candy.

"What the hell are you doing here Hooter?"

"Hi yah Captin'. I'm takin' a ride on a fancy big boat. How about you? You want one of these caramel things? Like Mr. Frog says they are delish." He stuffed a handful of candies in his mouth and swallowed with a smile on his face. Then Little Hooter puffed and the smoke rings disappeared with the prevailing winds behind the boat.

"Give me that stogie! Do you want to swim back to Jeffersonville? I know I don't."

"Okay Captin'."

Calvin crushed the butt, and then slid down next to Little Hooter. The wake of the Sergeant Floyd glittered like diamonds in the sunlight as the powerful engines hummed and clattered.

Froggy was right. With so much commotion and commendation not one person noticed that Captain Calvin Coolidge Johnson and Hoot Hollywood Gibson rode on the Sergeant Floyd on her trial run.

"Fifteen miles per hour, wide open," shouted the engineer through the bullhorn.

"Not a bad speed for a boat one-hundred-and-forty-feet long," Calvin mumbled as they stuffed their mouths full with caramel Modjeskas.

Little Hooter put the last of the red hots in his pockets. "Captin' don't this boat go real good?"

On June 30 the steel hulled Sergeant Floyd was officially launched. The United States Government purchased the ship for the Army Corps of Engineers for $21,000. She was one of the last oil-engine, screw- propeller passenger boats that slid down the ways at the Howard Shipyard. Her mission involved light towing, surveying, and assessment on the inland waterways under the authority of the Missouri River Division of the Corps of Engineers.

The job of hauling Brass around on the Missouri River sounded like as much fun as being captain of a Missouri River excursion steamer.

CHAPTER 14

FOURTH OF JULY

Babysitting this two-hundred-foot steamboat left Calvin with time on his hands, but not much money. As he walked to the post office he prayed that Billy Killebrew sent his paycheck.

"Good morning Arnold. Do you have mail for me?"

"Here you go Calvin, one letter. It smells real nice."

Whiffing the jasmine on the pink linen stationary he smiled and tucked the letter carefully in his pocket to read after calling Billy Killebrew. An update of the finances of the Hubbard was overdue.

Calvin walked down the street to the pay telephone at Schimpff's Confectionary. The candy kitchen smelled wonderful as he perused the cases. "Gus, there's two dollars on the counter. I'm making a call to St. Louis." Calvin dialed the operator. "I want to call St. Louis. Number 921."

RING. RING. RING.

"Killebrew here."

"Hello, Mr. Killebrew. I'm glad I caught you in the office. How are things going? I'm running out of money. What?"

Billy Killebrew explained.

"The bank wants more information about the boat. They're concerned about the Hubbard's age and history. The

Howard Shipyards won't be refurbishing paddle wheelers much anymore so we might have to try a different yard for the work."

"So what should I do?"

Billy talked so loud that Calvin moved the black telephone away from his ear.

"Look Calvin, getting financing takes time. I'm not just sitting on my ass around here. Yesterday I got a good lead on a financer named Double R Markle. He's been promoting showboats on the Ohio with his friend, Matt Swallow, an oil man from West Virginia. Their investments include famous showboats like the Sunny South, and the Golden Palace. Double R is interested in financing the Hubbard with the right profit incentive. Be patient. It'll just be a little longer, Calvin. I believe Mrs. Goodwall wired your money today. Keep in touch." Click. The telephone went dead.

Calvin was overwhelmed. He wondered if he should check Western Union for money, but instead he bought a bag of cinnamon red hots. He slowly walked down to the docks to see Baby Wildcat III, his Thompson fish boat with a conversion to make it look like a miniature cruiser. Baby Wildcat was his most reliable gal. Actually Christina was his favorite gal, but communication with her was limited to a few letters.

When Calvin felt down in the dumps he took Baby Wildcat on an excursion to Louisville. The short ride cleared his head. Today he pulled his boat out of the water so she wouldn't get knocked around by boat wakes. Next to the dock his eyes fell on a gleaming twenty-footer and an even bigger thirty footer tied up at the dock. He walked around the big boats for awhile, then crossed the cobblestone wharf to Main and headed up Fourth Street.

Louisville was a nice town, but Calvin was homesick. Slowly he walked passed Zapp's Grocery. The smells of food followed him down the street. At the elegant Crutcher and Stark's Clothing Store Calvin admired the stylish attired mannequins in the windows. He remembered that Christina loved to buy the latest fashions. She looked great in them. Christina would love these beautiful clothes. Finally at the Five and Dime he stopped and bought two pairs of white cotton socks and a red Japanese folding fan. Calvin planned to send the fan to Christina with a letter reminding her the Fourth of July was just around the corner.

His last stop was Benedict's. Calvin spent his last dime on a single chocolate éclair and savored it on a bench outside the store. Thoughts of Christina played in his head as he pulled out her pink envelope from the post office. Calvin planned to savor every word. First he inhaled the aromatic pink linen stationary with a whiff of jasmine. Christina wrote mostly about art school and her new friends. She never mentioned coming to Jeffersonville for the Fourth of July. He wondered if he should call her (which he really couldn't afford), or just wait to see if she would take the train to town to surprise him. Christina loved surprises. Calvin put the letter in his pocket. He continued walking down the street daydreaming and wiping his sticky fingers on his pants.

A flowing patriotic banner and flags outside Soupy Sikennette's Boat Store caught Calvin's attention. Hitch Smith stood in the street front of the building, carefully detailing an already gleaming mahogany Hacker motorboat on a trailer.

"I saw that gorgeous step-hydroplane in the water this morning. Does it belong to Soupy?"

"Yep. I just brought Kitty Hawk to the store to clean her up Calvin."

"She looks fast. What does she do?"

"Soupy says she does fifty."

"Hackers are known for their fine craftsmanship. That sleek V-bottom design allows for greater speeds at lower horsepower."

"I don't know about that. All I knows is that Soupy wants Kitty Hawk looking real pretty so he can show her off at the regatta. The meeting on the big race is happening in the store right now. Check it out."

"Thanks. I'll do that."

The door bell jingled as Calvin stepped inside the boat store. In the rear of the building sat a bunch of boisterous men around Soupy's big mahogany table. Soupy looked up and waved for him to join the group.

"What's going on, Soupy?"

"We're planning a big regatta for Louisville for the Fourth. Sit down. The town's hot for inboard step-hydroplanes."

"Yeah, I saw your Kitty Hawk outside. I didn't know you owned a hydroplane."

"I bought it from a friend in Mount Clemens, Michigan. Dudley's been involved with the custom-built, innovative Hacker designs for more than three years."

"I like those step-hydros souped up with Hispano-Suizas," added a big man with a double breasted suit. Calvin thought he looked over-dressed for the warm, late June day.

"I love Hispano-Suizas. In St. Louis I rode in a hydro with a converted airplane motor power plant."

Soupy put his arm around his shoulder. "Cal, I want you to meet Ed Waddell. He's the mayor."

"This must be an official meeting if the mayor's here."

"It sure is, young man. We're planning the biggest celebration Louisville's seen in years. The Fourth of July is the most important holiday for sales, next to Christmas."

"Celebrations on the Fourth bring in thousands of dollars to the businesses downtown," remarked George Garfield. "I own the Furniture Store on Fourth Street, Cal. With the boat races on the levee I can sell as much merchandise in July as I do at Christmas."

"Powerboat races in St. Louis brought cash and big crowds to the waterfront too."

"Do you know the fastest boat on the Ohio today?" asked George.

"Is it Kitty Hawk?"

"No Cal, she's the classiest."

"Okay. Then it's got to be the flashy thirty-footer at the Louisville Landing."

"Right you are! The boat's powered by a big Liberty and it's called the Kentucky Colonel."

"Kentucky Colonel is the king of the heap," boasted the mayor.

Soupy frowned. "That boat's a sure winner until she stands up on her transom and flips over."

"Let's get back to business. We need a plan. What kind of race will accommodate all types of boats regardless of horsepower?" asked Bobby Sikennette, Soupy's thoughtful older brother, and co-owner of the boat store.

"I saw a Bang and Go Back Race on the Big Sandy last year," said George.

"How does that go?"

"Well, everybody starts out from the dock wide open. When the judge fires the gun, all the boats turn around and dash back. The theory being, the fastest boat is farthest away.

So when they're turned around all the boats get back in a dead heat."

"That kind of a race sounds pretty chaotic. Let's try something else."

"How about a balloon race?" added the mayor. Jeb Willis and his crop duster could turn balloons loose over the river. We can put some dollar bills in them or advertisements from the downtown businesses."

"I like that!" shouted George and Soupy in unison.

Bobby stood up and took a contract out of his pocket. "Benny Barton and the River Bottom Ramblers agreed to play. They're gonna set up in the riverfront park at the bandstand."

Soupy interrupted. "Did you see what the River Bottom Ramblers travel in nowadays? It's an outrageous limousine Benny calls the Circus Wagon. It's painted red and gold with wheels that'll make you dizzy."

"Benny said we could use it in the parade," added the Mayor.

"I've seen it a time or two. Despite its flashy paint job it looks familiar. What do you think Soupy?"

Soupy frowned at Bobby. "Packard limousines are hard to come by."

Calvin interrupted. "Let's get back to the boat races. I love boat races."

"Cal, how would you like a temporary job running a big boat?" asked Soupy.

"Sure. I've got time and I need the money. What do you have in mind?"

"Well, it might include some odd jobs too."

"Great," Calvin added, hoping the jobs entailed driving Soupy's Kitty Hawk.

"Here's my Aunt Susan's business card. She's an interior decorator with an office just down the street. She needs help with the houseboat that she bought. Have you ever hung wallpaper?"

"On a houseboat?" Calvin studied the business card with his mouth wide open.

Bobby slammed down his empty coffee cup to get everyone's attention. "Gentlemen, let's get back to the regatta. We've still got some organization to do. What about putting together a cruiser race?"

The mayor took out a cigar from his pocket and lit up. "It could be a real crowd pleaser."

George frowned. "Last I counted there were only six cruisers in town."

Soupy got up from the table. "It won't be much of a race. Everybody knows that Itaska Joyce is the fastest boat around. That twin hull Scott ACF cruiser can run over eighteen miles an hour."

"Do you need more cruisers? I can enter my mine."

"Are you talking about that little Thompson that's beached on the landing?" asked Bobby.

"Yes, that's Baby Wildcat III."

George held up an official form from the table. "To race you must have all the items on this checklist."

"Just give me the list, the time and the place. I'll be there and I'll be official."

George handed Calvin the forms. "Be at the Louisville Landing, three o'clock Saturday.

"Yes, sir."

"Don't forget Aunt Susan, You can walk down to her office and introduce yourself."

"Soupy, I don't know about this job. I've never hung wallpaper before."

"She needs an able worker and you need the money. I have confidence that you'll do fine. I'll call her up and tell her you're coming."

"Thanks. See you on the Fourth."

Calvin walked out the door and glanced at the business card for Aunt Susan's address. Two doors down from the boat store stood a brick building with a sign that read Susan B. Steinhaus, Interior Designs. The office looked pretty impressive as he opened the door. Wind chimes tinkled. The gold brocade drapes covered the windows. His nose twitched with the strong smell of incense. The room was decorated with fine French provincial furniture. Artwork lined the walls. A Tiffany dragonfly lamp reflected greens and golds on a fancy desk. Calvin approached the well-dressed, gray-haired woman with bobbed hair working feverishly at an adding machine. Calvin was mesmerized by her long, red fingernails and bright red lipstick. He stood quietly next to her desk.

"May I help you, young man?"

"Hello Miss Steinhaus. I'm Calvin Johnson."

"What do you want? Can't you see I'm busy?" She continued to work.

"Soupy sent me." She looked up at Calvin above her rhinestone spectacles. "You have a lot of very nice pictures in here."

"These are more than pictures. This is art, young man. I have collected some of the finest examples of realism in Louisville today. In this room alone, there are important canvas by Thomas Hart Benton, Edward Hopper, Grant Wood and Leon Kroll. If you look on the far wall, there's a Hibbard, a Wyeth and one of Pippin's pieces. Horace Pippin is one of the foremost Negro primitive painters." She looked

Calvin straight in the eye. "You seem young to be a friend of Sebastian."

"Uh. Yes."

"Call me Aunt Susan. On the telephone Sebastian told me you're dependable. I don't like to dally when there's work to do. Take the wallpaper in the corner. The paste is on the boat. Get started. You can't miss my houseboat. It's moored at the landing. It's white and pink with the name, Lady Susan, in script on the back. Fifty dollars should be adequate for the job. Can you drive a boat?"

"Yes, I---"

"Good. I'm hosting a mah jongg party on the upper deck next week. I'll need a driver, Calvin. Thank you. See yourself out." Susan waved him out and continued to work.

Rolls of wallpaper stood near to the door. Calvin scooped them up and walked out. "Thank you for the job. Good bye, Aunt Susan." Whistling, he counted his money as he headed down to the landing.

Lady Susan was a scow of a houseboat with tongue and groove siding with exposed two-by-fours in the inside on two-foot centers. The boat was completely opposite of Aunt Susan interesting office. Calvin struggled with the paste, but finished wallpapering in a couple of hours. It didn't take much skill to match seams. The wallpaper looked like a pattern you'd find in a colonial-type drawing room in a mansion on Portland Place in St. Louis. It certainly looked out of place on this boat.

After wallpapering Calvin motored home in Baby Wildcat. The river was calm with only small ripples along the shore. Looking into the water as he moved across the river Calvin spotted schools of minnows gliding along together in giant clouds. The orange and pink from the setting sun cast a magenta light over the water where outlines of cottonwood trees dotted the Kentucky shore as the river fog rolled in.

The wind in Calvin's face fanned out his hair in a reckless fashion. Before he realized it, the City of Louisville was running along side. It was white and steaming upstream. He heard the hum of the engines and the smell of the smoke from the stacks. People on the decks looked down and waved. Calvin waved back to the mail boat and tried to stay out of its wake. Wildcat bobbed, rocked and tipped. The waves diminished as Calvin neared the Hubbard. He secured Baby Wildcat to the stern of the steamboat, and then he climbed over the side, landing on the lower deck. His nose caught a whiff of something usual. He sniffed again. It smelled like turpentine.

Calvin followed the acrid fumes into the galley. Cautiously he lit a lantern. Lining the galley walls from one end to the other were hordes of bright colors. There were oranges, reds, blues, greens, squares, circles, and something that looked like a school of goldfish. Or maybe it was a bowl of exotic fruit, or a basket of dancing clams. He stepped back in disbelief, stumbling over a row of paint cans.

Calvin stood up and squinted at the mural that extended the entire length of the galley. Was this the work of shanty boaters? If it was, their vandalism was in poor taste. Could this monstrosity be the work of Froggy's spooks? He collapsed in a chair wondering what to do. An envelope stood prominently in the middle the table. Next to it was a vase with a single red rose. As he looked closer he noticed the pink linen envelope had his name on it. He whiffed the jasmine scent first, and then opened it. It read:

My Dearest Calvin,

How do you like my wonderful surprise? Madeline and I spent all day expressing our inner state. We used our art studies to fuel our enthusiasm.

At sundown we walked down to her house. Madeline Howard lives in the big brownstone behind the brick wall on Market Street.

Tomorrow we are going to Arctic Springs for a picnic and to paint the clear, cold water flowing majestically from the rock ledges. Madeline says this beautiful brook runs in and out of the flower-filled woods, and finally disappears mysteriously into the river. We should certainly fill all our canvas with many subjects of nature.

Calvin Dear, I hope you like our electrifying mural. We painted objects from different points of view like the great masters did.

Your tired old boat certainly required our exhilarating painting to infuse new life. Those tall pipes on the top deck were particularly challenging to paint. Is that little house on the top of the boat your outhouse? I painted it primitively to reflect the wildness of riverboat life.

Love and Kisses,

Christina

P.S.--Since Mr. Howard sent a limousine to pick up Madeline and me in St. Louis I used your money for all this glorious paint for your boat.

P.S. again --Madeline said the Howards always have a splendid fireworks display on the 4th. I would love for you to join me for the party.

P.S. again and again-- Madeline and I are leaving in two days for France. I know this is short notice but we have an incredible opportunity to study expressionism and cubism with Georges Rouault and Emile Antoine Bourdelle in Paris.

The next morning Calvin drank his coffee and studied the mural that filled the walls. As much as he tried to appreciate Christina's art, he just couldn't. Colorful was the best Calvin could say about it.

Froggy walked into the galley. "Good morning, Captain." He stared at the painting with his mouth wide open. "What the hell happened to your boat? Did you do this after some bizarre jag? I don't think I like it."

"I don't like it either. And I didn't do it."

"What do you mean? You didn't paint all this?"

"No. I do plead guilty of bizarre behavior like wallpapering Soupy's aunt's houseboat, but I didn't do this."

"I didn't know Soupy had an aunt. Wallpapering? Why in the hell would anybody do wallpapering? You know Captain, this painting work could be your spooks. But it's hard to believe them ghosts have such poor taste in decorating." He poured a cup of coffee and frowned at Calvin across the table.

"This isn't the work of spooks, Froggy. It's the work of real live people."

"Well, these people must be crazy. I guess you ain't seen the stacks yet?"

"What stacks?"

"The stacks you got on the top deck of your steamboat. Stacks are perfectly good painted black, they don't need to be bright yellow like a wild canary. Worst of all, your pilot house looks like a god damn circus outhouse."

Calvin sighed. "I haven't seen the work on the top deck."

"These people have gone too far. What kind of excursion boat's is this gonna be? Right now it looks like a carnival's come to town."

"Froggy, a friend from St. Louis painted the boat to surprise me."

"Well, are you surprised? I sure the hell am," snorted Froggy as he eyed the galley walls. "Looking at this galley wall pitcher while I'm eating is mighty disgusting. Do you like this?"

"No."

"Good. I got some white paint in my shed. We can cover it over this afternoon."

"I can't do it. Christina would never speak to me if I covered her art work with white paint. She considers this a mural expressing her inner feelings."

"My inner feelings are telling me that this is travesty done to a fine old steamboat. How long is your girl friend gonna be in Port Fulton, Captain?"

"Christina's going to be here a couple of days. So we can't do anything about the art work right now."

"If that's what you want Calvin. The white paint has been sitting around in my shed for months so a few more days won't make any difference. But believe me, we gotta cover over this travesty before the next brew party. Johnny and the boys don't understand art work."

"When's the next party?"

"The Fourth will slow production some. I'd say there'll be enough brew in about three weeks."

"Three weeks is plenty of time to cover the paint job. Christina's leaving for Paris, France in a day or two."

"What kind of a woman would do this to a man's boat?"

"Painting's important to her. She goes to an art school in St. Louis. I don't really like the mural, but I like Christina."

"Calvin, art's supposed to be a pitcher, ain't it?"

"It is for me."

"You'd be better off if them spooks did the painting. Then we could use the white paint to fix it right away."

"You're probably right."

"I don't think this girl's gonna work out for you. Where is she anyways?"

"She's staying at the Howard place with her friend, Madeline Howard. Mr. Howard's limousine brought them here from St. Louis."

"Well, la-de-dah. She sounds pretty fancy, Captain. When's this lady painter coming back to see your derelict old steamboat?"

"I don't know. It won't be today because she going to Artic Springs to paint nature."

"I hope she's not contaminating the springs with them wild colored paints!"

"Forget about Artic Springs Froggy. I got a dilemma."

"What kind of dilemma?"

"Christina invited me to the fireworks at the Howards'. But I signed up for the cruiser race at the regatta in Louisville on the Fourth. What should I do?"

"Fireworks at the Howard's is like fireworks anywheres else, but a boat race is a special. I'd choose the race. But Calvin, how can you run in a cruiser race when you ain't got a cruiser?"

"I consider Baby Wildcat III my cruiser."

"The officials may not see it your way."

"I've got an official list from Soupy. It has all the things I need for Baby Wildcat to qualify for the race."

"Let me see the list." As he perused the paper Froggy continued his conversation. "Sometimes old man Howard races the Little Captain at the Louisville races. He's won a silver cup or two."

"Does he have a cruiser?"

"Nope. Little Captain's a speedboat. Howard doesn't like to lose."

"How about helping me get Baby Wildcat ready for the regatta? She's tied off the stern right now."

"Since we ain't painting, I got nothing better to do. I'll get the trailer and we'll work on your cruiser in Pat's garage."

On the day of the race, Froggy and Calvin brought the officially outfitted Baby Wildcat III to the Louisville landing. They watched the races and drank some brew. The Hissos engines were winners. The Kentucky Colonel gave quite a show, but like Soupy predicted, it flipped over at the end.

Finally a loud voice boomed through the bullhorn on the bank. "Cruisers line up. Ten minutes."

"Time to go, Captain. I'll be rooting for you."

"Thanks Froggy. Calvin slicked back his hair and untied Baby Wildcat. In a minute he drove out to the starting line and bobbed around with the other boats.

The judges' boat quickly approached Baby Wildcat. From the bow one sharp-eyed fellow stared at the sixteen foot boat. "Son, are you sure you're in the right place? This is the cruiser race."

"Yes. I have the paperwork for my Thompson cruiser with a Johnson Giant Twin," Calvin answered handing the judge the official forms.

"That little boat of yours is not a cruiser. You can't run."

"It is a cruiser. A miniature outboard cruiser."

"There are specific rules for cruisers. First of all, you've got to be able to sleep on a cruiser."

"No problem. The seats fold down." Calvin demonstrated the fold down position. "Plenty of room for two people to sleep. I've done it myself."

The judge frowned. "Where's your cook stove?"

Calvin reached under the seat, pulling out the stove and an Army mess kit. "This single burner sterno stove's not fancy, but it works for me."

"Where's the head?"

"Never needed one. I always use the starboard side, except when there are ladies present. Then I make a landing and find the nearest tree."

"This is not a cruiser. It's missing a head for sure, and the other items are marginal to say the least."

"Calvin," called Soupy from the stern of the second judges' boat. "Catch!" As Calvin looked and waved, Soupy tossed him a porcelain thunder mug. "You got a head now."

Calvin caught the mug from Soupy and held it up for the judge to see. "Baby Wildcat's officially got a head, so Baby Wildcat's officially a cruiser."

"Well, you do have a head."

"And he's got everything else too, Pete. He looks like a cruiser to me," shouted Soupy through the bullhorn.

"Okay. Go ahead."

"Thanks judges." Calvin put the mug under the front seat, and then lined up for the start.

When the gun sounded, Baby Wildcat moved out quickly, avoided the wash of the six planning inboard cruisers. The course was short to keep the race in view of the spectators that lined the landing. Before the first turn Calvin clearly lapped the other cruisers. Baby Wildcat took the checker flag far ahead of the competition. Smiling and waving he headed toward the dock.

Froggy met him on the dock when the awards were handed out. "You're a winner, Captain."

"Baby Wildcat's the winner." Calvin beamed as the chairman presented him with an unusual looking award.

"Mr. Johnson, we would like to present you with the new Outboard Cruiser Award. This silver thunder mug will have your name engraved on the bottom."

"Thank you. Can I give you a suggestion for next year's race?"

"What might that be Mr. Johnson?"

"Have two divisions for cruisers; one for inboards and one for outboards."

"The committee will take your suggestion under advisement," said the chairman as he filled his thunder mug with beer from a silver pitcher.

Soupy slapped him on the shoulder. "Come on, Cal. I'm having a party at the boat store. We have platters of food and more beer for your silver mug."

"I sure do like parties. Let's go, Froggy."

Balloons floated up from the landing and glowed in the setting sun as Froggy and Calvin laughed and skipped down the street and through the doors of boat store.

"It's Cal Johnson, the winner of the cruiser race. Come on in and join the party. Aunt Susan told me you did a fine job wallpapering her boat."

Calvin looked across the river. "Thanks Soupy."

"Are you okay Cal? You seem kind of quiet for a winner."

"No, I'm fine. I think a party is just what I need. Why didn't you tell me your real name was Sebastian?"

"Soupy is the name that sells boats."

After drinking too many brews from his silver thunder mug Calvin stumbled into an empty corner of the boat store and fell asleep on the floor. It wasn't until the following afternoon that he woke up with the sun glaring through the boat store window.

Calvin rubbed his eyes, slicked back his unruly hair, and stumbled down to the landing. Baby Wildcat was tied at the end of the pier. The Ohio was like a mill pond so his trip back to the steamboat was uneventful. Calvin slipped quietly over the side of the Hubbard. He walked with uncertain steps to the galley for a headache remedy. Propped against his coffee cup was a pink linen envelope. "Oh, No!"

Calvin sat down and opened the envelope slowly.

My Dearest Calvin,

I am sorry I missed you, but the last few days have been too exciting for words. Staying at the Howard house was breathtaking. It's a Romanesque Revival mansion built of brick and limestone with terra cotta adornments on the outside and elaborate woodwork on the inside. There are twenty two rooms on three floors. It has elegant mahogany furniture, gorgeous chandeliers with hundreds of dangling prisms and many paintings. A study by my favorite painter, Georges Roualt is hanging in the formal dining room. I could hardly believe it!

The rooms have their own names like Morning Glory Room, Pansy Room, and Chrysanthemum Room. (That's where I stayed.) My bedroom has cream colored walls and chrysanthemum flowers everywhere. It was like being in a garden. The Howard home is elegant with so much space. It makes my home on Broadway in north St. Louis so small in comparison. They even have a stable with horses to ride.

I looked for you on the Fourth. Mr. Howard sent balloons up at sunset. They were striped red, white, and blue and expanded when the wad of excelsior inside them was lit. They sailed above the trees into the setting sun. The fireworks display was oh-so-wonderful. We sat out on the benches near the fountain. The display started with pinwheels that hissed and made iridescent circles of color.

Next the Roman candles and giant firecrackers exploded one after the other. Sometimes bright fountains of colored spray lit up the yard.

Madeline and I are catching the train to New York at ten o'clock. From New York we booked passage on the steamer Grand Voyage to Normandy, France. We'll take a train to Paris. I'll write you after we find an apartment. Art is my life. Good luck with your steamboat venture.

Love and Kisses,

Christina

It was a sad. Christina had been Calvin's girl for four years. They met when he helped her one icy December night. She was driving her father's car when it slid down the embankment at the St. Louis Art Museum. She was sixteen, beautiful, and enamored by a handsome college guy who came to her rescue. Last year when Christina enrolled in art school at Washington University she had little time for him. Her life became her artsy, fartsy rich friends who traveled all over the world. Calvin was broke. The only way he could see Europe involved joining the U.S. Army. Calvin put his head down on the galley table.

CHAPTER 15

EXCURSION STEAMER TO TWELVE MILE ISLAND

An excursion steamer called the City of Memphis ran nightly trips from Louisville to Twelve Mile Island and back. Built in 1913 and named the Verne Swain, the side wheeler operated in the Pittsburgh to Wheeling packet trade. Swain boats were intended for use on short trips in placid waters. In 1922, the Verne Swain was sold and renamed City of Memphis. The boat was refurbished for excursions and dance cruises on the Ohio much the way the Streckfus Company ran the St. Paul on the Mississippi.

Froggy's friends, Elmer and Jake, borrowed Calvin's lifeboat once a week for an evening trip on the City of Memphis. The men rowed to the steamer after it left the Louisville landing at sunset. It was Jake's job to hang on to the rail of the side-wheeler, while Elmer climbed up to the main deck and tied up the yawl. Quickly both men clambered aboard for an evening of dancing and drinking free beer. Like clockwork before the excursion boat returned to the landing the men leaped over the railing to the lifeboat. They rowed back to the Hubbard before sunrise.

Tonight the distinctive steam whistle of the City of Memphis sounded like a wild cat caught by the tail. It echoed across the Ohio, awaking Calvin from a sound sleep. After that he stared at the ceiling for an hour. Finally he walked down to the galley for a hot toddy. On the lower deck he was surprised by Jake tying off the lifeboat. Elmer waved as he climbed over the side, water pooled up on the deck under his feet. His left shoe was missing.

"What happened to your shoe Elmer?"

Elmer wrung out his shoulder length, matted hair with both hands. "If you're aguessin we was atakin' a midnight swim fer fun, you'd be wrong."

Jake continued. "Captain, we was having a kick ass good time on the dance floor when all of a sudden this new mate notices the yawl tied up to the stern cleat."

"Right away he blowed his whistle. He started acuttin' the line when I grabbed his shirt and slugged him."

"Naturally the guy got up and called Elmer some unflattering names. Then he hit Elmer with a chair. So naturally I jumped on top of him and choked his neck. That's when all hell broke loose."

"We was awinnin' when four more big guys appears. A whistle screeches. I covers my ears and watches as one guy finishes acuttin' the line on the yawl. Well, I grabs him. But before I could do any good, two other guys threwed both of us right over the side."

Jake shook his head. "It's a good thing we was good swimmers because the boat caught the current and headed toward the sandbar."

"It was a long swim but we finally gots in the boat. We paddles round in the dark. I knowed we seen this same dead tree a hunderd times."

"It's because we was going in circles, Elmer. Finally I headed toward them government lights on Towhead. We was rowing good until this here snake crawls into Elmer's boot."

"I gots skeerd. Real skeerd."

"Elmer you fell outta the damn boat!"

"Jake, I just lost my balance and my boot."

"So I flung that damn snake over the side and kept rowing to Towhead. Elmer leaped back in when he noticed the snake swimming next to him."

"My friend Bubba keeps a shanty boat on Towhead so I knowed we could rest there. He gives us hot coffee at and heads us the right way. Ever try aridin' the City of Memphis, Captain. It's excitin'."

"Sounds too exciting for me. Elmer."

"There's a lotta pretty women," Jake added.

"There's a lotta dancin'. Ifin you dance."

Jake patted Calvin's shoulder. A lotta pretty women will do you good, Captain. We heared you got your heart broke by a crazy woman from St. Louis."

"My heart's just fine, boys." Calvin handed the men towels. "I've got no time for fun right now. I've got a job to do for Soupy's aunt in Louisville on Sunday."

"That won't take all day, will it? City of Memphis goes downstream Sunday afternoon, not to Twelve Mile."

"A ferry runs to Louisville. You ever takes the ferry?" asked Elmer.

"Didn't you hear me? I don't have time to ride the City of Memphis. I've got a job to do Sunday and I need the money."

Elmer dried his hair with the towel and ignored Calvin. "If you changes your mind, you can catch the ferry at the foot of Spring Street by the Staus's Hotel."

Jake stood up. "My cousin, Amos, is captain of the W.C. Hite. Amos lets me ride the ferry for free, but it'll cost you a nickel."

"What kind of a job are you adoin' for Soupy anyways?" asked Elmer.

"I'm not working for Soupy. The job is for Soupy's Aunt Susan. She's paying me to drive her houseboat while her ladies' club plays mah jongg on the top deck."

"Majon? What the hell is majon?"

"A game I think."

"Are these ladies lookers?" asked Jake.

"Aunt Susan is like my mother. What do you think?"

"I thinks majon don't sound American," added Elmer.

"You can make the afternoon cruise if you don't dilly-dally around with them old ladies."

"Lotsa pretty women on the Memphis ifin you dance. I'm gettin' tared and cold Jake. Let's go."

"I could use some dry clothes myself. Have a good trip tomorrow, Captain."

Early Sunday morning Calvin headed to Aunt Susan's houseboat. He drove his jalopy down the steep dirt road to the foot of Spring Street to catch the ferry. Cars, buggies, and a bulky hay wagon waited. The W.C. Hite docked and then unloaded. Calvin joined the line of vehicles that jolted across the wharf boat and onto the ferry. He paid a nickel to the toll taker and parked near the bow.

Soon the gate raised, bells rang in the engine room and the boat moved out into the river. Effortlessly, the ferry moved underneath the Big Four Bridge as Calvin stood at the railing. He noticed the Burlington Northern freight train chugging across the bridge overhead. Sometimes the Ohio was placid pond, but today the rains upstream made it wide and roughened by the strong current. In about twenty minutes the ferry lined up at the Louisville landing and maneuvered into place. Calvin braced himself for the big bump as the ferry hit the dock. The deckhands jumped up to tie up the boat with big hemp ropes. Walkers moved onto the cobblestone landing, and then vehicles started moving off. Calvin watched the scoop of the Ohio River Sand Company work as he waited his turn. The machine seemed to take giant bites of the crumbly mountain, loading the golden sand into nearby railcars. Squinting past the sand mountain, Calvin watched the ladies on the top deck of the Aunt Susan's houseboat.

"Hey buddy. You with the old Ford. Move off, I gotta ferry to run here."

"Sure." Calvin cranked up his jalopy and drove across the cobblestone wharf.

On Fourth Street he parked next to Benny Barton's colorful limousine, and then walked down past the Coast Guard boat landing. At the City of Memphis wharfboat Calvin noticed tickets for half price for the afternoon cruise. He counted his money and then optimistically bought a ticket. He couldn't pass up a bargain.

Twelve portly ladies waved to Calvin from the top deck of Aunt Susan's scowl of a houseboat. They ignored Calvin's safety recommendation that no more than eight people should stand on the roof of the houseboat at one time. Calvin thought about taking the boat out, giving the wheel a fast turn, and flipping the women into the harbor just to prove his point. That was only a passing thought since Calvin needed the money more than he needed to make a point about safety issues.

"Good morning, ladies," Calvin saluted from the dock. He looked handsome in his uniform borrowed from Captain Duffy and his own jaunty captain's hat.

"Calvin, you're running late. We're ready to leave," bellowed Aunt Susan through a bullhorn from the top of the boat. "Untie the lines."

"Yes, madam."

As Calvin started to untied the ropes, he noticed the biggest, blackest cloud hanging over the Lady Susan. A cold wind blew. Calvin retied the lines. Quickly he climbed the gangplank and hung on to a beam under the deck roof as brisk winds picked up the tables and chairs. Soon rain, small hail, and mah jongg tiles pelted him from above. Susan and the ladies squealed and tramped inside.

It was a short-lived thunderstorm, but Aunt Susan canceled the trip. After the ladies departed Calvin helped Aunt Susan clean up and collected his money. It was fate. Calvin would be early for the bargain priced Sunday cruise on the City of Memphis.

It was a short walk to the boat. At a stand on the lower deck Calvin bought a sandwich, and then climbed to the top deck to listen to the River Bottom Ramblers playing patriotic songs. Soon the engines began humming loudly as the deckhands pulled in the gangplanks. As the City of Memphis moved the boat's high-pitched whistle sounded again and again. Calvin looked around. The channel buoy stood straight ahead the boat.

"The City of Memphis isn't in the channel! Why is the pilot ignoring the buoy?" Calvin sputtered to the man standing next to him at the rail.

"Don't mind it, fella. The pilot knows where he's going. He's been piloting the Ohio for most of his life."

"Jonesy been piloting a ferry boat most of his life," added another man.

"Going back and forth from Louisville to Jeffersonville don't take much thinking."

Suddenly a loud crash shook the City of Memphis. The bow jutted up like some giant hand pushed it from underneath. Water poured over the stern. People screamed all around. Two guys jumped over the rail into the river. Immediately the pilot made a quick turn and beached the bow on high ground near the Sand Company. Benny Barton and the River Bottom Ramblers waded through low water carrying their instruments on their shoulders. Calvin followed the orderly stream of passengers to the road back to Louisville. Walking back to his car he noticed activity at the Coast Guard landing.

A man in a neat blue uniform with lots of gold braid stepped out of the Coast Guard building. "Ahoy there, Mr. Johnson."

Calvin waved and walked toward him. "Good day, Commander Whitesides."

"Mr. Johnson, were you aboard the City of Memphis this afternoon?"

"Yes, I was."

"What happened? We got a call about an emergency on the river, and then it was cancelled."

"I think the City of Memphis hit something. The bow's on the bank and everybody made it ashore. No causalities."

"I guess there's no need to send out a boat?"

"No need, Commander."

"Thanks Mr. Johnson."

Calvin continued walking to his jalopy. He was disappointed that his trip on the City of Memphis was cut short. Sweating from the hot humid day, he bumped his Ford onto the ferry for an uneventful trip home.

On Monday big talk at Pat's garage was the fate the excursion boat.

"I heard the City of Memphis ran into some trouble Sunday," said Pat.

"Zach Jones got a ninety day suspension for making a bad judgment," reported Froggy.

"I was there. He took too many chances. Probably not his last mistake."

Next week Calvin picked up the newspaper. This time the mighty Ohio took charge. The Jeffersonville Evening News read:

City of Memphis sank just below the Falls with a good load of passengers aboard. All 321 persons were saved.

Captain Zachariah Jones was unaccounted for and presumed dead.

City of Memphis

CHAPTER 16

RIVERBOAT RIDER ON THE OHIO

Froggy's Victrola played peppy tunes on the deck of the Hubbard. He whistled as he painted the stacks and the pilot house. Calvin stood on one of the pews to paint the outside walls. Froggy swiped his brush along to the strains of a catchy tune called Let It Rain, Let It Rain, Let It Rain.

Hopping off the church pew Calvin stepped back to admire his work. "You got a song about sunshine. I'm tired of all the rain stuff."

"Sure Captain." Froggy hopped over and changed the record on the Victrola to You Are My Sunshine. "How about this song Captain?"

"I like it and I like this paint job."

"Yeah. This white paint from my shed works real good. The Hubbard looks more like a boat and less like a circus. Are you ready to slap some paint over that ugly pitcher in your galley, Captain?"

"No, not yet. It reminds me of the good times with Christina."

"La-de-dah. Ain't you over that woman yet? She didn't even see you when she was here. Look Calvin, your boat has to be free of this here artwork for the brew party in two weeks. Get over that woman and get on with your life."

"That's hard."

"Look Captain, there's nothing that helps a man get over a woman quicker than a boat ride. My friend, Captain Teddy Tobin, is taking the Revonah to Madison tomorrow. I'm sure we can bum us a ride."

"I don't think so."

"Look Calvin, a boat ride is a good way to clear your head."

"Okay. Okay."

The next day Froggy and Calvin took a short ride to the Coast Guard landing in Louisville to check out the packet, Revonah. After beaching Baby Wildcat, they walked up the cobblestones to the wharf boat.

"This wharfboat is a wreck. The Hubbard looks better than this."

Packet Revonah

"This wharfboat is really a wreck. It's the hull of the steamboat Wilmore Jones. The steamer went down near the Falls ten years ago. On the lower level is the cargo warehouse and on the upper deck is a place for passengers to wait. Packets contract with these wharf boats for freight and goods."

"That packet must be at least a hundred feet long."

"Revonah's a hundred and twenty feet long with a twenty foot beam. She has a four-cylinder, direct-reversing Kahlenberg oil engine. Nice and smooth. Today she's going to Madison, Indiana. I'll tell Teddy you'd like to know more about the business and we won't have to pay." Froggy waved as they approached the bow. "Good Morning, Captain."

"Hello Froggy. Welcome. Who's your friend?"

"Teddy, this is Captain Cal Johnson. He wants to learn the packet trade. We'd like to ride along today."

"Sure. Go anywhere you want on the boat, but stay clear of the rousters. They stay busy the whole trip. Packets are goods and chattels, gentlemen. This is not a ship of state, but more like an ark."

Calvin added. "Captain Appleby told me pilots are contractors. He stipulated his own terms and made a lot of money."

"That's a true statement. I'm a contractor myself. I do four trips a month. I have a steersman and a crew of twenty. I've heard of Captain George Appleby. He was known for his extraordinary memory, steady nerves and an uncanny ability to read any river and anticipate its tricks."

"I know Captain Appleby is quite a talker."

"Don't sell him short Cal. He knew how to make big money. That's what made him a legend on the river."

"Where do we sit?" Calvin asked looking around at the crowded deck.

Captain Tobin frowned. "This is a packet, not an excursion boat. Make yourself comfortable on the hay bales or the crates of chickens in the stern. Lunch is at noon. Check out the pilothouse afterwards. I'm cubbing a new steersman. He'll give you a few pointers about the business."

"Thanks, Captain."

The steamboat shuttered as it fired up. Calvin watched the action in awe. The engineer busied himself around the oil engines as a steward gave directions to four colored boys. The cook rolled carts into the galley to store up vegetables and meats. Deckhands fixed fire hose lines and lifeboat tackle. Three men put fire-axes in holders and swept the decks.

"Let's head to the stern, Froggy. It's too busy around here. I don't want a job." Calvin led the way, climbing over boxes and barrels, past a couple of unfriendly mules tied to a post and squealing pigs in a fenced-off area.

"Lay me a gangway!" bellowed the mate.

Calvin and Froggy moved out of the way while hand trucks rumbled over steel decks from the wharf boat. They clattered on the sheet-iron rollways, and thundered to the decks of the Revonah. The rousters sung and jibed at one another as they worked. The first mate directed the rousters.

Calvin watched the action. "I can see that these colored men are hard workers."

"Roustabouts work hard for a dollar a day. They sleep on a pile of freight and eat out of a tin pan."

Froggy scratched his head. "How do you keep track of everything that going on?"

"It might look chaotic to you, but there's a plan. The bulk of the tonnage must be moved in precise order and stowed with the gifted knowledge of the boat's trim and exactness. I'm Mr. Burns, the first mate. I'm in charge of all the details including landings.

"Do you ever make mistakes?" Froggy asked.

"I must execute all the details at all times; otherwise, I'll find myself out of a job."

Calvin scratched his head. "When do you know when to pick up cargo?"

"We stop at designated wharf boats or when a shipper hails the boat from the bank."

"You mean this boat would stop for a cow or a barrel of lard anywhere along the river?"

"You bet. That why you must stay clear of the rousters. They are always moving."

When the packet began her journey Calvin and Froggy watched the action from a hay bale. Revonah made three stops before noon. A wave of a white handkerchief at the Reedsville's farm stopped the boat for fifteen cases of eggs. At Rabbit Hash the rousters worked relentlessly unloading the unruly pigs by hand to a farmer on the shore.

The last stop was a wharf boat at Carrollton. Captain Tobin opened up with the landing whistle. He blew one long, two short and one long blast of a familiar note. The terminal signal was longer. It blew over a minute and fifteen seconds. Roustabouts worked like a horde of ants loading two dozen barrels of cider and fifty bales of cotton. Calvin was glad he took the first mate's advice and stayed clear of the rousters. Froggy missed most of the activity because he sprawled out behind the hay bales in the sun and fell asleep.

CLANG! CLANG!

A rouster waved. "Times to et. Don't wait. Food be gone."

Calvin poked his friend. "It's time to eat, Froggy."

Froggy bounced to his feet like a jack-in-the-box. "This cook puts out a spread. Let's go."

Calvin followed Froggy's sprint into the galley. The cook and his helpers laid out a plentiful meal on a long wooden table. There was a stew of meat and potatoes, sliced raw tomatoes, cucumbers in vinegar, green beans cooked with pork, homemade bread, New Orleans molasses, rice pudding and black coffee.

"A spoon will stand up in Cookie's coffee. Don't forget to cut it with some cream," suggested Froggy.

Calvin loaded the black coffee with cream and grabbed a compartmental metal plate.

Froggy gave Calvin a shove. "Put that down. Those are rouster pans. We sit at the table. The waiter will deal us some shells."

Quietly Calvin put the pan down and followed Froggy to the table. They sat on the bench across from the crew. In front of Calvin was a freshly baked loaf of bread. He grabbed a piece of bread off the top of the plate and slathered it with butter. The deckhands across the table snickered.

Froggy elbowed Calvin in the side. "Don't eat the bread off the top of the stack!"

"Why? It looks good. I'm starving."

"A good boatman never takes the top slice of bread. He takes the next one in the deck."

Calvin shoved the entire slice in his mouth and swallowed. "I don't understand. This bread is good."

"Look Cal, you need to learn steamboat etiquette. It's also better for your health. The top piece is the roof for the flies to land on. The sugar bowl is covered for the same reason."

Calvin grimaced as the deckhands continued to chuckle. Calvin felt sick to his stomach. The waiter appeared with a tray of food. He dealt them six individual dishes each filled with different foods. Each dish was about the size of a canary bathtub. Calvin inhaled the fragrant smells and woofed down the bites without a second thought. The waiter continued to serve the men until they were full.

"Cal, this is the first time I've seen molasses and butter worked into a paste and put on bread. I like it."

"Despite my mistake with the bread, this was the best meal I've had in weeks."

"I'm full too. I could use a walk."

"Do you want to check out the pilothouse?"

Froggy wiped his chin on his bib overalls. "Okay. Moving around will keep me from napping."

It was a short climb up a ladder to the pilothouse. Calvin and Froggy peered inside and watched the small, but intense young man at the big mahogany wheel. His shoulder length hair was tied back. He stood on a box so he could see over the top of the wheel.

"Good Afternoon. I'm Cal Johnson and this is Froggy Woodson."

The young man kept his blue eyes riveted on the river ahead as he spoke. "My name is Walter Foster. I am Captain Tobin's steersman."

"I'd like to train as a pilot myself. Can I watch?"

"Of course. Step right up next to me. You can get a better feel from here. Conditions are pretty easy right now. Do you want to feel the power of the river?"

"Sure," Calvin answered stepping up to the wheel. Since he was over a head taller than the steersman he ignored the box.

"Just hold her steady."

Calvin took the wheel. Walter moved his box and stood next to Calvin looking out into the river.

"This is exciting. Is there a time when your job gets hard?"

"Yes. When the water's up it gets more complicated. Especially when we have to dodge the sawyers. They're submerged trees, you know, nearly waterlogged. They have just enough buoyancy to rise up and down. You never know how big they are under the surface."

"You can move the boat out of the way of the sawyers, can't you?"

"Sometimes. It can be a disaster for a boat if you get caught on one. Snags that float out of the water are easier to avoid." Walter moved his box up to the wheel. "I'll take it now."

"Thank you for allowing me steer."

"Walter, what's this here thing sitting behind the door?" asked Froggy running his hand over the knots in the tall pine box. "It looks kind of like a coffin."

"It is a coffin."

Froggy backed away from the box. "What's a coffin doing in the pilothouse?"

"This is one of the coolest spots on the boat. The corpse needs to stay cool on a summer day."

Calvin stared at the box. "Doesn't having a dead man in here make you nervous?"

"Not really. A dead man can't hurt you."

"Where's the body going?" asked Froggy.

"The man's name is Colonel Malcolm O'Brien. He's going to be interred in a cemetery in Monterey on the Kentucky River. We'll drop him off on the trip tomorrow."

"Ain't it bad luck to have a dead guy up here?"

Walter laughed. "Like you, Captain Tobin's superstitious too. He likes a shot of whiskey every half hour while he's up here at night. I've got a bottle right here in the drawer. Do you want some?"

Froggy looked worried. "No. It'll take more than whiskey to keep me up here. Where's the head Walter? I gotta pee."

"There's a lard can right here and a toilet seat hanging off the stern."

"I'm going to the stern Calvin."

"Thanks for the lesson," added Calvin.

Calvin and Froggy made their way to the stern and stayed out of the way of the crew. They napped on the hay bales until sundown when the Revonah made it back to the Louisville landing.

Calvin smiled as he rope started Baby Wildcat for the ride back to Port Fulton. "Froggy, you were right. That was a great boat trip. I feel pretty good."

"Did it make you forget about that crazy painting woman?"

"A little. But mainly I learned that packets aren't my forte."

"You got to admit Calvin, the food was great."

"Yes. It was the best part of the trip."

"What did you think of that toilet seat hanging off the stern?"

"Drafty."

They both laughed.

After the experience on the Revonah, Calvin watched boats from the shore with more boatman knowledge. Most excursion boats were Kentucky-owned with the "brag boat" of the Ohio River being the Gilded Lily. At the Louisville landing every night from April to October, the Gilded Lily ran moonlight cruises with dancing and an orchestra. It was a fancy-pants version of the City of Memphis. The steamer's calliope, associated with the showboat and excursion life, echoed from shore to shore. This steam piano operated from a keyboard with twenty-six to thirty-two brass keys connected to whistle valves. It was exciting to hear the lively, hair-raising melodies like There's a Bonnie Lass in Scotland echoing throughout the Ohio River valley.

Relaxing on the top deck on his newly acquired pews from the Depot, Calvin watched the steamer, Tom Greene, traveling majestically up the river. She had a regular run between Louisville and Cincinnati. Captain Lenard Greene and his mother, Captain Mary Greene worked the boat. Froggy told him all about the boat including the description of the exclusively outfitted forward cabin on the texas deck that was Mary Greene's luxurious private apartment. Calvin liked becoming an experienced riverman and wondered what it would take to ride on that boat.

CHAPTER 17

TOM GREENE AND BETSY ANN

Sunday Calvin took the ferry to Louisville. He wanted to check out the steamer Tom Greene. Froggy said the Greene line painted its wharfboats with red and white trim with the town name above the middle doorway, so the bright, cheerful wharfboat was easy to spot. Calvin walked through the doorway and peeked into the office window. Inside was a small cubical with a stove and a cot. A whiskery faced old man pulled blankets up around his neck on the cot. Since boats blew their begging whistles miles from Louisville the wharfmaster had plenty of time to get ready for action. Calvin knocked on the door of the shack.

"What do you want this early? I'm tryin' to get some shut-eye."

"Do you know where I can find the captain of the Tom Greene?" asked Calvin through the office window.

"Who's askin'?"

"I'm Captain Cal Johnson of the steamboat John W. Hubbard. We're anchored near the Howard Shipyard waiting restoration."

Opening the door, the old man squinted at Calvin. "Greene Line doesn't work Sundays. Captain Mary is a devoted Baptist and believes Sunday is the Lord's Day. Come on in. I'll get you some coffee and you can tell me what's on your mind. I'm Seth, Mary's cousin." Seth handed

Calvin a cup of coffee from the pot on the stove. "Why are you wantin' to talk to Mary?"

"I'm learning about piloting and I thought the captain might give me pointers about the Ohio River. My experience has been on the Mississippi. I'm from St. Louis."

"Mary Greene and her son work the boat, but Mary's pretty much in charge. She got her pilot's license in '96 and her captain's license in '97. Her husband, Gordon, died last year. She's been puttin' in a lot of time since then."

"Isn't it unusual to have a woman piloting a riverboat?"

"Maybe, but she's real good. It's no trophy license, kid. Mary's been pilotin' steamboats longer than you've been alive."

"I didn't mean any disrespect. I'm interested in knowledge about steamboating."

"Mary's done many a hard job. Taking the H.K. Bedford between Cincinnati and Louisville during low water in '97 was a remarkable task for any pilot."

"She sounds skillful."

"Yes sir, she's both skillful and classy. Captain Mary's boats are always popular for their dependability and their air of refinement."

"Mary Greene's been piloting awhile. Does she have a favorite trip?"

"I think Mary's biggest moment was when she took the Greene Line's side-wheeler Greeneland from Pittsburgh to the St. Louis Worlds Fair."

"She went up the Ohio and the Mississippi all the way to St. Louis. Hot damn! I'll bet the crowds went wild."

"They sure did. I remember every moment. I was on that trip. Did you hear about the great Ohio River race between the steamers, Chris Greene and the Betsy Ann?"

"No. What happened?"

Seth opened the newspaper to the front-page headline. "Read this son."

Calvin took the paper and read the article aloud.

"The contest between the steamboats Chris Greene and Betsy Ann on the Ohio was more than a twenty mile race between rivals. It was not the great speed which contributed to the joy and excitement of racing, but the quality of the contestants in the struggle. The boats evoked stirring recollections of the romance of the river. Thousands of enthusiastic well-wishers lined the Ohio on both sides, waving flags to the patriotic music echoing on the Cincinnati levee. Dreams and memories reflected what travel on the Ohio means. Everyone who saw this contest between two worthy rivals hoped this spectacle might again become a common experience on the beautiful Ohio River."

Seth smiled. "The words are almost as excitin' as the race."

"The paper doesn't say who won."

"The Greene boats always win. Did you hear there's been talk about a race in Louisville next Thursday?"

"Who's running?"

"The Tom Greene against the Betsy Ann."

"Hot damn! We could use some excitement around here. I hope it happens."

After a chatty morning with Seth, Calvin rode the ferry back to Port Fulton. As he walked back to the Hubbard he stopped on the corner of Spring and Main Streets. He noticed the bold headline on the newspapers piled under a rock. It said: *The Steamers Tom Greene and Betsy Ann*

Reenact Historic River Racing Classic Thursday in Louisville.

"Hot Damn!"

Thursday's temperature was hot and humid 98 degrees as Froggy and Calvin stood shoulder to shoulder on the Louisville levee. The whole city was centered on two steamers moored at the cobblestone waterfront with the greenish mauve-colored water of the Ohio eddying around them. Just feet away from them, Captain Frederick Way of the Betsy Ann and Skipper Greene of the Tom Greene put on their captains' caps and shook hands.

"Look at all that gold braid standin' around us. You think all these guys are boat captains?"

Calvin adjusted his borrowed cap. "Maybe. Maybe not."

People started crowding onto the boats for the run. Youngsters selling Louisville newspapers made piles of money hawking them. Artists lined the levee, sketching the captains and anyone else who wanted their portrait made for a quarter. As they got in line to board the Tom Greene, Calvin noticed a flop-eared brown dog wandering near the water. His eyes followed the dog through the crowd, but he lost sight of him behind a wharfboat.

Froggy pulled Calvin up the gangplank by his arm. "Come on, Captain. Let's get aboard and find a place while we can."

As the crowd flooded the lower deck, the fans circled lazily, but they made no impression on the oppressive August heat. Sweat dripped into Calvin's eyes from his jaunty captain's cap.

It was four thirty. The Ohio River waters did their best to sparkle, but all Calvin could think about was the sweat profusely leaking through his fresh white shirt. The stokers checked their gauges on the boat while pretty girls moved chairs closer to the rail.

"Let's stand closer to the lovely ladies," said Froggy as he pushed Calvin up behind the girls. Suddenly the steam popped off. The Tom Greene trembled like a sprinter anticipating the gun. "The Ohio River is stagin' a comeback. This is the most excitin' thing that's happened in years."

Calvin felt pretty sticky and sweaty, but added an enthusiastic, "Hot damn!"

At five o'clock black smoke poured from the stacks of both boats. People waved from the levee. Five bells, three whistles, and then up came the gangplanks. At first the Tom Greene slipped backwards in the river with the force of the powerful current. She strained against the remaining line that held her. Suddenly her paddles turned as the roustabout dropped the rope from a spile and she moved forward.

Five pistol shots announced the start of the race. Tom Greene and Betsy Ann pushed upriver. Several dozen boats filled with officials, newspaper men, photographers and race fans darted through the water like dragon flies alongside the steamers. A plane circled overhead.

"You know Froggy, this is almost as thrilling as riding a hydroplane at the St. Louis Regatta!"

"This race is important to people in Port Fulton. It means the Ohio River's coming back to life again," shouted Froggy hanging onto the rail.

"Who's the favorite?"

"The Greene boats always win."

At seven fifteen Tom Greene crossed the finish line. Betsy Ann finished two minutes later. A cannon fired on the Jeffersonville shore echoed across the river. Firecracker rockets exploded as Benny Barton and the River City Ramblers serenaded the boats on the Louisville levee as passengers disembarked.

"This has been a long day for this old man."

"It's been a long, but exciting day for me too. It's time to get back to Port Fulton." As the sun slipped behind the Kentucky hills Froggy and Calvin clambered onto the W.C. Hite ferry for the trip home.

It was a sweltering August night as Calvin climbed the gangplank of the Hubbard about midnight. The night was warm and sultry and not a breeze rippled the river. He fanned himself and stood out on the deck. Not a breath of air stirred. Mosquitoes buzzed in his ears. He walked into his cabin and took off his pants to cool off. Calvin stretched out on his bunk and finally dozed off from exhaustion.

During the night the wind picked up. The thunder rumbled. Calvin awoke to a noisy thunderstorm that broke the heat. Calvin nervously watched as the stern of the Hubbard pushed out into the Ohio River. One cable became taut. The strain on the line made a creaky sound. The wind and the current pushed. Could the cable take the load? Calvin rushed onto the top deck just in time to watch the cable snap. Immediately the Hubbard caught the current and drifted several hundred feet sideways into the willows on the Kentucky side of the river.

Calvin watched and worried on the top deck until sunrise. At least the steamboat stayed in one place. Remembering what Tom the watchman from Towhead told him about getting help, Calvin waited for the steamer Tom Greene to appear for its morning run. Calvin brought out Tom's red tablecloth and frantically waved it back and forth. The Tom Greene whistled back.

"Ahoy, there," shouted a woman's voice through a bullhorn as the steamboat pulled alongside.

"I need some help back to Jeffersonville."

"Don't worry. We'll get some ropes on you and tow you back."

Calvin was mesmerized with the sight of the beautiful white steamer. "Thanks," he shouted over the drone of the engines.

The ropes were secured by the deck hands and the John W. Hubbard was towed back the Indiana shore. It wasn't the way Calvin would have planned it, but he finally met the Captain of the Tom Greene.

"Hot Damn!"

CHAPTER 18

THE SAGA OF THE STEAMER SOUTHLAND

One sunny Saturday Calvin noticed a flashy white steamboat anchored downstream from the Hubbard. She looked like a mysterious, beautiful woman standing in the shadows of the evening sun. The name Southland stood out in bold letters on the side. Could Southland be another stern-wheeler waiting for repairs at the Shipyards? As Calvin approached the gangplank, a small-framed young man waved to him. The sailor was seated on the bow polishing his fancy leather boots. Dressed in a neat and tidy blue uniform, he looked a few years older than Calvin.

"Ahoy there! This is a beautiful boat. Are you awaiting repairs at the shipyard?"

"No sir. The Southland's in fine shape just as she sits. We're anchored here to save on docking fees. Captain Ian McCardy and his jolly Scotch-Irish crew are aboard. I'm Sean O'Keefe. I'm the steersman. Come on up."

"Thanks." Walking up the gangplank, Calvin was enamored by the boat's ambience. "I'm Captain Cal Johnson from the steamer John W. Hubbard. My boat is anchored upstream a quarter mile or so. We're waiting for financing for restoration."

"You seem young to be a captain. I'm cubbing the Southland and working on my second class pilot's license. I'm glad to meet you."

"I've read books about river piloting."

"You don't need books. The only thing you need to know is the river itself," interrupted Sean. "Piloting is more art than a science. Captain McCardy says it's taught by word of mouth and reinforced by hands-on training."

"Captain McCardy sounds like a task master."

"He certainly is. His pilot's pay is among the highest on the river. $750 a month gives him the right to be uncivil to anyone he wishes. Would you like to meet him?"

"Sure."

"Follow me to the pilothouse." Calvin followed Sean up the ladder to the top deck. As they entered the pilothouse Calvin stood behind the steersman, just in case Captain McCardy was in one of his uncivil moods.

"We got a visitor, Captain. Meet Cal Johnson from the steamboat John W. Hubbard anchored upstream."

A stocky man with bushy hair and a red handlebar mustache enjoyed a cup of tea in a comfortable leather chair. He got up to stoke the Katy stove that snapped and crackled, and then he extended his hand to Calvin. "Good morning lad, I'm Ian McCardy."

"You have a fine looking boat, Captain."

"She's strong and has a good crew."

"Are you in the excursion business?"

"We do excursions sometimes. What can I do for you?"

"My partners and I envisioned the Hubbard as an excursion steamer. Of course, we need major renovations before we get into the business."

"I don't need more competition."

"We won't be competition. The Hubbard won't be cruising on the Ohio. We plan to run the Missouri River from St. Charles to Jefferson City."

"I've seen your boat downstream from the Shipyards. It's too big to run the Missouri. That river's fast and unpredictable. You might reconsider other options. Who's your pilot?"

"His name is Captain Michael Muldoon. He's very experienced. And I'm going to be the relief pilot."

Captain McCardy stroked his mustache and chuckled. "Ah Laddie, I know Captain Mike Muldoon. I don't think he'll find river navigation where he left it thirty years ago. If you're going to be the relief pilot on the Hubbard, you'll need to learn about river cruising today."

"What do you suggest I do?"

"You'll need river experience Laddie. Lots of river experience. Tell you what I'll do. We're going to Madison, Indiana on an excursion for Clark College. Since your boat's laid up, I'll give you a job on the Southland. I won't be paying you, but you'll be getting good experience. Do you want to come along Laddie?"

"I sure do. When are you leaving?"

"Tomorrow at daylight."

"Do you think I could work with you or the engineer for my river experience?"

"O'Keefe's cubbing with me, but there's plenty to do. It'll be a long ride. To make money we've got to conserve coal. We won't be hurrying."

"That's fine with me."

Captain McCardy looked out the window to the ice crystals around the moon. "If the winds die down there'll be a fog. I'll pick you up at dawn."

Walking back to the Hubbard Calvin noticed the winds were calm. Little wisps of vapor rose from the water.

All night long the Hubbard and the Southland lay shrouded in a blanket of thick fog. When Calvin awoke at five o'clock he couldn't see any farther than the deck rail. He pulled on his pants and grabbed two stale biscuits from the galley, and then headed to the top deck. Using a lantern he tried to spot the Southland in the soupy fog.

Suddenly Calvin heard big engines humming and chattering. The paddle wheel splashing echoed in his ears. Then a creaking, cracking, scraping sound reverberated along the side. The outline of the Southland appeared. A whistle tooted and a bell sounded. A bump on the riverside of the Hubbard knocked Calvin to his knees.

Captain McCardy's voice boomed loudly. "Ahoy, Laddie, are you ready to board?"

Calvin grabbed onto the railing. "Yes I am, Captain."

"Grab him Centerpole." Out of the fog came a disembodied arm. "Hang on!"

Calvin grabbed the huge, muscular arm and a man with the strength of an ox lifted him over the railing to the deck of Southland. "Welcome to the Southland, Colonel. I'm Centerpole," said the deck hand as he effortlessly placed Calvin on the deck beside him.

"Glad to be aboard. I'm Cal Johnson."

"Captain says you stays with me."

"Fine." Calvin sat next to Centerpole as the Southland drudged along at three or four miles an hour in the fog. "Is Captain McCardy usually this cautious?"

"Yes, sir."

"I guess he's dead serious about saving coal."

"Yes, sir."

After an hour or so with the non-conversational Centerpole, Calvin made his way to the pilot house. As he peeked in the door he noticed McCardy sitting in his comfortable chair, above the fog, checking landmarks on the banks with his binoculars.

"The fog's disappeared. What happened Captain?"

"When we have fog on the river it's always clear up here, Laddie." Captain McCardy walked across the room and called through his communication tube to the engineer's department. "John, give her a little more steam. We won't make Madison by noon if we don't get a move on." McCardy looked at Calvin. "Do you want to watch an ace pilot at work?"

"Yes, sir."

"Then sit down and pay attention."

In ten miles, around Utica, the fog lifted completely. Now the steam was up. The Southland puffed and huffed. At noon the steamboat ran her bow up onto the gravel banks at Madison. While a deck hand dropped the anchor, Centerpole and another colored boy pushed out the gangplank.

Calvin walked with Captain McCarty to the top deck. He blew a piercing whistle that made Calvin cover his ears.

"That whistle's loud enough to wake up the whole town."

"I only hope it's loud enough to wake up those college kids."

The crew buzzed around securing the boat. In about ten minutes, the students from Clark College dribbled down the hill to board the Southland. The band members, napping on the lower deck, proceeded to set up their instruments on the texas. They tuned up. Soon music lit up the Madison levee with joyful excitement.

Centerpole waved to Calvin. "Come on, Colonel. Doggie's laying out a spread. Time to gets some food." Calvin nodded and followed Centerpole.

In the galley Doggie Cross, the cook, looked like a veteran of years of river travels. His face was lined and shriveled. His forearm carried a tattooed and vivacious figure of a naked female trapeze artist. Calvin couldn't take his eyes off Doggie's tattoo.

"You like her son?"

Calvin just smiled. He was at a loss for words and just nodded yes.

"Aphrodite is an emblem of my wandering life. I've cooked for packets and for circuses. I've traveled on showboats along the lagoons of the south, and worked steamboats on a dozen waterways." Doggie put down a platter of ham and cheese sandwiches. Calvin started to grab for one when a herd of college students pushed by him and gobbled them all down with gusto.

"Come on Colonel. We're gonna open the soda bar on the top deck," added Centerpole. "There's food up there."

"I'm supposed to get valuable river experience with Captain McCardy or the engineer."

"Captain tells me to use you where we needs you. Right now, we needs you on the top deck. Soda jerks gots nice hats."

Calvin frowned and followed Centerpole for his river experience.

About two thirty the Southland engines hummed. Deck hands untied her ropes and she steamed upriver for the cruise. The kids left the soda bar and headed to the dance floor where a five piece band played a loud, raucous version of The Charleston.

Calvin took off his red soda jerk hat and grabbed a Grape Nehi. He climbed down to the dance floor to watch the kids wildly stomp and dance. The movement involved in dancing fascinated him. Calvin's mother sent him to dance classes in high school, but he never accomplished more than the two step. For a mechanical guy Calvin just couldn't coordinate the mechanics of movement to rhythm of music.

Doggie brought the left-over sandwiches from the dance floor to the top deck. Calvin eagerly gobbled down two. "I'm heading for the engine room guys," he called as he disappeared below deck. Shooting the bull with the engineer seemed more interesting than watching kids dance. Calvin followed the rickety ladder to the bowels of the boat.

The door to the engineer's room, propped open with a crowbar, made Calvin look in. The engine room appeared crisp and clean, definitely the showplace of the boat. The floor was red-leaded, with the bulkheads painted white, and the carlins overhead painted green. The maze of hot pipes covered with asbestos and banded with brass stood out prominently. Other pipes coated with aluminum lit up the room. The cylinders and upper works gleamed. All the naked steel rods and fittings were rubbed up and sandpapered so they appeared zebra-like alternating dull steel with the glittering steel look. A balding, burly man snored with a smile on his face in a big chair in the corner. On the desk was a placard with the words, Chief Engineer in bold letters. Calvin tapped the sleeping fellow gently on the shoulder.

The man jumped up and grabbed Calvin. "Who the hell are you? Are you one of them college kids? You're not suppose to be down here!"

"No. Captain McCardy invited me on this trip. He said the engineer could give me some pointers. I've got some engine experience myself."

"Engines, huh." He shoved Calvin into a chair. "Where'd you get your engine experience?"

"A lot of places. Right now, I'm working on the steamboat John W. Hubbard anchored in Port Fulton. I'm Captain Cal Johnson." Calvin didn't think it would be to his advantage to tell him that the engines on the Hubbard failed years ago.

"Those college kids give me a headache with all that loud music and jumping around. Cal, you look kind of young to be a captain."

"I'm not exactly a full-fledged captain. I'm in training. The Hubbard's laid up right now waiting restoration so Captain McCarty took me on this trip to improve my river experience."

"Experience on Captain McCarty boats is always worth it. The more the merrier."

"Well, since the frivolity with the college kids picked up, I was hoping to find a quieter place in the engine room where I could learn about steamboat engines."

"Next to the engines is the best place to be. It's not always the quietest. I'm John O'Malley, the chief engineer. If you like the percussion music of the engines, sit down."

"I love the sound of engines, chief. How many pounds of pressure do you have?"

"Two-hundred-and-ten."

"Hot damn!"

Creak! Twang! Snap! Suddenly the pipes above their heads began swaying up and down. Soon the engine room filled with steam.

"She's blowing a joint. Come on Cal. I'll give you some real hands-on experience."

"Blowing a joint sounds serious. Are we going to explode?"

"No, this happens all the time with steamboats. The packing is being forced from around the cylinder head by steam pressure." O'Malley handed Calvin two rolls of packing. "Hold this and give me some when I ask for it."

"Yes, sir."

With the dexterity of a surgeon O'Malley clipped, slit, hammered and punched things, while Calvin stood by with packing when the engineer called for it. Finally O'Malley wiped his hands. "That should hold her." He looked up at the pipes above their heads as they flexed and squeaked. "I wish those kids would slow down. The deck's vibrating like a drum head!"

"It's a popular dance."

"Jumping in the air every five seconds is too much action! As you probably know, the deadliest risk in steamboating is a boiler explosion. With cast-iron boiler heads, loose rivets and weak internal flues, a lot can go wrong without having those kids jumping and loosening the system."

Calvin looked overhead, wondering what would happen to him if those tired old wooden decks and pipes collapsed. "Chief, that eight-inch steam pipe from the boilers to the deck is moving back and forth a foot or two."

O'Malley looked up and frowned. "That's not a joint. If it breaks it means a hot water bath for us. Let's move out of here." He quickly rang up the Captain. "McCardy, as long as those college kids are jumping like kangaroos, I mean dancing, the engineering department will be on the top deck. Let's go, Cal." The men climbed up the ladder and found a couple of chairs in a quiet corner of the top deck. O'Malley sat in one and put his boots on the rail. Then he took two Cuban cigars out of his pocket. "Try one."

"Thanks, Chief." Calvin took a match from a box in his pocket and struck the head off the bottom of his boot. He lit both cigars effortlessly.

"You got to be careful with boilers. When a critical boiler component fails, there's little warning, only concussion, flame, scalding water, and searing steam. There's a saying on the river. If you can't put out a fire on a boat with a bucket of water, you better look to getting ashore."

"That's when swimming skills come in handy."

"True, but passengers and crew aren't killed outright in explosions. They drown or worse."

"What can be worse?"

"The unthinkable horror of being entombed in the rubble of the burning, sinking steamboat is a lot worse."

"If working on a steamboat is so dangerous, why do you do it?"

"I love engines and my time on the river."

Suddenly there was a blast of steam that blew out of Southland's starboard stack with such force that it drew all the draft from the other stack. Calvin looked up and wondered if he'd be practicing his swimming skills soon. The boat shuttered. The music stopped. The only thing Calvin heard was the syncopated heartbeat of the engines. O'Malley continued to puff on his cigar. "Chief, should we be worrying?"

"Not this time Cal. It's a boiler blow off."

After another minute that seemed like an hour, the music began again. This time the band played a slow waltz.

"I got some fresh stogies, Chief. Want one?"

"Sure. We got more than an hour before we land in Madison."

From the top deck of the Southland the Ohio River looked like picture postcard. With every turn fresh river vistas opened, the spectacles of the river showing more life than the shore. Swallows followed the boat. Wild ducks spattered along the river surface like seaplanes before a take-off. Kingfishers and herons patrolled the shore along the sycamores.

At five o'clock the steamer tooted and landed. The college kids exited with enthusiasm. The gangplank was quickly raised and Southland headed back downriver. As the city of Madison dissolved into the background, Doggie appeared on the top deck with a half platter of sandwiches.

"Good evening, gentlemen. How about some tasty leftovers?"

Calvin nibbled a sandwich. "Why didn't we stop? It might be nice to walk around for awhile."

"Are you kidding? The captain can't stop so you can walk around." Doggie scowled. "That would make this a two day trip for the Southland and then we really wouldn't make any money."

"Extra time takes all the profit out of the operation," added Captain McCardy grabbing one of Doggie's sandwiches. "That's good information for you to know for success in the excursion business, Cal."

Later that evening as the moon lit up the Jeffersonville skies the Southland slid up next to the Hubbard. As the boats touched, Calvin climbed over the rail.

"Thanks again, for the valuable river experience."

The next week Calvin read an article in the Louisville newspaper that made him question his new career.

STEAMBOAT BURNS ON THE OHIO

The steamer Southland burned near Evansville, Indiana. Captain Ian McCardy made an abrupt landing and upset the Katy stove in the main cabin. The Southland caught fire and burned quickly with the old wood and thick paint feeding the blaze. It took only fifteen minutes for the Southland to burn to the waterline.

Thanks to the quick thinking of Sean O'Keefe, the steersman, and Monroe "Doggie" Cross, the cook, the entire crew escaped safely.

The Southland sunk to the bottom of the Ohio River in less than one hour.

CHAPTER 19

NOBODY BUYS COAL IN PORT FULTON

From the top deck of the Hubbard, Calvin watched the Alice Brown as the great gilded anchor swung jauntily between her stacks. She was the popular stern wheeler of the William H. Brown fleet. This afternoon the Alice Brown pushed coal barges upriver. People in Port Fulton talked about passing coal on the Alice Brown as more an honor than a job. Transportation by barge was the cheapest way to transfer coal from the mines in Pennsylvania, West Virginia, and Kentucky to towns along the Ohio River. Often these crudely built, one-way barges to New Orleans sank, paving the rivers with coal. For the barges that landed in Jeffersonville the wagons from the Rose Coal Company carried the coal to the yard at Eighth and Wall Streets.

Froggy informed Calvin that nobody in Port Fulton brought coal. There were more creative ways to harvest it. For instance, Butch and Hitch Smith lashed up two yawls so there was only about a six to eight foot gap between them. Together the boats drifted slowly toward the coal barges anchored near the bank. Between the two yawls the men dragged a long wooden rake. An efficient team like the Smiths' raked enough coal in a week to last all winter.

The preferred method of coal harvesting was hijacking. Coal barges laid along the banks for weeks in low water on the Kentucky side of Towhead Island. Men took boats downstream to the barges. Reaching up, they lifted off chunk after chunk of coal. The watchmen on the barges ignored the practice as long as the men didn't leave obvious holes in the stacks.

One autumn afternoon Calvin stretched out his lazy body across one of the comfy pews and napped in the warm sun. Calvin awoke with a smile on his face as Elmer shook him.

"Wake up Captain."

"Damn it, guys. You interrupted a dream about sexy women and excursion boats."

"Me and Jake needs to borrey your lifeboat. How about it?"

"Aren't your days of dancing and drinking over?"

"What do you mean? We ain't givin' up drinkin' and dancin'. The City of Memphis don't run til spring."

Jake put his arm around Calvin's shoulder. "Me and Elmer need your boat for something really important like hijacking."

"Hijacking what?"

"We need your lifeboat to hijack coal off them barges. That big boat of yours could hold enough coal for the entire winter in one trip."

"I need coal to keep warm this winter too. I'll go along."

"You don't needs to go. Me and Jake can gets the coal fer all of us. Since we're usin' your boat we'll gives you a share."

"I still want to go. Remembering your reckless midnight rides, I'd prefer to keep an eye on my boat."

Jake smiled. "Whatever you want Captain."

The truth was Calvin was getting bored and looked forward to the excitement of a clandestine operation like hijacking. "You guys get the boat set up and we'll start out after lunch."

At three o'clock all three men set out toward Towhead Island in the Hubbard's yawl. Elmer sat in the middle and rowed powerfully. Jake sat in the stern and supervised Elmer. Calvin relaxed with the wind in his face, smoking a fresh cigar.

Elmer moved the boat along at a pretty good clip while Calvin dozed. In an hour they pulled up to some shanty boats on Towhead Island.

"Come on Captain. It's time to stretch your legs."

"Jake, what in the hell are we doing here? Aren't the coal barges in the opposite direction?"

"Bubba gots a fire agoin' under his big iron pot. Before we do all that hard hijackin' work we needs some grub. Don't you agree?"

"I'm not hungry."

"Bubba's stew is real tasty," added Jake.

Elmer and Jake put their arms around Calvin and pulled him toward the fire on the beach. The three men sitting on the log next to the cast iron pot waved.

"I forgots somethin'." Elmer ran back to the yawl and pulled a jug from under the seat, and then joined the men back by the fire. Everyone was quiet as the aromatic smells wafted from Bubba's black pot.

Bubba gave Elmer a friendly tap on the shoulder. "I gots your favorite recipe acookin'."

"Delish. I smells it clear across the river."

Bubba stared at Calvin with his piercing blue eyes. "Try this," He handed him a bowl of his concoction and a spoon.

"What's in it?" Calvin asked, tasting it reluctantly.

"Riverbank rabbit, taters, onions and carrots and a little flour fer thickenin'."

Elmer licked his bowl clean, and then took a swig from the jug. "Been awritin' much?"

"Yep."

"Captain, Bubba's awritin' a book. I never learns to read so he's been areadin' it to me."

"How many times I gotta tell you. It ain't no book Elmer. It's a log like them riverboat pilot's write."

"I tried writing a log on Baby Wildcat once. I ran out of words in two days."

"I never runs out of words."

"Bubba, this here is Captain Cal. He lended us his big boat to pick coal."

"Howdy," said Bubba. The other men just waved.

Calvin smiled at the men. "Do all you guys live here?"

"No. Me and my brother lives in that shanty boat over yonder. I'm Gilpin Clink."

"I'm Gilmore Clink. Just call us, More and Pin. We poled down from Cinny awhile ago."

Calvin scraped the bottom of the bowl with his finger. "How do you get the fresh vegetables?"

"I growed me a garden. Vegetables from the garden be best fer your health."

"I heard some people think shanty boaters are bad?"

Bubba stared right at Calvin with his piecing blue eyes. "They ain't unless they is provoked."

More Clink interrupted. "Look Captain, there's good shanters and there's wretches who take stuff."

Bubba continued to stare at Calvin. "Sometimes people needs to take stuff to live. Good shanters are God fearin' people."

"I don't like them city people," added Pin Clink.

Calvin passed the jug, but he didn't drink. "Jake, we should leave. We need to pick coal while it's still light."

"Rains acomin'. I seen a red sky this mornin'."

"If it's going to rain that even more reason to leave now."

"Captain, you ain't no fun." Calvin shrugged and continued walking toward the boat. The boys followed.

Immediately they rowed for the coal barges on the other side of Towhead Island. As they approached the barges, Elmer and Jake picked chunk after chunk of coal from the bottom of the coal piles. Calvin sat in the bow supervising. It didn't take long for chunks to fill the bottom of the boat. Calvin felt the boat sinking to the gunwales. "Our freeboard disappearing, boys. I think we've got our limit."

"Hell, no! This boat can hold lots more," shouted Jake as he continued flipping big chunks into the boat.

Calvin put his fingers into the water. "Only inches separates us from the river!" Suddenly a cold wind from the west made him shiver. A bolt of lightening lit up the sky and a rumble of thunder reverberated along the bank. "Boys, listen to me. The river's almost in the boat and there's a storm coming."

"Don't worry, Captain. We knows about coal."

"Believe me, this big boat can hold lots more," interrupted Jake.

Elmer looked up at the sky. "That storm's aways off. No rain yet."

Lightening lit up the sky again. Boom! Bang! The thunder bolts grew closer and louder. "I'm chickening out. I want to go back."

"What do you mean? We can still pick more."

"Look Jake, you fill this boat with a ton of coal, but first, drop me off on the mainland. I'll take the ferry to Jeffersonville. I want to go back. And I want to go back now."

"Okay Captain. Don't get your pants in a twit. Elmer sit down we're heading to Louisville."

Elmer scowled. "We're losin' time we could be apickin'."

The men were silent as the yawl approached the Louisville levee. Calvin jumped off. Sloshing through ankle water, he waved. "I'm depending on you to bring back my boat safe and sound."

"No problem Captain. And we'll have plenty of coal for winter," shouted Jake.

Calvin watched the yawl leave, and then stumbled along the Louisville landing. The lightening lit up the sky. Thunder roared. As the rain came down in sheets, Calvin ran up the gangplank of the ferry. He hid out of the wind under the lower deck. It was a rough crossing with the waves splashing over the rails. Calvin hung on tight as the rollers battered the ferry. He was glad when the W.C. Hite arrived at the landing on Spring Street. In a steady rain he walked back along Market Street. Calvin was soaked to the bone as he approached the boat ramp near Froggy's place. Men in raincoats and wide brim hats stood along the bank. Some pointed toward the river.

Gus Shapiro, in a brown trench coat, motioned for Calvin to come over. "Cal, I'm glad you're alright. We heard the lifeboat from the Hubbard went down."

"My yawl sunk? What happened to Elmer and Jake?"

"Jake swam right up to the bank about fifteen minutes ago. Froggy took him to his place. He was drenched, but doing fine."

"What about Elmer?"

"Nobody knows."

"Did he drown?"

"Elmer's a strong swimmer, don't count him out."

"What happened?"

"Jake told me they were picking a big load of coal when it started raining."

"I was with them for awhile. When I left, the yawl didn't have much freeboard."

"Jake said he knew that the boat was at the point of sinking, so he started throwing chunks overboard to lighten the load. Elmer stood up to help, but his shift upset the balance and water poured in over the stern."

"Is that when it went down?"

"Not exactly. It went down when Elmer caught his foot and fell backwards. The yawl sunk on the spot with Elmer's foot wrapped around the anchor line. Jake jumped clear."

"Elmer got his foot wrapped on the anchor line? That doesn't sound good. Where did the boat go down?"

"We heard it sunk in forty feet of water near Towhead."

"I was afraid something bad like this might happen. Can I do anything?"

"Not right now Cal."

"Then I'm going back to the Hubbard for some dry clothes and a slicker. I'll be back."

As Calvin walked back to the steamboat in the steady drizzle many scenarios played in his head. He pulled off his clothes in the galley and laid them on the warm stove. Calvin shivered and felt kind of feverish, so he filled a cup with whiskey and water. It went down slowly and tasted good, but it made his head heavy. He plopped down in a chair. Soon he rolled onto the floor naked and fast asleep.

In the morning the sun brightly lit the galley. A barking dog on the bank woke him up. Calvin uncurled himself from the floor. He was cold and his head ached.

Woof! Woof! Woof!

WOOF! WOOF! WOOF!

Finally Calvin pulled on his pants and stumbled to the rail.

"Bonjour, my friend," called a familiar voice. "Jean Claude and I are lost. The river looks very much the same everywhere. Calvin, isn't it too cold to be sleeping without a shirt?"

Calvin squinted into the sunlight, down the gangplank. "Anne Marie is that you?"

"Oui."

Calvin grabbed the red tablecloth and wrapped it around his shoulders. He walked to the gangplank. His eyes focused on the flop-eared dog and the chestnut haired beauty standing on the bank. She wore a flamboyant shiny pink and white flowered dress that emphasized her long shapely legs. "Seeing you here is really a surprise."

"We meet again Calvin. It must be our destiny."

"What happened to your job on the showboat?"

"I was fired. Invite me aboard and I'll fill you in."

"Of course. Come on aboard. I'll grab my shirt and make some coffee."

"We'll be right there." Anne Marie and her dog walked up the gangplank and sat down in the galley.

"What happened?" Calvin asked pouring two cups of coffee.

"Three months ago I got a job on the Golden Palace showboat. Remember?"

"Of course, I remember. It was just before the Sergeant Floyd was launched. I hated to see you leave."

"It was a wonderful job, Calvin. We traveled up the Ohio as far as Madison performing melodramas. Everyone enjoyed our performances. Last week I argued with the producer, Double R Markle, about money he owed me. He didn't see it my way and fired me. That same afternoon he dumped me and Jean Claude on a sandbar with a leaky boat and a ten dollar bill."

"What a terrible man!"

"I learned too late that Markle was a crook."

"Markle's a crook." Calvin thought back to his conversation with Billy Killebrew. Didn't he mention Markle in the financing of the Hubbard?

"Calvin, there was talk on the showboat about all of Markle's boats going broke. That wouldn't surprise me. Double R Markle doesn't pay his people and he cuts corners on safety issues."

"You should be glad you're free." Calvin wondered if this incident was a precursor of things to come for the Hubbard.

"Calvin, fate has always been on my side. Yesterday when Jean Claude and I landed the boat in Westport, I ran into an old friend again. Billy Bryant was looking for actors for his showboat. I met Billy and his family when the Golden Palace stopped in Louisville for the steamboat races."

"I thought I saw Jean Claude walking around in the crowd."

"I should have stopped by to see you, but I was painting to earn money. The last hour before the Golden Palace headed upriver I did a sketch of Violet Bryant for her husband. Billy Bryant seemed impressed with my talent. He paid me ten dollars!"

"He's the man you met in Westport."

"Yes. I met Billy Bryant in Westport yesterday. He offered me a job as the understudy for Violet in their new show called At the End of the Road. He told me to meet the Golden Palace in Brandenburg on Friday."

"Then why are you in Jeffersonville?"

"Well, Jeffersonville wasn't my destination. I was heading to Brandenberg when this storm came up. It blew Jean Claude and me downriver. As you know, my sense of direction has never been very good. This morning when I looked around to see where the storm had taken us, I saw your steamboat. I couldn't believe my good luck. And here we are." Anne Marie continued to stare at the galley wall. "What is this monstrosity?"

"It's a mural my friend painted for me. I guess you don't like it?"

"No, mon chère. It's too big, too modern, and very ugly. Get rid of it."

"You're not the first person to recommend that."

"By tomorrow night I must meet the Princess in Brandenberg. Calvin, I need your help."

"Relax. The steamer Queen City is going downriver today. Do you have money for a ticket?"

"I have ten dollars."

"That should be enough. The Queen City wharfboat opens for tickets at noon."

"That's wonderful!" Anne Marie looked around at the boat. "I don't want to be mean, but your steamboat is not very pretty, Calvin."

"I know it's not much to look at right now, but my boss is getting the financing for a complete restoration. By next year the John W. Hubbard will be a fancy excursion boat on the Missouri River. I'm going to be training to be the pilot."

"What a fabulous opportunity!"

Calvin looked at his pocket watch. "Make yourself at home for a couple of hours, and then we'll check out the Queen City schedule. Right now I've got to find out what happened to my friend. I lent him my yawl and the boat went down in the storm last night."

"How terrible! Did he survive?"

"That's what I need to find out. Have coffee on the top deck. You can get a view of the river and escape my galley monstrosity. I'll talk to you later."

"Thank you, Calvin. I hope you find your friend."

"Me too." Calvin waved to Anne Marie and walked to Froggy's place to get the latest news about Elmer.

In the willows, near Froggy's boat ramp Calvin stumbled over something. When he checked it out he found it was a body of a man covered with mud and debris. It looked like Elmer. Calvin touched his face. It felt cold. Calvin jumped back when he snorted and sat up. "Hot damn, Elmer! You're alive!"

"Ah-choo! Ah-choo! AH-CHOOO!" Elmer wiped mud out of his eyes with Calvin's sleeve. "Captain, your boat sunk. It filled with water before I could do anythin'.

Jake gots clear, but I gots pulled underwater. I holded my breath and thought abouts heaven and hell!"

"You could have drowned. What happened?"

"I gots stuck! I told you! I gots stuck! My foot gots tangled up in the rope. I went straight to the bottom of the river, before I gots enough slack in the rope I saw them catfish swimmin' by. I thought I was a goner."

"Everybody's been worried."

"I'm not finished, Captain. When I gots to the surface I swimmed all the way to Towhead. And I'm alive thanks to Bubba and the Clink boys.

"What do you mean?"

"The boys saved me. They found me on the beach and brought me back to life at the shanty. Bubba wrote abouts my adventure. I'm real proud to have my name in his book."

"Let me help you. Let's see if Froggy's has some dry clothes for you."

"Thanks Captain." Calvin and Elmer staggered up the bank to Froggy's house.

"Did you swim back to Port Fulton?"

"Nope. Pin Clink rowed me here."

It took three days for Elmer and Jake to make a complete comeback from their ordeal. With dry clothes and a cold, the fierce twosome turned up on the lower deck of the Hubbard on Sunday.

"Captain, we knows where your lifeboat went down," sniffed Jake.

"Ah-choo! How abouts alettin' us borrey Wildcat for gettin' coal."

"I don't think so. I'm buying my coal retail."

"I guess we'll have to talk to Froggy abouts usin' his boat. So long Captain."

"So long guys."

"You don't know what you're missing," they chanted as they walked toward Froggy's place.

As for Anne Marie, well, she and Jean Claude caught the Queen City for Brandenberg, Kentucky. Her note listed the dates of the shows on the Princess. She bought two gallons of bright yellow paint with instructions to cover-over the monstrosity on the galley walls. She placed the cans on the front deck next to a watercolor she painted of the Hubbard. Her picture of the steamboat looked like a restored John W. Hubbard. The picture, hanging over Calvin's bunk in the captain's cabin, was Calvin's dream for the future. He had to squint at the details of the boat since Anne Marie's canvas was only eight by ten.

In the morning Calvin carried the yellow paint to a cabinet on the lower deck with good intentions of covering the monstrosity.

CHAPTER 20

RIVER LOGS BY BUBBA SMITH

May 5

The paddle wheel steamboat Tennessee Belle hauled my shanty from Buffalo Bayou to Towhead Island on the mighty Ohio River. Captain Joe Bob is kin so he don't charge me except with quips and quotes he taked as payment fer the pull. I bank tied my summer quarters to Towhead and set out to deweed my old garden plot on the bottoms. Today is a tad cold but worken the garden comes over me every year round this time. I loves the musty smells of dirt floaten up to my nostrils. It speaked to my brain of all those tasty vegetables that growed here before.

May 6

I was surprised when my cousin Catfish McCoy comes acalling. He rowed over from Louisville with a jug of brew. He gots a bullet hole in his shoulder that's healed up. Sez its from cleanen his gun. I knowed Catfish all my life and he don't usually tell the truth. After we drinked his brew he sez that old steamboat near Howards gots gold on it. Asked me if I wants to be rich. Sure I sez. Let's go gold hunten he sez. In the dark we rowed over to the steamboat. It was a bad time rights away fer me when my foot gets stuck. That deck is fallen apart. We didn't find no gold just a guy on the boat with a gun. He shot at us. Catfish almost gots shot in his good shoulder. Jumping overboard in the dark is scary. I thinks this story of gold is a figment of Catfish's imaginashun. From now on I am sticken to growen vegetables.

July 4

Elmer borreyed a rowboat. He talked me into going with him to the Louisville boat races. It was a big 4th of July celebrashun with fancy food, fast boats and a band callen theirselves the River Bottom Ramblers. Me and Elmer watched Froggy playing the harmonica and dancing with the band. The River Bottom Ramblers gots them a flashy car. Them spinning wheels on that car makes me dizzy. Near dark we seen red, white, and blue balloons flying pretty as you pleze over the river. Froggy drinked lottsa brew and went to sleep in the street. Me and Elmer taked Froggy home. Then we rowed to the shanty to eat and watch fireworks that looked like shooten stars.

July 13

I sees a full moon tonight sleepen on the deck when I heared shouten. I looks up and sees a boat. It was Elmer and Jake. They was rowen like crazy round and round. Come here. Come here I sez. I gets them outta the water and gived them some coffee. Elmer sez they gots tossed off a dance boat. They was real tired so they sleeped on the bank. Then the boys rowed home. Elmer and Jake is good friends.

July 14

I watched two big guys come a push poling their wood shanty boat to the bank. They anchored downstream aways. I starts to get that piney feeling, so these new shanters banken in close up to me makes me smile. Was they good shanters or bad ones? That won't make no never mind anyways cause they is what they is and that is that.

July 15

My gardens growed good this year. I put in some taters, carrots, beans, onions, cukes, and some tomata plants. Them pesky rabbits been eaten my beans and tomatas. Maybe its time to catch me one of them critters fer supper. I wonder if the new shanters gots a trap?

July 16

I catched me three big channel cats on red wigglers. Ivy rowed over from the green houseboat and she traded me some fine ears of corn fer my green beans. I shucks corn and grinds it up on a hollow rock. Mashed up corn tastes good with them cats. I fixes up them cats by rollen them in corn and slow fryen them in the grease of a possum who gived hisself up to me. Soon I heared shouten and holleren and such going ons down the new shanters way. I heared lotsa cussen and splashen in the water. Not being one of them busy bodies who noses into other peoples business without an invite, I just let them new shanters by theirselves to figure things out. Soon my fish entices them boys by sending out the best smells down wind so they stood at my fire introducen theirselves as Gilmore Clink and Gilpin Clink of Rising Sun, Indiana. Them brothers liked being called More and Pin. Would you guys like some supper I sez. Sure they sez. Them fish tasted delish. Them Clink boys sure do talk lots about nothen.

September 5

When I sees this red sky this morning I knowed rain is comen so I makes a fire early to cook my stew. More and Pin walks over to help me cut up the fixens fer my iron pot that has lots a flavor soaked into it. That pot gives up a little bit of flavor to every batch of cookens I puts in it. More is real good at catchen critters. Today he brings me this fine river bank rabbit that he skins and slices up fer my pot. I adds taters, onions, and carrots. Then I adds water and a little white flour fer thickenen. I puts my pot on a slow fire to cook to what I call a stick your finger in kind of temperature. Me and the boys sits and jaws while it cooks.

What a surprise. Elmer and Jake rowed up in a big boat. With them was this Captain fella from Port Fulton. He sez he lives on that old steamboat near Howards. His voice sounds familyyour to me. He don't seem to enjoy shanty food as much as smoken them stinky cigars. And he gots some queer ideas about shanty boaters. I thinks maybe this Captain fella was the one who shot at me and Catfish when we was looken fer gold. He don't have no patience and wants to gets the coal fore the rains comes. Yep I sez, its gonna be a soaker. I smell the rain already. When the boat leaves Pin and More pulls up chairs on my shanty. More plops them tired feet of his up to the rail. Soon the rain comes. We set a spell and watch the storm run its course.

There ain't nothing more breathtaken than a lightenen storm on the river. More sez its the force a nature meeten with the hand of God. The air gets heavy. The sky gets dark and scary. The air smells musty like a wet dog sitten in a spring house. The voice of the wind screams louder. The river answers by raisen up its wavy fist in angry protest. Not to be out did the sky turns a nasty green and starts moanen and groanen. Waves foam and leap up to spit in the eye of the storm. Pin sez that lightenen makes the sky look as pretty as fireworks on the 4th of July. After awhile the storm can't bully the river no more and moves on.

When the winds stops howlen More points to somethen moven out in the river. Its a man walken right outta the river. Pin hops over the rail and drags him back. The man is wet and muddy but looks familyyour. He looks up at me and sez I is sure glad to see you Bubba. You looks awful Elmer I sez. I needs a towel and a bowl of stew he sez .O.K I sez. Soon Elmer curls up on the deck and falls asleep. In the light Pin takes him back in his rowboat to Port Fulton.

September 7

The natural self cleanen of the river sends lots of driftwood floaten in a silent parade. Them trees don't stop til a branch or a root or a sand bar yanks them from the grip of the river. Some of them swells up. They lay stuck just belo the surface to grab ahold of stuff. Sometimes damage is final like what happened to the City of Memphis. She catched a snag belo the Falls. Newspaper sez the steamer sunk and the captains missen.

September 30

I feels cold weather in my bones. The geese is flyen south. Days gets shorter and them trees turns pretty colors. A man can't tie up to a spot fer too long cause of the ever present danger of sinken roots. Thats not happening to Bubba Smith. Its time fer me and my shanty to move on. I likes my freedom and I likes to be warm.

October 15

More and Pin jaws about the cold. They don't like fall creepen down from the north. I sits in my chair and smells the cool in the night breeze. When them leaves shows their Sunday best colors old man winter wakes up just down the road. More points up to the sky. He spots more geese flyen south. I likes the fall cause the bugs leave and the nights turns crisp and clear. I sleeps in my bed better with a sweater on.

October 30

More and Pin needs to be moven on to. They pulls up the lines of their shanty and starts poling down to Memphis. They gots a brother with a house on Main Street with a warm wood stove fer winter. More sez Gilroy Clink and his dog Elvin don't mind company specially kin. I miss them boys already. It don't take no time to build a fire to warm your bones, but it taked time to build friends that warms up your soul.

November 20

Ifin I want to be warm now I needs to stoke up my stove with wood. The fire burns hot. It sure do feel good to the bones when that stoken heat gets to worken.

Elmer rowed over. He sez him and Jake shot them a bunch of ducks today. Elmer brout me a duck and a surprise. The surprise was a new tablet from the Five and Ten in Louisville. Elmer sez its fer writen down things fer my logs. Thank you I sez to Elmer. That duck and the last of my taters makes us a tasty supper. I reads my logs to Elmer as he helps me get ready to go. Captain Joe Bob comes tomorrey.

November 21

Me and Elmer sits on my deck awaiten fer Joe Bob's boat. I reads the last pages of my logs out loud to Elmer. All of a sudden Elmer stands up and points to this big white boat coming downstream. I heared people call them yauts Elmer sez. Its bigger than a ferry I sez. Abouts 70 feet Elmer sez. I sees a name on the stern. It sez Episode. Elmer sez that's a funny name for a boat.

Joe Bob's Tennessee Belle is acomen around the bend. I sees the smoke from the stacks behind the yaut. Soon my shanty will be headen down the Sippy to Buffalo Bayou. It's a long pull. Buffalo Bayou is a good place cause its warm and there is a bunch of shanters all in spitting distance. We gets together most winters. I gots lotsa stories this year to share with them river rats.

I wants to deadicate these logs to my friend Elmer Long who always gots time to hear me read.

CHAPTER 21

THE FINE ART OF DUCK HUNTING

It was a sunny, crisp November day when Calvin invited Pat Murphy and Chief Johnny Hillfinger to the top deck of the Hubbard. Shooting ducks from a steamboat with a rifle was as illegal as hell, but, like everything else in Port Fulton, people never worried much about the consequences.

In the comfort of his favorite chair Calvin surveyed the landscape. Pat snoozed on a vintage church pew with his feet propped up on another. Johnny sat next to him. He alternated between cleaning his gun and eating. A plate of ham sandwiches and homemade brew rested on a barrel between Calvin and the boys.

The sun warming his face felt good. Calvin rubbed his arms through his threadbare green sweater. "Isn't it a great day to enjoy the bucolic ambience of the mighty Ohio River?"

"What the hell are you talking about?"

"The day Johnny. It's a beautiful fall day. A little cool maybe, but real nice."

"Right." Johnny turned toward the river and raised his rifle. He looked through the sight, and then panned across the sky practicing for a flock of ducks. "I'm taking shots at any and all ducks that make the mistake of flying by. Hey Cal, I've been meaning to ask you. What kind of a crazy picture did you paint on the galley wall? Today's the first time I saw it up close in the daylight. It's really ugly."

"I didn't paint it. A friend of mine did it back in July. It's called modern art. She calls it Cubism."

"Cuba-ism? What the hell is that? Cuba-ism don't sound American. Get rid of it Cal. It looks sissy-like."

"I've been meaning to cover it. I even have the paint."

"What are you waiting for? It ain't no treasure."

Pat yawned. "Speaking of treasure Johnny, tell Cal what you know about the Hubbard's gold? It's a story only you can tell."

"Yeah, I do tell great stories."

"Tell me about the gold, chief."

"Well Cal, you know there's a lot of rumors about this old steamboat going around in Port Fulton," sputtered Johnny cleaning his gun as he wolfed down another sandwich.

"What kind of rumors?"

"First of all, the Hubbard's got a bad history."

"Froggy told me there were problems."

"It's more than problems. The Hubbard has bad Karma."

"What do you mean?"

"Years ago the Hubbard was a floating speakeasy with high stakes gambling. She made runs between Louisville and Cincinnati. The boat developed a dangerous reputation."

"What does a bad reputation have to do with the gold?"

Johnny sat back and put his shiny boots on the pew and stretched out. "The gold and the bad Karma go hand in hand."

"I'll be the judge of that. Tell me the story."

"Okay Calvin. Sit down and listen. The fate of the Hubbard started out one foggy night on a Louisville to Cincinnati run. The boat picked up some gangsters from Mooresville, Indiana to play poker. The men carried with them a suitcase full of gold Double Eagles."

"Didn't the front page of the newspaper tell about the robbery at the Indiana State Bank?" questioned Pat.

"The papers were everywhere, but people on the boat didn't connect Dillinger and Fat Charlie to the Indiana State Bank robbery. Two more players joined the poker party. They were well-dressed Mexicans. Four-Fingered Paco Diego was a big guy and his sidekick, Fast Felisco Fernando was considerably smaller and smarter. They put a sack of gold coins on the table to secure their seats. Sheriff Oscar Peabody was hired to keep the game honest."

"I heard Sheriff Peabody got jailed because people thought he killed the Mexicans."

"You're ruining my story, Cal."

"Yeah Cal. I love a good story. Continue Johnny."

"Well, as night turned to early morning this poker game became very high stakes. Lots of gold changed hands. The Mexicans were winning big time as the Hubbard started to tie up at the Cincinnati landing. Another steamboat came in right behind the Hubbard. It exploded. Sparks and fire from the boiler explosion spread throughout the crowded wharf."

"The Hubbard didn't tie up," interrupted Pat.

"The boats moored at the landing caught fire and burned to the water line. Since the Hubbard wasn't tied up, the pilot moved her back into the river. As the Hubbard crew put out fires on the deck, shots were fired in the saloon.

"I know the Mexicans got shot."

"Yes. When the lanterns relit the Mexicans were dead on the deck. Both men shot through the heart. Their gold vanished. The gangsters, John Dillinger and Fat Charlie were seen hightailing it downriver in one of the Hubbard's yawls."

Pat continued. "As you know, Oscar Peabody took the rap. He got charged for the crime of murder and robbery since bullets from his gun killed the Mexicans."

"People are always talking about the ghosts. Tell me about the ghosts."

"Calvin, the Hubbard's got bad Karma, not ghosts."

"People in Port Fulton say that on foggy nights the Mexicans search the steamboat for their gold."

Johnny frowned. "That's a lot of baloney Cal. You know as well as I do that all the gold on the Hubbard headed downstream in the rowboat with the Indiana gangsters."

"Did we come here to hunt or talk about non-existent ghosts?" asked Pat.

"Hunting was the plan." Calvin waved his revolver. "I don't think my gun will get any ducks, but if you guys shoot them, I'll cook."

Pat loaded his rifle. "Sounds like a good deal to me."

"Cal, I've been meaning to tell you, I like these pews. There's room for my ammunition and all my gear within easy reach."

Calvin put down his gun on the pew. "I've got a duck-hunting story. You guys wanna hear?"

Johnny frowned "No. You ruined my story. I'd rather be hunting."

"Does this story have good Karma?" asked Pat.

"Duck hunting stories always have good Karma," answered Calvin.

"Okay. Okay. We can shoot bull and then shoot the ducks. We have all day."

"Thank you, chief. Just this week Elmer told me I had a keen sense of duck behavior. Maybe that's Karma?"

Johnny snorted. "Maybe. But I've never considered Elmer Long an expert on any level."

"Elmer's has a lot of useful knowledge."

"Come on Cal. Are you going to tell this story or what?" asked Pat. "I want to bring some ducks home before dark."

"Sure. The story started when I took a ride on Baby Wildcat behind Towhead Island."

"Is this a duck story or another one of your damn boat stories?"

"Well chief, I guess it's both. I went out riding to clear my head when this huge flock of ducks appeared out of nowhere. There must have been a hundred!"

"This sounds like fiction."

"It's a true story, Johnny. Cross my heart."

"That damn loud noise of that outboard engine of yours flushed them out."

"Yeah, I'm sure the motor noise had something to do with it. The ducks took off in a big flock and flew out into the river. Their exit gave me an idea."

Johnny looked at Calvin with one eyebrow raised. "My idea would be to paddle out the next day and bring your gun."

"That was my idea too! The next day I took my boat out behind the island to scan for ducks. Jake and Elmer followed me in their boat with their weapons. They stayed downriver while I went up the river to sweep the ducks backwards toward the boys. They got off several successful shots. Needless to say, I cooked us all a delectable duck supper. And we put the rest on ice."

"Is that tactic legal?" asked Pat.

"Sure. I took a boat ride and I chased the ducks a little, but I didn't break any laws? Right, Johnny?"

"Well, laws are made to be adjusted. Cal, I have better duck hunting story. It showcases my expertise which is better than Elmer's useful knowledge. And if you've heard this story before Cal, just shut up or I might rethink the laws in your duck hunting story with Elmer and Jake."

"Okay, Johnny. Let's hear your story."

Pat yawned and closed his eyes in the warm sunshine.

"It was close to Thanksgiving I think. The weather was nasty. Everything Homer and I put into the boat stuck to the bottom. Tools, engine, gas can, decoys, even my boots. It was so cold the current under my boat was moving, but the water inside my boat was frozen solid."

"We had a lot of rain last November. The water was high," added Pat.

"That's right. The river was at flood. The sheriff and me started out early, running our boat wide open down the middle of the river, dogging six-foot twigs and sometimes whole trees. Then, without warning, we disappeared into this fog. It was so thick I couldn't see Homer sitting right in front of me."

"Ah Ha! It sounds like you and Homer were in a horror movie with Boris Karloff."

"Stop interrupting me Cal or they'll be consequences! Who the hell is Boris Karloff anyway?" Johnny gave Calvin a hard look and continued. "Homer and me continued downriver at full bore.

"Weren't you worried about going fast in the fog? questioned Pat."

"No, real men are lucky. They don't worry about small potatoes. Besides in less than a mile the fog lifted. A minor problem was the river splashing into the boat. It froze our clothes as hard as boards. My beard was filled with icicles."

"Did anyone mistake you for a duck hunting Santa Claus?"

"Stop interrupting or he'll never finish. I'm ready to hunt."

"Thanks, Pat. Homer and I were freezing our asses off as we got to the island and threw the anchor. I dug out six of them newly whittled decoys of Froggy's. Homer pitched them over the side. Unfortunately they all floated belly up!"

"Belly up? How come?" asked Pat.

"Froggy forgot to tell us to weight the damn things. I could hardly feel my fingers, but I netted all six. Homer put on some lead sinkers and we tried again. Most of our decoy flock straightened and faced smartly into the wind. The two ducks that were hooked backwards backed into the wind. One decoy got tangled on my ammunition case and they both sank."

Calvin smiled. "That doesn't sound like you were experiencing good Karma."

"Maybe not. I've had nightmares that were more pleasant. It was cold. It was windy. Then it began to snow. Suddenly out of the nowhere a skyful of ducks appeared. We shot. We shot all around them."

"Did the ducks fall out of the air? There were plenty of holes in it."

Pat chuckled, "Quack! Quack! Quack! Did you ever hear a duck laugh?"

"You guys are ruining the mood."

Pat and Calvin gave Johnny their best serious faces. "Okay."

"It was cold and our clothes were frozen. And worst of all, we didn't hit a single duck. Finally it was time to head home. Homer fumbled with the lines on the ducks. I thought he might be planning a new career with the circus as a duck decoy puppeteer!"

Calvin interrupted. "Johnny, Mark Twain once said there were three classes of lies: just plain ordinary lies, damned lies, and statistics. Which is this story?"

"What do you think?"

"Does it have anything to do with Karma?"

CHAPTER 22

THE EPISODE ESCAPADE

Calvin stirred up a can of yellow paint Anne Marie left on the deck. The crisp weather invigorated him into painting over Christina's mural in the galley.

Calvin reflected on his life as he swiped the wall with the yellow paint. Things seemed bleak. First of all, his four year relationship with Christina evaporated. Secondly, the excursion boat business was sinking in a river of red tape. Calvin called St. Louis collect weekly, but the telephone in Billy Killebrew's office just rang and rang. Calvin Johnson was running out of money and patience.

Life on the river in Port Fulton slowed down. Calvin had more time on his hands than he had hours in his day so the idea of a treasure hunt on the Hubbard intrigued him. Boy, could he use a pot of gold at the end of the rainbow! Calvin and Mud spent hours looking for the Hubbard's hidden gold. They investigated all the closets and crevasses. Unfortunately they came up empty handed when it came to the gold. However, there was no shortage of dead critters and dusty bottles filled with Dr. Park's Indian Corn Remedy.

Autumn was delightful with its sunny days and cool nights. Fall blossoms showed edges nipped by early frost. The tar paper on the texas deck frosted over some nights. Trees in Kentucky hills reflected vibrant colors of red, yellow and gold for miles. Calvin was thrilled with the pleasant weather and colorful leaves dotting the greenish surface of the waters of the Ohio River.

School bells sounding in Port Fulton signaled Calvin into organizing the boat for winter. After some maintenance, the hull was stronger and now a kerosene pump kept the bilges relatively dry with less work. When Mud and Calvin ran out of things to do, they took lazy sunbaths on the church pews on the top deck in this perfect Indian summer weather.

"This is the life," Calvin chortled as he and Mud gorged themselves on roasted peanuts and threw the shells on the deck. The shells blew away in the wind like swirling leaves.

"I loves eatin' peanuts like this, Captain. Especially since we don't have to clean up."

Late into the fall the boys from the orphanage occasionally dived and fished from the forward deck. On weekends Mud King invited Calvin on trips to the woods with the kids. Groves of walnut and hickory trees supplied Calvin with free snacks when peanuts ran out. They picked fruit from the finest stands of persimmons and pawpaws. Mud taught Calvin how to make a refreshing beer from pawpaws on the galley stove. The boys from the orphanage carried baskets of persimmons to Pat Murphy. He turned the fruit into a persimmon brandy in the still in his garage. The brandy was tasty, but powerful stuff that could spin your head around like a top.

Winter on the river brought many changes. The biweekly beer parties on the Hubbard adjourned to Froggy Woodson's basement. Parties happened as a sufficient supply of homebrew became available at three to four week intervals. Froggy's homemade Limburger cheese added to the regular menu of sausages and potato salad. Because of limited space, only Froggy's fiddle and an accordion player provided entertainment.

"The Hubbard's getting cold. I like these parties in your basement." Calvin said, snuggling up to the warm gas pipe.

Pat sized up Froggy's system. "Your unique gas-fired heating makes your place real cozy. I'd like to try your idea on my house. How's that jumper on the gas main work?"

"It's pretty simple, Pat. I put a pipe on three sides of my basement along the baseboards. The pipe, perforated with small holes about every six inches, connects to the gas main. When it's lit, tiny flames at six inch intervals make the room nice and warm."

"And it's cheap! Who figured out that connectin' the gas pipe between the meter and the street gets you gas for free?" asked Elmer.

Froggy laughed. "It was some retired ace carpenter and his ingenious buddy with larceny in his heart. I heat my whole house for free by leaving the basement door open."

While it wasn't warm enough for big crowds at night, during sunny days the galley of the Hubbard was acceptable as a meeting place for the guys at the store.

"Thanks for letting us use the galley, Calvin. It's too cold to meet under the awning," said Red Fredricks.

"I'd like to think my cast iron cook stove provides cheery warmth. But probably you should thank Elmer Long for the ample coal supply."

"Think nothin' of it, Captain. Me and Jake owes you since we sunk your boat."

Calvin stared at Red as smoke filled the cabin. "What are you smoking? It smells like burning garbage."

"I roll my own cigarettes. Use genuine Sears Roebuck Catalog papers and burly leaf tobacco, ten pounds for a dollar. Wanna try one?"

"No. That smoke makes me light headed."

"Don't bother me none. I salvage the tobacco crumbs from the butts and roll more cigarettes. When the crumbs get too dry I moisten them up with brew."

"That doesn't sound tasty." Calvin hoped Little Hooter didn't find out Red's recipe.

The Ohio River seldom froze solid enough to interfere with navigation. The fogs in early morning were frequent and low-lying. They never surrendered their hold on the river. When Calvin looked from Green Hill, all he saw was a pilot house and two smoke stacks drifting above the eerie low-lying fog.

One morning as Calvin enjoyed his morning coffee he caught a glimpse of a wispy figure running down the lower deck. "Hoot, is that you?" He got up and followed, but the figure disappeared into the bank of fog at the stern. The squeaky hatch to the engine room opened and closed so Calvin trotted to the hatch and opened it. "Hoot, if you're in there, come on out. Hoot? Hoot? I've got some fresh stogies. Do you want to try one?"

A voice called from the gangplank. "Hey, Captain. I'd like one of those stogies, providing they're not the Italian ones. Would you like some company for breakfast? I brought some fresh corn muffins."

Calvin turned around to see a blurred figure in the fog. "Good morning, Froggy. Sure, I'd love a muffin. I'll meet you in the galley.

Froggy took two hot muffins out of a paper sack on the galley table. He handed one to Calvin. "They're from a recipe Minnie wrote down for me."

Calvin popped one in his mouth, and then stopped chewing. "Did you fry these in lard?"

"Sure. Minnie fries everything in lard and I followed her recipe. Do you want another one? I've got a sackful."

"One is plenty for me. Did you see Little Hooter on the way over?"

"Nope," said Froggy chomping on his second muffin.

"Did you see anybody run passed you?"

"No. You must be seeing things?"

"Someone opened the hatch to the engine room, and then slammed it shut. I thought it might be Hooter sneaking around for smokes."

"I didn't see a thing. Besides ain't Little Hooter in school right now?"

"You're right. Hoot wants to read and do arithmetic."

"Could the slamming around be your spooks?" Froggy questioned. "Spooks haunt around in the fog. Do you want the rest of your muffin?"

Calvin nodded no. "You told me there's no such thing as spooks, Froggy."

"Yeah, I remember. Hey, I got a great story for you. You wanna hear?"

"Is it about spooks?"

"No. Spooks are make-believe. My story's true. It's about my friend, Ivan Smith, and how he got his nickname, No Bottom in one of these soupy, Ohio River fogs."

"Sure. I got nothing but time," sighed Calvin. "Let's take our coffee out on the deck and enjoy the full effect of your fog story."

"Good idea, Captain."

Calvin and Froggy got comfortable on the pews on the deck as the fog surrounded them.

"My story begins when Ivan, or Smitty we called him, was a lowly deck hand. He was assigned to the forward end of a leading barge in the fog. His job was to keep sounding with a lead line on the front of the barge. The pilot could see the bank on both sides above the fog, but couldn't see the river ahead."

"Yeah, I experienced that phenomenon myself on the Southland."

"Well, Smitty sat out at the edge of the barge alone with his lead line. In the fog he chimed for hours rhythmically, 'No Bottom! No Bottom!' Finally the pilot anxiously called up to the Captain. Sir, we're going to have to tie up. We're not making an inch. The Captain leaned out on the top rail. A big tree sticking out of the fog didn't move. The Captain said you're right. Tell Smitty to tie up."

"So what happened?"

"Inside of a minute another deck hand rushed back to the Captain with a silly grin on his face. Sir, you can shut off the engines. We don't have to tie up. We're not moving an inch and we won't be for a longtime."

"I don't understand Froggy. What's going on?"

"Smitty was out there on the end of the barge with a lead line and a jug of brew, singing out. 'No Bottom! No Bottom!' He kept drinking and calling without actually checking his lead line until the boat was fifteen feet into a dry cornfield."

"What a mess! I'll bet no one let Smitty forget that."

"Not on your life. And that's a true story, Cal. Hey, the fog's clearing off. I can see Louisville."

Calvin got up and walked to the rail just in time to see a large, handsome yacht motoring downstream. It was up on plane, running effortless with a smooth rooster tail of water behind it. "Hot damn! Look at that!"

Froggy crowded him at the rail and waved. "That boat looks a magnificent white swan."

"She's at least seventy feet."

As they admired the gorgeous boat, it made a U-turn. It headed right for the Hubbard. Froggy and Calvin looked at each other.

The boat slowed and slowly pulled up alongside the steamboat. The skipper called through a megaphone. "Ahoy! Can we tie alongside?"

Froggy waved as Calvin scrambled for his bull horn. "Come right ahead. I'll tie you off. You can stay as long as you want."

"The crew of the Episode thanks you, Captain."

Froggy and Calvin tied off their lines. Then they watched the crew feverishly secure the Episode so that it floated alongside the Hubbard.

"Come on aboard." Calvin called.

The men waved.

Calvin helped three well-dressed men over the rail. The older man stepped forward. "Afternoon mates, I'm the skipper of the Episode. Archie Packman's my name. This is my engineer, Clyde Jones, and our chef, Jacques Rubidoux."

"We're pleased to meet you. I'm Cal Johnson, the captain of the John W. Hubbard and this is my friend, Froggy Woodson."

Froggy stared across at the boat. "That Episode of yours is one of the most beautiful boats I've ever seen. Where are you guys from?"

"We've been based at the Columbia Yacht Club in Cincinnati all summer," answered Archie.

"We're on our way to Florida for the winter months," added Clyde.

Calvin stared at the boat bumping gently against the Hubbard. "Captain, what's it take to own such a magnificent boat?"

Archie laughed. "It takes a hell of a lot more money than I have. I'm her skipper, not her owner."

"We're the paid crew," interrupted Clyde.

"Yeah, her owner is R.J. La Fontaine," continued Archie. "R.J. has a machine tool manufacturing business in Cincinnati. He's been busy this summer and hasn't been able to use the boat much."

"It's not that he hasn't wanted to," snickered Clyde.

Archie sat back on the pew with his feet up. "As far as R.J.'s concerned, his crew's become proficient in the stalling tactic."

"What do you mean Archie?" Calvin asked.

"When the boss calls and wants to use her, I'd say: The engines are down for maintenance, or Clyde's got food poisoning, or the river's white-capping. The truth is we covered for Jacques. Our renowned chef moonlighted at a snooty French restaurant in Cincinnati. The Fantaisie paid a fantastic salary which we all shared."

"So where are you heading now?" asked Froggy.

"We got a telegram in Cincinnati to take Episode south. R.J. wants use her in a warmer climate during the winter months. This summer has been a dream. Extra cash, the use of a magnificent boat and a fine expense account."

"You're life sounds like a dream. Will you be here long?"

"We'll be here through the end of the month, Captain. Then we'll motor downstream to the Gulf. Our destination is the Cabana Royale Yacht Club in Miami.

"Monsieur Archie, I need to sharpen my culinary skills before Miami. I would love to prepare a gourmet feast for Christmas. Se faire comprendre?"

"I understand Jacques. Let's do it. I'll put the groceries and the drinks on the R.J.'s account. How about it, would you like to join us?"

Calvin couldn't believe his ears. "You want us to join you for a fancy Christmas dinner on the Episode?"

"Yes. Can you make it?"

"You bet." Froggy and Calvin answered together.

"And bring guests. I like big parties."

Froggy clued the crew into the local sights. Clyde and Archie took an interest in the girls at Catfish Mary's place while Jacques concentrated on organizing his elaborate dinner.

Five days before Christmas Calvin's father sent a letter with money for a train ticket to Granite City for the holidays. Calvin kept the cash and called his parents on the telephone collect. He wished them a Merry Christmas and told them he had an invitation to eat with friends.

December was the beginning of a milder than usual winter on the Ohio. On Christmas day Calvin pulled on some linen dress pants and a red wool sweater that his mother knitted for him last year. He looked in the mirror to slick down his unruly hair and decided against wearing his old worn coat. At noon as he climbed gingerly over the side of the Hubbard to the deck of the Episode. He walked through the large ornate mahogany doors into the opulent interior of the yacht. Fancy drapes, chandeliers, long dinner tables with silverware and elegant dishes and glassware overwhelmed his senses.

Froggy sat in a fancy brocade chair gulping a snifter of brandy. He wore an almost new pair of bib overalls and a clean blue and white checked flannel shirt. As Calvin walked toward him he noticed that Froggy smelled like flowery soap and Vitalis.

"Boy do you look fancied up Froggy."

"Hello Calvin. You got to try some of this tasty brew. I don't think it came from Johnny's still."

Calvin sniffed Froggy's drink. "Smells great. It's worth a try." He poured himself a glass from a fancy decanter with horses on it. Calvin sat down on the gold velvet sofa across from Froggy. "Did you ask Elmer and Jake to this extravaganza?"

"Are you kidding?"

"Archie said we could invite guests. I asked Pat and Minnie and the kids."

"I'm here solo Captain. Elmer and Jake wouldn't fit in around here."

Soon Calvin's guests, Pat and Minnie Murphy and their three children climbed aboard. Clyde ferried them out in the classy Episode lifeboat. Froggy and Calvin watched them enter the boat through the dining room. They were dressed up in their Sunday clothes. Minnie and thirteen year-old Patsy couldn't take their eyes off of the glitzy crystal chandeliers. Patsy touched the elegant dinnerware on the long table with the lace tablecloth.

"This is like reliving Pat and me's honeymoon dinner in a Black Bear Hotel in Louisville," remarked Minnie. "Thank you for inviting us Calvin. Being here is an amazing Christmas present."

"I'm glad you could come." Calvin took their coats to the closet. "There's some grape soda on the table. I can pour you some."

Minnie and Patsy sat on the velvet sofa. "Grape soda sounds wonderful Calvin. Thank you."

Buddy, the sixteen year old, and Pat walked with the skipper to the pilot house. Oscar Murphy, called Baby by his family, was the only reluctant guest. The ten year old sulked in the corner while he scuffed the mahogany walls with his floppy leather shoes.

Calvin walked over to Baby and handed him a bottle of grape soda. "This is tasty. Try it."

"Okay," Baby mumbled as he quickly drank down the bottle leaving a purple mustache on his upper lip.

"What do you think of this boat?"

"Nice, I guess,"

"Sounds like you'd rather be doing something else?"

"Yep. Playing outside."

"Would you like another grape soda?"

"Nope. This is boring. I wanna go home."

Clyde smiled as he passed Calvin and the ten year old. He wore a white French linen suit with a silk plum colored bow tie. The new crew members, LuAnn and Chantel, were draped on each arm. Calvin recognized the working girls from Catfish Mary's place. LuAnn, an attractive, long-legged woman with curly blond hair and a short red dress smiled at Baby. The cat-like Chantel looked fashionable with her bobbed black hair. She flipped her feathered boa around her bare shoulders and patted Baby on the head. The ten year old perked up, smiling from ear to ear.

"Isn't he adorable with that cute little purple mustache," flirted Chantel. "What's your name darling?"

The boy's eyes lit up and his face got red. "They call me Baby."

"What a cute name. You certainly are a very handsome baby. Come on, we'll show you the boat."

"Yes. . .Yes ma'm." Baby followed behind the giggling ladies like a lovesick puppy.

Jacques proved to be an excellent cook, producing a mostly American Christmas dinner that provided an outstanding culinary experience for the guests. The meal included roast turkey, ham with a honey glaze, yams, mashed potatoes and gravy, cranberry sauce, wild rice and a French dish with snails that Calvin and Froggy avoided. Desserts were plentiful and lavish. Calvin stuffed himself with slices of pumpkin and mincemeat pies. The extravagantly decorated five-tier chocolate torte looked like a work of art, much too beautiful to eat.

When the Murphys and Froggy left in the yawl with Clyde for the mainland, Archie and Calvin plopped down in comfortable chairs. "You want to stick around and shoot the bull Calvin?"

"Sure."

"Then we need R.J.'s favorite stash." Archie walked into the galley and brought back a bottle of French brandy and two glasses. "Come with me Cal."

"Sure."

Calvin followed him to an elegant parlor with Victorian furnishings. Archie filled their glasses and offered him a fine Cuban cigar from a locked gold plated humidor. After drinking the whole bottle of brandy and talking about boats with Archie, he passed out on the sofa.

In the morning Calvin woke up with the sun shinning through the porthole in one of the plush staterooms of the Episode. He was groggy with a big headache. He shivered. Where were his clothes? He looked around. The bed was lavishly large with red silk sheets and spicy potpourri in ornamental containers around the room. Calvin's clothes were neatly folded on a hassock. He pulled on his pants and red wool sweater, and then stumbled out the door.

Archie waved from the parlor. "Good morning Cal. Have some coffee. I want you to know we're leaving on Saturday."

"I'll hate to see you go, Archie. This has been a once in a lifetime experience for me. Is there anything I can do for you before you leave?"

"No, we've got everything under control. It'll be a long trip, so we've got to get moving before the winter weather gets rough."

LuAnn and Chantel walked in from the deck carrying armloads of new clothes. LuAnn paused to kiss Archie on the cheek. "These are beautiful. Thank you for your generosity."

"I'm glad you could find what you needed in Louisville." The girls waved and walked up the winding staircase in the aft of the boat.

"Are you taking the girls to Miami?"

"Sure, the dolls are a lot of fun. I've juggled a few names so Lou and Charlie will be on the payroll as deckhands for the trip."

Calvin chuckled. "Good luck on your trip south. I've enjoyed every minute the Episode spent here in Port Fulton."

It was after the New Year when Calvin got a postcard from the crew, it said:

Buenos Días Calvin:

We made it safely to Florida before winter set in. The dolls jumped ship in Miami to work for the mob in a fancy speakeasy. R.J. called and decided to base the Episode in Cuba for the winter so we've got a long trip ahead of us. Fortunately Clyde found two new deckhands at the Miami Blue Moon. The dolls, Gloria and Carmen, are lookers and smart too. They even speak Spanish. We're leaving for Havana in the morning.

Feliz Año Nuevo.

The Episode Crew

CHAPTER 23

WINTER COMES TO PORT FULTON

As sub zero temperatures of February approached the Ohio River occasionally froze overnight. In the morning a thin, glass-like sheet of ice about an eighth of an inch thick formed. When the first boat of the day moved through the water, the ice cracked bank to bank. It made a delightful tinkling sound like throwing bricks through a greenhouse window.

The crackling ice was not a hindrance to navigation, but deadly on the hulls of wooden boats like the Hubbard. As the glass-like ice drifted by wooden hulls, each sharp, jagged-edged particle removed a small sliver of wood along the water line. Individually, these slivers didn't amount to much. Collectively, they could conceivably saw the Hubbard in two at the water line.

The captain's cabin was heated by an old-fashioned kerosene heater. As the winter temperature dropped below freezing, keeping the place warm was expensive. The colder the weather became, the more time Calvin spent doing business in the Murphy's kitchen. As nights grew frosty, Calvin slept at the Murphy's too. One night when the thermometer dropped below zero, he carried his bag and feather pillow into the Murphy's house to stay until the weather moderated.

"Thanks for taking me in. The boat's like an ice box. There's no way to stay warm."

"Close the door before the cold wind puts out the stove," groaned Buddy Murphy.

"You're certainly welcome here," said Minnie. "This ain't no fancy steamboat, but there's always room for a friend. Patsy and I sleep here in the bedroom. Us girls need our privacy."

Pat put some blankets on the threadbare couch. "Cal, I'm sleeping on the featherbed in the corner with Baby. He's got kind of a peeing problem some nights and I hate to pawn him off on a stranger."

"Good thinking. Where do you want me?"

"You'll be bunking with Buddy. He sleeps on the pull-out couch. He's kind of a restless sleeper, but I'm sure you'll work something out."

"Thanks Pat." Calvin put down his bag on the cold linoleum floor. Looking down he watched Buddy who already pulled out the bed and snuggled up under the woolen blanket. "You look toasty." Buddy grunted and turned over.

"And Calvin, these below freezing temperatures mean I'll be getting calls about starting cars. Get a good night's sleep. I'll need your help in the morning. Sleep well." Pat blew out the lantern and slid under the covers of the featherbed.

"I guess you and me are sharing the bed, Buddy."

"Yep," he mumbled from underneath the covers.

Calvin kept his socks on and slipped his shoes under the bed. "You don't pee in the bed at night or anything, do you?"

"Nope. Don't pee. I kicks. That's why Papa lets me sleep by myself."

"Okay. Well, we'll work things out," Calvin slipped off his pants and folded them neatly next to the bed. After slipping on another pair of thick socks over his long underwear, Calvin slid under the blankets.

Buddy snored loudly while Calvin stared at the cracks in the ceiling. The kid bucked and pushed. Calvin moved as far over in the double bed as he could, but Buddy scooted over too. Soon Buddy pushed him right over the side and onto the cold linoleum floor. Plop! Surprised, Calvin got up on his hands and knees. He looked up at Buddy who snoozed comfortably curled up on Calvin's side of the bed.

"Move over Buddy. Move over." Calvin gave him a gentle push, but the kid didn't move an inch. He walked around to the other side of the bed and crawled in. "Now I've got three quarters of the bed for myself for the night." Calvin pulled up the covers and finally closed his eyes.

At sunrise a voice whispered in Calvin's ear. "Wake up. We've got a job. I got a call from Byron Van DeMeer. His National won't go and he's got an important business meeting in Louisville this morning."

"What?" Calvin sat up dazed and rubbing his eyes.

"We've got a job to do for Van DeMeer and we've got leave right now."

"Okay. Okay. Let me pull on my pants. You got a heavy coat I can borrow?"

"Check the closet. I'll meet you at the truck."

When Calvin stumbled to the garage, Pat already backed up the truck. "Boy, I'm glad you got a thermos of coffee and two cups. This old pea coat of yours is not stylish. Does it make my butt look too big?"

"Shut up and get in."

"Is Van DeMeer the only call?" Calvin asked as he closed the door.

"No. We'll be working on Millionaire's Row most of the day. Van DeMeer's is my only regular call when the temperature drops below zero, but we'll check the cars in the neighborhood while we're up there. The mansion owners got these big fancy cars, but they never learned the technique of starting the monsters in low temperatures."

The men drank coffee quietly on the drive up the Utica Pike. Pat's truck arrived at the row of Victorian mansions facing the highway.

"Where's the car?"

"Grab the tool box Cal and follow me."

As the winter sun peeked over the holly bushes lining the driveway they walked up the sidewalk to Van DeMeer's estate. Calvin followed Pat to the back of the house and into the huge garage.

A distinguished, gray-haired gentleman looked up at them from behind the hood of the Sterns. "Who are you?"

"I'm Pat Murphy, Mr. Van DeMeer's chief mechanic. Cal Johnson is my assistant."

"Thank goodness you're here. I'm Dunbar Donovan, Mr. Van DeMeer's chauffeur. I can't get the Sterns to turn over and the National won't start either. It must be these bloody cold Indiana winters. Mr. Van DeMeer has a stock holders meeting in Louisville this morning."

"I know. Don't panic. I got orders to work on the National. Mr. Van DeMeer never tries to start the Sterns with temperatures below zero. In cold weather that car won't turn over even with the spark plugs out. Where's the National?"

"It's over there."

Pat and Calvin walked to the rear of the garage where the National stood with its hood propped up.

Calvin put down Pat's tool box and walked around the National. "Boy, what a beauty!"

"Stop prancing around, Cal. We've got work to do. Open all the petcocks on the cylinder head. I'll spin the motor over a couple of times to loosen the oil film."

"Okay boss." Calvin opened the petcocks and then stood back while Pat tried to crank over the engine. "This is not working. What's wrong?"

"It's too cold. I guess we'll have to prime half the cylinders. Get the can of ether and gasoline out of the truck."

"Yes, sir."

Pat primed the cylinders and closed the petcocks. "Try it now Cal."

Calvin cranked it up. This time it fired roughly.

"Hot damn! We're in business."

"Let it buck and snort for awhile until the exhaust manifold warms up. Then I'll prime the other half." After Pat's final maneuver, the National ran like a Swiss watch. "Hey Dunbar, the car's ready to go to Louisville. Grab the tools Cal. The next stop is the Walkers."

"Yes, sir."

Pat drove the truck down the street to the gleaming white mansion with art deco columns. The huge garage was behind the house. Pat opened the unlocked garage door. Calvin followed behind him.

Calvin stopped behind Pat as soon as they got in the door. "Is that another Pierce Arrow?"

"Yes. That's Walker's new toy. It's a challenge to start in cold weather. The engine has no petcocks."

"What? No petcocks? How do you start it?"

"It's tricky, but two people working together can it done. I'm going to work on the starter and controls at the wheel. Your job is to give the starter a little help by manning the crank shaft out front."

Port Fulton

"Okey-dokey Boss."

As Pat cranked Calvin ducked. The Pierce Arrow's custom-made radiator ornament was a gold-plated Indian girl with a bow and arrow. Every time Calvin came up with the crank, the sharp point of the arrow on ornament rotated just passed his nose.

"Keep cranking Cal, she's ready to turn over!"

"I could put my eye out on this damn thing!"

"Keep cranking."

VOOM! Voom! Voom! Pat put on the brake and jumped out of the car.

Out of nowhere a neatly dressed Negro with a chauffeur's cap appeared. He opened the door of the Pierce Arrow and slid into the driver's seat. A gray-haired man in a trench coat carrying a valise followed him and hopped into the back seat.

VOOM! Voom! The Pierce zoomed out of the garage. The old man waved to them.

"Have a good trip Mr. Walker," called Pat as the car accelerated onto the street, and up the hill.

"We make a good team, Pat."

"Of course we do."

"I'm glad you got that Pierce going before I got impaled on the hood ornament."

"Me too. I'd hate to lose such a good partner this early in the day. Cal, let's eat the ham sandwiches in my lunchbox before we go to the Howard place. Starting his Cunningham will be our last job."

"That sounds fine to me."

In the truck Calvin unlatched the lunchbox. He handed one of the sandwiches wrapped in wax paper to Pat as they continued toward the Howard mansion at the end of the circle. The house was as big as an elegant southern plantation house on the cover of Look Magazine.

"Hot damn! A five-car garage! Does he really have enough cars to fill it?"

"Howard collects cars. There's another garage behind the first. Let's go." Pat jumped out of the truck, grabbed a blow torch, and then headed for the open garage door. "Come on, Cal. I'll need you as a lookout."

"What do you mean? We're not doing anything illegal, are we?"

"No, we're not doing anything illegal. It's just that Howard is persnickety. He doesn't want a blow torch around his precious Cunningham. He doesn't realize this car would be dead in its tracks on cold days without my secret weapon."

"That blow torch is a secret weapon?"

"You bet. The Cunningham doesn't have petcocks. I'll have to warm the intake manifold to start it. Your job is to make sure no one comes close until I fire her up."

"You can depend on me, partner."

Calvin stood out in front while Pat worked on the car.

"I feel like a bank robber lookout. Are you about done?" Finally the car chortled and sputtered. VOOM! VOOM! VOOM! Calvin walked over to Pat. "What a sound!"

"My secret weapon starts this car every time. Get in the truck, Cal. We're going to tell Howard his prize is ready to go."

Pat and Calvin jumped in the truck and headed to the front of the house. Pat walked over to a wiry fellow with thick eyeglasses wearing a beaver hat. He looked cold with his hands in the pockets of his raccoon coat. The old man smiled and handed Pat a roll of bills. Pat handed Calvin ten dollars. "We're heading home."

The snow started to fall on the windshield as they reached the Utica Pike.

"Pat, do you start these fancy cars regularly?"

"Every winter more than once. Actually most of the chauffeurs could start the cars just as well as I do. I could teach them."

"Why don't you then?"

"It wouldn't smart business. It won't put cornbread on my table. My motto is: what you don't know, you'll pay for."

"What you don't know, you'll pay for sounds like it could be a motto for the steamboat business too."

"Actually it works for all businesses. I made up that saying years ago when I worked on my cousin's car. Jack limped his Maxwell into my garage one cold Sunday in October. I tried one thing and then another to get the car going. I fiddled around with it over an hour with Jack sitting in the driver's seat giving me his opinions. Finally I switched two spark plug wires. It ran perfectly. Jack was happy. He gave me a family hug, paid me a fin and took off for church."

"I don't get it. You're a great mechanic. Why didn't you spot those wires right away?"

Pat gave Calvin his broad Irish grin. "If I'd have changed those wires without fiddling around awhile, cousin Jack would have gone away resentful. He might have thought he was stupid for not having spotted the problem himself. This way we got some family time and he gets a cheap price. The next week Jack tells everyone I'm a genius because I fixed his car and he wasn't even late for mass."

Pat and Calvin laughed all the way to Port Fulton as the snow piled up on the Utica Pike.

CHAPTER 24

HARD TIMES AHEAD

The winter of 1928 was long and hard for the people of Port Fulton. When Calvin walked the decks of the Hubbard in the still of the morning air, a peculiar tinkling sound caught his attention as a ferry broke through the ice field on the Ohio River. It sounded like muffled sleigh bells, only more hollow and crystalline.

Calvin tried writing a letter to Christina, but a cold breeze whistled through the chinks in hull freezing the ink in his fountain pen. Calvin thought it must be a sign, or like Johnny said bad Karma. He folded the stationary into a fine paper airplane. He took it to the rail and let the wind catch it. It flew gracefully down the river and out of his life.

Work tapered off at the garage, so Pat took a full time job at the Depot to make ends meet. Calvin didn't think he could abandon the Hubbard or he would have signed on at the docks too. Pat knew Calvin was strapped for money so he invited him to join the Murphy clan for meals. Minnie always made enough for one more. Calvin brought over coffee, cornmeal, flour, and other leftover staples from the steamboat.

"Calvin, I want to thank you again for the cornmeal."

"It's just gathering weevils in the Hubbard's pantry Minnie. My skills in the kitchen are terrible. Now I wish I would have I paid more attention to my mother's cooking."

"Sounds like you got a hankering for something from your mother's kitchen. What is it Calvin?"

"Cornbread. I remember how good my mother's melt-in-your-mouth cornbread tasted. It was my favorite."

"How abouts I make you some cornbread like your mother done?"

"Really? I can hardly wait, Minnie. Thank you."

"Scoot on over and stay warm while I fixes some of Minnie's melt-in-your-mouth cornbread."

Calvin moved his chair next to the iron stove to keep warm. Sipping a cup of hot coffee he watched as Minnie prepared her cornbread. First she combined the cornmeal with some eggs and milk. Next she took out her iron fry pan and covered the bottom with a liquid from a can on the sink. When the liquid got hot on the stove she poured in the cornbread mixture. It sizzled and smelled like burned bacon.

"Minnie, I think my mother baked cornbread."

"I hear some people likes to bake their cornbread. But Minnie's melt-in-your-mouth cornbread is more flavorful fried up in bacon grease."

"Is that what's in the coffee can on the sink?"

"It's my secret ingredient Calvin."

Calvin smiled sheepishly and hoped Minnie's cornbread tasted better than it smelled. He peered into the corner. "What's in this milk crock? It's got a funny gray color. Do you eat it?"

"We sure do. I call it rabbit scrapple. When I fries it up, it's delish."

"Do you serve it for supper?"

"Of course Calvin."

A cold draft whistled through the kitchen as the front door opened. Pat took off his coat and hat. "Hello, everybody. I'm home."

"Pat, how many rabbits did you get this year?"

"None for me, but Buddy shot two hares in the woods last week."

"Then I guess we ain't had much rabbit scrabble this year."

"This is the first batch. Minnie's rabbit scrapple lasts us a fortnight, but it has to age like mountain dew before she cooks it up."

"Pat, you can't compare my rabbit scrabble to aging brew!"

"Sure I can."

"What's in rabbit scrabble?"

"Well, first I cuts up two rabbits, after they is skinned of course. Then I puts the parts in a big pot and boils them until the bones work out. The next step is kneading the meat with cornmeal. Then I adds salt, pepper, lemon, and vinegar and puts it into a milk crock to solidify for a couple of weeks. For meals, I slices it, rolls it in flour, and fries it in lard. How does that sound, Calvin?"

"I'm not sure. Yummy I think."

"Good, because we'll be having it soon with greens I've canned up."

"I remember the taste of those nineteen kinds of greens you cooked up last summer."

"My greens are even tastier when they're canned up and aged some."

"I can't wait. Rabbit scrabble and nineteen kinds of greens canned up and aged. It's time for me to check on the

Hubbard." Calvin slipped on his coat and headed for the door to get some air. "I'll be back in awhile."

"Don't be too long Calvin, or else you'll miss my delicious melt-in-your-mouth cornbread."

It wasn't until the next day that Calvin came back over to warm up in the Murphy's kitchen. Pat sat silently stirring his coffee at the kitchen table. His face looked tired.

"How come you're not at work?"

"I took the day off because I didn't get much sleep. Minnie got sick. She had severe abdominal pain."

"It might have been that cornbread. My stomach got queasy just watching her fry it up."

"No Cal, this is serious. About midnight I drove her over to Dr. Renski office. Doc looked her over and thought her problem was acute."

"What's acute mean?"

"It means he wanted me to take her to the hospital in Louisville. So I packed up some of her clothes and put Buddy in charge."

"Why didn't you come and get me?"

"There wasn't time. She was in terrible pain. When we checked in at the hospital, the doctor said she had appendicitis. He recommended an operation right away. She came through it, but she'll be in the hospital for ten days."

"Don't worry, Pat. She's in good hands."

"I know the hospital people are good, but I'm overwhelmed. This operation is going to wipe out our savings. How can I do the housekeeping, watch the kids and work at the Depot? Cal, I need some help."

"I don't have a surplus of cash right now, but can I help you some other way?"

"Yes. Could you take over housekeeping and watching the kids?"

"I don't know," Calvin sputtered. "I'm not really good at housekeeping and I have no experience taking care of children."

"Look Cal, I'm between a rock and a hard place. I can't afford to take off from work anymore."

"How long would the job be?"

"The doctors say she'll be as good as new in ten days. The kids will help you with the house. How about it?"

"Sure, why not."

Doing Minnie's job was a difficult ten-day stint for a guy who knows little about housework and nothing about children. Calvin's cooking skills consisted of opening cans, so cooking was a problem too.

One night Calvin tried frying up some rabbit scrabble according to Minnie's recipe. "How about trying some rabbit stuff?"

"It smells bad," said Patsy. "I like mom's cooking better than yours." Buddy and Baby turned up their noses and refused to try it.

Calvin just about gave up cooking when he found a continued renewable source of protein that even he couldn't mess up. In the back of the garage Minnie kept three ducks in cages. They produced eggs regularly. Calvin scrambled them. He fried them. He boiled them. He poached them. It was easy, even for a guy who couldn't cook.

"Are we having duck eggs again?" asked Patsy. "We had them four times this week. I'm sick of them."

Calvin ignored the complaint and put the plates on the table in front of the three children. "I like duck eggs. They're easy to fix and good for you."

"They taste like fish," said Baby. "I just want hominy."

"Me, too," said Patsy. "And put lots of raisins in it."

"When we getting some meat?" asked Buddy.

"Meat's expensive, but your father's bringing us a treat from the Depot today. Plank steak's on sale."

Buddy scrunched up his face. "Plank steak is as tough as a boot heel when mother fries it up. I hope you got a better recipe."

"My cooking is getting better," Calvin snickered as he adjusting his flowery pink apron. "Meat, even plank steak, is good protein. Did you ever eat jerky? It's good for your teeth."

Pinch-hitting for Minnie was more difficult than the repetitious duties on the Hubbard. Even though cooking was tough, the hardest thing was getting the children to help around the house. Laying down rules to children wasn't something Calvin did effectively.

"Kids, I don't mind watching you and cooking for you, but we've got to work out dishwashing."

Patsy stood with her hands on her hips. "Dishwashing is getting done. You don't see no dirty dishes, do you?"

"There aren't any dirty dishes because I'm doing them. I've been cleaning and cooking and working my fingers to the bone. I'm tired of it! Starting tonight, if you kids don't wash your dishes, I won't be cooking your next meal. Do you understand?"

"Yes, sir," the kids said in unison as they shook their heads.

With grins on their faces, Calvin thought they might not be taking him seriously. Sure enough, after supper all three of them giggled and disappeared, leaving Calvin the job of washing the dishes again.

For supper the next day Calvin cooked a mess of duck eggs for himself. He sat down to eat them at the table. When the kids came in from school they took off their coats and looked around the kitchen for their dinner plates.

Patsy stood in front of him." Where's our food Calvin?"

"You don't get any."

"What do you mean? I'm hungry," wined Baby.

"None of you helped wash the dishes last night after supper like you promised, so you won't be enjoying any of my tasty duck eggs. There's some cold hominy in the icebox to tide you over. Wash up your dishes when you're done eating." Calvin put his plate in the sink. "I'm going in the living room to listen to the radio."

The children grumbled, but they ate the cold hominy at the table. Calvin peeked into the kitchen later. Patsy was washing the dishes in the sink while Baby dried them and Buddy put them away.

The ten day job at the Murphys seemed like ten months. Finally Pat brought Minnie home from the hospital on Saturday afternoon. Everyone fawned over her, but no one was happier than Calvin to see her back. Walking back to the Hubbard that evening, Calvin felt a heavy weight lifted from his shoulders.

It was the middle of March and the thaw began. Spring was on the horizon so living full-time on the Hubbard was getting easier. Pat's five dollar salary for Calvin's stint at housekeeping started his life back to normal.

After Calvin's housekeeping escapade he splurged and ate out a few times. He loved not having to do the dishes. When the ferry began its operation again Calvin discovered a chain of little stands in Louisville called Oyster Bars. They reminded him of the St. Louis White Castle stands. For a nickel Calvin bought a huge oyster, batter dipped and fried and then served on a napkin. After rabbit scrapple, nineteen kinds of canned greens, and fried cornbread, he stuffed himself on these delicious delicacies until his money ran out.

One breezy afternoon, Mud King and Calvin sat on the top deck contemplating spring. The coal supply ran out, but luckily the temperatures were moderating. A few cakes of ice floated by, but most of the river was ice free.

"Hot damn! The Ohio's breaking up. Doesn't it look like a green cocktail with ice floating in it?"

"You're funny Captain. I gots a question for you. What's more important to you, drinkin' or bathin'?"

"What do you mean?"

"I think bathin' is more important. I really be glad when spring comes because I needs a bath."

"Are you serious?"

"Yes, sir, Captain. There's no runnin' water at the home."

"I forget that a lot of people don't enjoy the pleasure of warm water."

"Free water from street hydrants don't work good for baths in the winter. It'll be awhile until the river warms up."

"Pat lets me wash in the tub at his house once a week. I guess I'm lucky."

"You sure is lucky. I'm lookin' forward to takin' a bath in the river."

"The Rite of Spring in Port Fulton."

"It's a wonderful time. Ain't it Captain?"

CHAPTER 25

HUBBARD R.I.P.

The rains upriver never let up. High water inundated Port Fulton. Acres of wood streaming down the Ohio caught against the hull of the Hubbard. Calvin worried as the driftwood accumulated against the bow. His anxiety increased when he noticed a very large cottonwood tree jammed between the paddles. Calvin talked to the local boys to help. They walked the driftwood raft in search of firewood, preferably oak or chestnut. Calvin tried to get them to haul off the big cottonwood, but they weren't interested. Cottonwood burned too hot and too quickly. As days went on, he wondered if his steamboat days were ending. Would the cables on the bow of the Hubbard hold under the tremendous load? It was time to think about personal safety as flooding on the Ohio River became more desperate.

One rainy morning Calvin rowed to the foot of Green Hill. He tied up the rowboat to a shrub half-way up the hill, and then walked up to Spring Street to Schimpff's Confectionary.

"Hello Gustav. Can I use your pay telephone for an important call? Calvin handed him his last two dollars from his sock.

"Sure thing, Calvin. I just made some fresh caramel Modjeskas. Try one. No charge. They might perk you up."

"Thanks." Calvin savored the tasty candy then he sat down to call Billy Killebrew. Lots of things crossed his mind as the telephone rang and rang and rang. He was just about to hang up when he heard the click.

"Good morning, Mr. Killebrew's office."

"Boy am I glad to hear your voice, Myrtle. This is Calvin Johnson from the John W. Hubbard steamboat in Port Fulton, Indiana. Remember me?"

"No."

"Remember, Billy Killebrew is working on financing to restore the Hubbard as an excursion boat on the Missouri River. Can I talk to him? I need advice."

"First of all, Mr. Johnson, my name is Miss Goodwall to you. Secondly, Billy is in Chicago on business. He won't be back for a week."

"I need advice right now. Can you give me some advice concerning the boat?"

"No."

"But I need advice right now. We're experiencing high water on the Ohio River. There could be big problems with the steamboat. I'm worried about safety issues. What should I do if the boat breaks loose?"

"Look Mr. Johnson, I can't tell you what to do. You'll have to call Billy back in a week or so. He makes the decisions around here."

"I need to talk to him right now."

"The best I can do is take your number. He'll call you when he gets in."

"This is a pay telephone in a confectionary. I can't be here all the time. Please Miss Goodwall, there are issues with the steamboat that need to be discussed today."

"Mr. Johnson, I'm sorry, but I've already told you I can't help you."

"Okay Miss Goodwall. I'll call back. In the mean time, I'll do what I can do to secure the boat." The phone line buzzed, clicked, and went dead.

Calvin worried about his situation as he rowed back to the Hubbard. All night long he listened to the cables creaking with the load. As he fixed his morning coffee Calvin made up his mind on a plan to insure his safety.

By noon Calvin walked down to the orphanage to enlist Mud King for a full-time job helping him secure the Hubbard. Calvin made arrangements with the caretakers for Mud to live with him for an unspecified time period. Calvin underscored the dire consequences. Immediately Mud packed his bag with his clothes and his books and they headed down to the steamboat.

"I'm relieved you'll be able to help me out, Mud. The high water's put a strain on the Hubbard's cables."

"What can I do Captain?"

"I don't know how much longer the cables will hold, so we need to be vigilant. While I sleep, I want you to be my second set of eyes."

"Yes sir, Captain."

At sunset Calvin and Mud climbed over the tree limbs to check the cables. "Mud, I'm worried. There's a lot of debris pushing against the boat."

"I knows Captain. The cables are creakin'. This big cottonwood is causin' a lot of strain."

"I know. They could snap at any time. We're going to take turns sleeping tonight. I'm the boss and I'm really tired, so I'm sleeping first."

"That'll be fine with me. What should I do while you sleeps?"

"I want you to watch to see how the boat reacts to the strain on the cables. Wake me up if you notice anything unusual."

"Do you cares if I read?"

"No, I don't care. Just stay alert. By the way, when did you learn to read Mud?"

"I learns at the orphanage. I reads good."

"What kind of books do you read?"

Out of his sack Mud pulled out four books. "I like history about America and scary stories like Mr. Ed Poe writes."

Calvin scanned the dog-eared books Mud placed carefully on the deck. "You've got some great horror stories by Edgar Allen Poe here."

"I reads them over and over. They're all great. The Pit and the Pendulum, Murders in the Rue Morgue, and The Fall of the House of Usher are my favorites."

"I could never read books like that at night. They'd scare the devil out of me."

"I loves horror stories. They don't scare me. They keeps me awake."

"Awake is what we need Mud. You read your books, stay awake and pay attention to what's happening to the boat. I'll get some shut-eye."

"I'll keeps one eye on my book and the other eye on the cables."

"Good plan."

"What happens if we breaks loose?"

"You don't really want to know Mud. It'll be a dangerous situation with this fast current. Downstream there's a bridge and an open dam. If we get loose and by some miracle we get under the bridge, the dam will do us in for sure."

"You gives me a very important job, Captain. What happens to us if we breaks loose?"

"We've got to be ready to leave quickly. I've put my camera, my gun and most of my valuables in Baby Wildcat. It's all gassed up and tied securely to the side. If things get bad, we got ourselves a way to escape."

"I'm curious Captain. How do we knows it's time to escape?"

"I'll show you, Mud. Come with me." They walked over to the forward window of the captain's cabin. "Look out here, Mud. We're high enough up and the stern's swung out in front enough that we can see the street lights in Port Fulton. They are all lined up in a neat row."

"Yes, sir."

"Keep an eye on those street lights, Mud. When they no longer line up, it means the boat's loose. Then it's time for both of us to climb over the side and make a quick getaway in Baby Wildcat."

"I don't likes leaving the boat."

"I don't either. But if our lives are on the line, we'll have to abandon ship."

"I understands. Don't worry, Captain. If those lights don't line up, I'll wakes you right away."

That night was peaceful. Mud read while Calvin slept soundly. Lady Luck smiled down on them day after day. Over the next week a wind shift moved about two acres of driftwood off the bow of the Hubbard. The people downstream had to deal with the logs, but Calvin and Mud were greatly relieved.

Water was still running high, but with the load off the cables, Calvin felt safer. He took his personal belongings out of Baby Wildcat and put them back aboard the Hubbard. The water continued to drop so two weeks to the day Mud returned to the orphanage.

Later Calvin motored over to Froggy's boat ramp. Froggy helped him back down his trailer and load up the boat. They parked it on dry land in Pat's front yard. By the end of the week life on the Hubbard got back to normal.

It was cool and windy Saturday on the top deck when Mud came back to visit. "Good morning Captain."

"Good to see you Mud. I got a dollar for your help during the high water."

"Thanks Captain. I was wonderin'. Could I use your rope ladder? It's still a little cold, but I thinks today is a good day for a bath."

"My rope ladder is on the deck, but these winds are fierce, Mud. Wait until late this afternoon. They usual die down about sunset."

"No matter, I can wash in the mornin' or afternoon. I gots some peanuts for eatin' while we wait," added Mud taking a big sack out of his jacket. "You wants some?"

"Great! We'll eat until it warms up and the winds die down."

Mud opened the sack of peanuts on the pews when the wind shifted and blew the bag over the rail. A big gust hit the boat from the shore. Next to the bank another old cottonwood tree with its root system weaken by the rains and high water, creaked and then crashed across the front cable of the Hubbard. The falling tree snapped the bow cable like a matchstick. The boat twisted and broke the anchor line. In a matter of seconds the Hubbard floated free. Calvin rushed to the rail just as the boat caught the current.

"Mud, I'm going to try to steer us clear of these logs. There's another anchor in the engine room. See if you can tie it off and throw it out. Dragging it might slow us down."

"Yes, sir. I'll finds it."

Calvin fought the wheel. For awhile the Hubbard hovered in the middle of the river caught up in a backwater, but soon the current grabbed the boat and sucked it downstream. The winds shifted again, and the steamer lurched toward the shore. Calvin struggled to keep the boat in the river. Finally the gusty March winds caught the boat again and pushed it toward the lowlands along the bank. Calvin sighed as the Hubbard came to rest in the sticky mud along the bank.

"Mud, you can forget the anchor," shouted Calvin.

"Captain, I needs your help down here. There's water comin' in."

"The hull always leaks. Let's secure the boat first."

Mud stuttered and shouted. "It's really comin' in, Captain. Water's everywhere. And there's a big tree sittin' right next to me!"

"Oh, Oh! If we got a tree in the bilges, we got problems." Calvin rushed down to the engine room.

Unbeknownst to Calvin, a huge, three-pronged stump drifted underneath the Hubbard in the downstream struggle. It got tangled in the paddles and under the hull. When the winds pushed the boat into the reeds and cattails, the Hubbard settled on top of the stump.

"I'm over here Captain," called Mud, frantically treaded water. He waved with one hand and hung onto the prong of the huge stump with the other. "I usually swims good, but I'm havin' trouble. This water is cold."

Calvin climbed on top of the engine and pulled him up. "Are you alright Mud?"

"My legs are numb, but I'm okay."

"I got a bucket of concrete over here. Let's try to build a cofferdam around the stump."

"Captain that concrete ain't goin' to do us no good. I tried prayin', but prayin' ain't helpin' neither."

"A good prayer couldn't hurt."

"Prayin' won't fix the split in the bottom."

Suddenly the creaking noise stopped and the rushing water made a sucking sound as all three prongs of the stump poked up through the hull. Calvin and Mud hung onto the engine as the boat shifted. River mud squirted up like a fountain next to them. "Now we're on the bottom. Let's get out of here."

"One thing's lucky. We're in walking distance of town Captain."

"Let's swim over to the ladder and get out of the water."

As they headed to the top deck Mud added. "I thinks your days being a boat captain is over. What you gonna do tomorrow?"

"Tomorrow, Mud? I guess I'll telephone Billy Killebrew to tell him what happened. Thanks for all your help. I'll talk to you later."

"See you Captain," called Mud as he sloshed back to the bank soaked to the bone. Calvin watched him go and changed to his rubber boots. It was a long walk to the pay telephone at Schrimpff's. The water was shallow, but the sticky mud slowed Calvin down. Finally he hobbled through the door into the confectionary.

Gus Schrimpff looked up as he organized some fresh candies in the case. "You looks wet and peeked Calvin. Did you fall in the river?"

Calvin sighed. "Not exactly. The Hubbard sunk. I need a new job."

"That's too bad Calvin. Wanna try some red hots? I got a fresh batch right here."

"No thanks, Gus. I need to clear my head and use your pay telephone. I've got an important call to make, but I don't have any money. Can I owe you? I'm calling St. Louis. It might be a long call."

"It's okay. Use my chair if you're making a long call. You might as well be comfortable."

"I really do appreciate this. Thanks Gus." Calvin wrote the number from memory on a tablet on the counter. He wasn't sure how to explain this fiasco to Billy. He thought hard about the right words. On the third ring Billy's voice answered.

"Killebrew here."

"Hello Mr. Killebrew. This is Calvin Johnson."

"Nice day Johnson. What's up?"

"I've got some bad news about the Hubbard."

"Well, I've got a ton of bad news for you too, Calvin."

Calvin sat back in the chair and took a shallow breath. "Bad news? Okay, tell me your bad news first."

"It's simple. Getting a loan for restoring the Hubbard fizzled out. Double R Markle ran into financial problems with his own boats so he doesn't have any money for new ventures. To make matters worse, we don't have a master pilot. Captain Mike's dead."

"Captain Mike's dead? What happened?"

"Mike drowned. According to his friend, Mike fell off his boat netting a ten pound river cat and was swept downriver with the current. They still haven't found his body. What's your news, Calvin?"

"Well, I guess I've got good news as well as bad news. Which one do you want to hear first?"

"Give me the good news."

"The good news isn't that good. Today a high wind caused a tree to snap the Hubbard's cables. She floated free and caught the current. The good news is that she settled in the lowlands a few hundred yards downstream."

"Okay. So what's the bad news?"

"The bad news is a three-pronged stump that had been stuck underneath the hull and in the paddles poked a hole through the bottom. The Hubbard sunk."

"It's sad, but it doesn't matter. We're out of business Calvin. The Killebrew Navigation Company is kaput."

"Kaput?"

"The company is finished. We're bankrupt."

"What should I do now?"

"I guess you can scavenge what you can from the boat. Sell the stuff and keep the money and we're even. So long Calvin. Good luck in your next venture." The line clicked and went dead.

Calvin sighed. "Scavenging? What next venture?" He hung up the telephone dazed. "Hey Gus, I want to stuff my face with a big mess of chocolate candy from your fancy cabinet. Put it on my bill."

Gus slid out a tray of dipped chocolates from the glass case. "Take what you want Calvin. It's on the house."

"Do you have a whiskey chaser to go with them?"

CHAPTER 27

THE BEGINNING OF THE END

Calvin spent the next couple of weeks scavenging useful things he could sell. Calvin needed to sell enough stuff to get money to get back to St. Louis. When he called Granite City collect his father said his old room was available on a temporary basis.

Pulling items out of the muddy water was a cold and messy job. Pat let Calvin borrow his rubber waders so he could slosh around for hours without his legs cramping in the frigid Ohio River water. Mud was strong and didn't mind carrying things to town. With the help of a wagon Mud hauled the Hubbard's clean sheets, linen, and the galley paraphernalia to Pat's house.

One afternoon Pat and Buddy dragged off the last three dry mattresses from the passenger's quarters. "Minnie won't believe our good fortune. Now we'll all have our own beds. Thanks Calvin."

Mud enlisted kids from the orphanage to take the books as well as old quilts and bedding. The banged up steamer trunk was so heavy that the boys hauled it to a horse drawn wagon to tow it home.

Calvin organized his things in the captain's cabin when Little Hooter showed up at the door.

"I'll miss you when you goes Captin'."

"Hello Hooter. I'll miss you too."

"Captin', do you cares if I checks around for stogies?"

"Go ahead, but pick up the dry ones only. Smoking butts sitting in river water could make you sick."

"Okay Captin'."

"Stay dry," Calvin mumbled as he continued to organize his clothes, and the pictures of the people and boats of Port Fulton in his travel sack. He pulled out Christina's letters from a box under his bunk. They smelled nice. He took a long whiff of the flowery envelopes, and then stuffed them in the trash.

Hooter stopped at the desk to peruse Calvin's magazines. "I likes these books of neked ladies. Are you takin' them with you?"

"I won't need them. Go ahead. Take them."

"These magazines got better pitchers than my school books. Thanks." Hoot gave Calvin a quick hug and stepped back.

Calvin patted Little Hooter fondly on his head. "Good luck. Don't forget to keep going to school Hoot."

"I will. Seeya, Captain," called Hoot as he scrambled down the gangplank with his pockets full of butts and his arms filled with magazines.

On Monday Calvin sold the ship's whistle to American Car and Foundry Company in Jeffersonville. The pilot's wheel became the property of the LeRose Theater on Spring Street. Michael Switow, owner of the movie palace, converted the elaborately carved wheel into a fascinating chandelier. The Howard Shipyard bought the bell and the engines for scrap metal.

It was the end of the week when Mud and Calvin climbed through the debris on the top deck for a final sweep.

"Mud, I'm going to check the pilot house. Give me a few of minutes."

"Sure, Captain. I'll be next door pullin' up the carpet. I thinks it will be nice on the icy floors in the bunk room."

"You might need my tool box. Take it." Calvin shoved the box next to Mud, and then opened the door to the pilot house. He just started to evaluate the papers in the desk drawers when a blood curdling scream made his hair stand on end. Calvin dashed next door to the purser's office. Mud was lying under the desk. He looked up at Calvin without saying a word. His eyes were wide as saucers. "Are you okay Mud?"

"Captain, you got to see this." Mud got up on his knees and rolled up the carpet. "Look at these!" He opened the box to reveal hundreds of shiny gold coins.

Calvin squatted down next to Mud. "Gold coins. Gold Double Eagles! Hot damn!"

Mud kept shaking his head as he pried the foot-rest box off the floor with the crowbar. "I can't believe it."

"I thought we checked every nook and cranny on the boat. The gold was in the foot-rest all the time. Holy Cow!"

"I ain't ever seen this much gold."

Calvin grabbed two handfuls of the coins from the box and let them run through his fingers. "All these lovely Double Eagles. What made you look here Mud?"

"I just kind of stumbled on to it Captain. When I rolls up the carpet for the home, I sees this box underneath. It says Property of the U.S. Army on it. I thinks maybe its guns or something we can sell, so I pries open the box. There it was. All these gold coins in neat stacks."

"Hot damn!" Calvin scooped up handfuls of coins and stuffed them into his pockets. "Hot damn! We're rich, Mud!"

"We can't take this, Captain. It don't belong to us."

"You can't be serious."

"It belongs to the U.S. Army. It says so on the box."

"I don't understand you. Being rich is a dream of a lifetime."

"Captain, we can't keep the gold. It's not ours. We needs to take it to the police so they can give it back to the U.S. Army."

Calvin sighed. "Are you sure that's what you want to do? I vote for keeping it."

"Giving it back is the right thing to do Captain."

Reluctantly Calvin put the coins back in the box. "You're right, Mud. I've been poor for so long that the thought of being rich overwhelmed me. Sure, we'll turn in the gold coins. I hope there's a reward."

"There's some dry flour sacks in the galley. We can put the coins in the sacks and tie them up. It'll make them easier to carry."

"Good idea Mud. You take care of the coins. I'll go to the Murphys and borrow Oscar's Radio Flyer so we'll roll them to Johnny's office."

Sloshing to land in his rubber boots was slow. Calvin trudged along the bank and up Green Hill where he spied the red wagon next to the house. No one was around. He grabbed the handle and took off running. Calvin ran frantically with the wagon bumping along behind him to the bank near the Hubbard. "I'm back Mud. Throw me the bags."

"Okay Captain." Carefully Mud pitched Calvin sack after sack from the top deck. Calvin caught them, and then loaded each one into Oscar's wagon. Mud leaped over the railing after the last one and landed on his bare feet next to

Calvin. "Come on Captain." Mud grabbed the handle and pulled the loaded wagon at a brisk pace toward town.

"Wait for me!" Calvin slipped and slid behind Mud and the wagon. "I've got to catch my breath."

"I'll slow down."

Mud trotted at a slower speed along the bank and over the hill, and then headed for Main Street. Calvin huffed and puffed behind him. In front of the police station they stopped to rest. Calvin coughed and bent over in exhaustion.

"Are you okay Captain?"

"I'm a little winded, but I'm fine."

"You smokes too much. It ain't good for your breathin'."

Calvin looked annoyed. "My health's just fine. What are we going to tell Johnny?"

"Just tell him the truth, or I guess, you can make up a story. You're always good at tellin' stories."

"Okay. Let's go." Calvin opened the door as Mud pulled the wagon into the middle of the room. The shade near the rear of the office was pulled down. The room seemed empty. As they looked around a buzzing, chortling noise startled them from the dark corner. It was Johnny. He snored loudly in his chair with his freshly oiled boots propped up on the desk. A gust of wind slammed the door.

BANG!

The buzzing, chortling noise abruptly stopped.

Johnny drew his gun and aimed it right for Calvin's heart. "What the hell is going on Johnson?"

"Don't shoot!" shouted Mud, stepping out from behind Calvin.

Calvin waved sheepishly. "We need to talk. Put your gun away."

"You scared the daylights out of me boys." Johnny put his gun back in his shoulder holster and stood up. "Mud, why in the hell did you bring that wagon and crap into my office? Take it outside."

"Johnny, we found something important and we need to ask your advice."

"It's not a cut up corpse in those bags, is it?"

"No, it's nothing like that."

"It's gold," exclaimed Mud enthusiastically as he opened one of the bags in the wagon. He handed Johnny a handful of shiny coins. "We found them on the boat."

"Well, I'll be. The rumors were right. That old boat did have some treasure."

"The box said the gold belongs to the U.S. Army," added Mud. "I'm worried."

Calvin sat down in the chair. "It's probably the gold the Mexicans stole from the government payroll. What should we do with it?"

Johnny sat down in a chair across from Calvin. He rubbed his whiskery chin and studied the bags of coins. "What do you want to do with it, Cal?"

"Well, I wanted to keep it, but Mud thinks we ought to be honest and turn it in. The box we found it in had the U.S. Army marks on it. Do you know if there's a reward posted?"

Johnny pulled down all the shades in the room and closed the door. He sat down and looked Calvin straight in the eye. "Who knows about this gold?"

"Mud and me, and now you."

"You know boys, I ain't seen no official paperwork saying the Army lost any gold that I know of."

"Then you think we could keep the coins?"

"I don't see why not, Cal. Those Double Eagles are just as spendable today as they were ten years ago."

Mud bit his lip nervously. "If we keeps this gold, won't the U.S. Army put us in jail?"

"No, I think we're safe. It's been more than ten years. Records were lost, probably. You know what I think we ought to do?"

"Your opinion is why we're here, chief."

"Why don't we divide the gold, say three ways."

"What?" Mud and Calvin said together.

"Cal, you're going back to St. Louis. Take your share and spend it a little at a time. Mud, put your share in the bank and use it for your education. As for my share, well, I'll be putting my Double Eagles in a safe deposit box at the Louisville Bank for retirement. I always wanted a ranch in Montana."

Suddenly the door popped open. Jean Claude charged in. He sniffed the contents of the wagon and lifted his leg. Anne Marie walked in behind the dog. "Sit, Jean Claude." She put down her valise on the floor in front of Calvin. "Did I hear you are going back to St. Louis?"

"Probably Anne Marie. Do you need a ride?"

Her eyes stopped at the four flour sacks filled with gold coins in the Radio Flyer. "Is there something you want to tell me, mon chère? Are we rich?"

"How about a four way split Johnny? Mud and I don't mind sharing."

Johnny gave Calvin a mean look. "Who is she?"

"Chief, this is Anne Marie. She's a fine artist and actress with marginal navigational skills. Her dog is Jean Claude. I wouldn't fool with either one of them. They're dangerous."

Jean Claude growled low and snarled.

"I guess one bag will be plenty for my retirement."

Anne Marie smiled and slipped one of the sacks into her valise. "Jean Claude and I will ride back to St. Louis with you whenever you're ready to go."

"Where's your easel and paints?"

"I left them next to you car and boat trailer."

Baby Wildcat III and Ford

CHAPTER 28

EPILOGUE

To the people of Port Fulton only the stacks and the pilot house were visible as the John W. Hubbard lay peacefully on the river bottom north of the shipyard.

In the thirties a plan for the improvement of the Ohio River was modified. It eliminated Dam 40 which was to have been built fifty two miles upstream from Louisville. The existing Dam 41 at the Falls was to be raised to provide a nine-foot channel all the way to the Markland Dam sixty-four miles upriver. This new dam would permanently inundate the lower end of the ways at the Howard Shipyards. After the tough economic years after the 1929 stock market crash, ship building changed. Jim Howard thought this was a good time to make changes himself. The Howard Shipyards bought four more city blocks northward from the yard for expansion.

The economy was looking up. The states repealed prohibition. Beer returned in April, 1933 to Indiana.

The Howards moved to a more spacious residence in Louisville, and the old brick mansion in Port Fulton lay empty for years. The city fathers finally converted the building to an Ohio River museum.

Earl King completed his education at the Taylor High School in Jeffersonville, and then continued at Lincoln University in Jefferson City, Missouri where he earned a degree in business. With ties in Indiana, he returned to invest in real estate in Jeffersonville. Mud cashed in the Double Eagles from a safe deposit box at the Clark County State Bank. As an industrious businessman he bought many of the river front buildings, including the orphanage for expansion. He helped co-sponsor the North Pole Eskimos Baseball Team with Doc Kehoe, a local merchant. His most significant investment was a library for the children where he contributed over two thousands books from his private collection.

Anne Marie and her dog drove back to St. Louis with Calvin. With their share of the gold, the water taxi service became a reality on Laclede's landing. Anne Marie enjoyed buying expensive things. Her real extravagance was purchasing a beautiful twenty-eight-foot wooden boat from Will Chambers to give to Calvin. They called the new boat Baby Wildcat IV.

Anne Marie put her acting and painting career aside and learned the boat business. Calvin wasn't surprised she had a real talent for balancing the books as well as driving fast boats.

In 1933 Anne Marie and Calvin got married at the Old Cathedral on Walnut Street in St. Louis. They had a wonderful honeymoon taking their new boat, Baby Wildcat IV, up the Illinois River to the World's Fair in Chicago. That year Calvin got a deal from an old steamboat captain. It was a big brick house on Bissell Street off East Grand. People talked about the ghosts of the Bissell House, but since Calvin had experience with spirits in Port Fulton he bought the rundown old mansion overlooking the Mississippi River anyway.

Finally the Howard Shipyard cleared their new property to add another building on the riverside of the Pike. On December 5, 1933 the John W. Hubbard, which had been deteriorating in the willows, was torched. It coincided with the big party in Port Fulton celebrating the repeal of prohibition. The ghosts of Port Fulton were laid to rest and the gold was used for good purposes.

The Hubbard made a magnificent bonfire.

Baby Wildcat IV at the Mound City Boatyard